ELIOT GRAYSON

THE ROYAL CURSE

TWILIGHT MAGES
BOOK ONE

Cover by Fiona Jayde

Interior Formatting by BreathlessLit

Published by Smoking Teacup Books

Los Angeles, California

ISBN: 9798867927608

CHAPTER ONE

"Absolutely not. Look at me! I don't need a nursemaid. I'm a mage, a perfectly competent adult, I'm, I'm tall, for fuck's sake—"

"You're a mage who can't use his magic, and you're a prince, which means you require a royal guard if you wish to stray outside the gates. Don't even get me started on what your height has to do with it. And you hardly need me to tell you any of this, Nikola."

Philippa didn't bother setting aside her correspondence or so much as glancing up at me, her pen continuing its steady, if obnoxiously scratchy, journey across the paper on her desk as she spoke. A long, shining coil of hair the same mahogany shade as mine hung down over her silk-clad shoulder. My fingers twitched with the desire to reach over and give it a good, hard yank the way I would have fifteen years ago.

Well, all right. Ten years ago.

A few weeks ago. Whatever.

Instead, being a grown man of twenty-eight in the presence of the crown princess of Surbino, I gritted my teeth to keep in a reply that would've been beneath my dignity—and more to the point, have badly undermined the argument I needed to make—and strode to the window, turning my back to her so that she wouldn't see my red cheeks if she deigned to look up after all.

That I was now blocking the light and making it harder for her to finish her letter could be considered a happy coincidence.

A deep, put-upon sigh from behind me made my lips twitch. I opened my mouth, wanting to say something teasing, but the words died on my tongue. If I opened my mouth, I wouldn't tease. I'd say something Philippa didn't deserve.

Breathing deep, I gazed out at the garden beyond Philippa's window, a sea of bright green peppered with the orange and pink and white of the mild winter's small crop of out-of-season roses. They'd been lovingly nurtured by a palace mage with a botanical bent, and they practically glowed in a flood of honey-golden sunlight. Lovely. Everything within the palace walls was lovely, right down to the polished brass curlicues of the ornate frame holding the windowpanes and the high sandstone walls around the garden that glittered with flecks of mica.

In short, every part of my cage gleamed and sparkled, for my mother the queen would have it no other way.

Although no one else appeared to mind their circumscribed lives, from Her Royal Majesty all the way to the smiling kitchen maids. Everyone in Surbino seemed disgustingly happy to remain there indefinitely.

And why wouldn't they be? Good harvests, thriving trade along the coast and across the mountains, strong but just rulers, and half a century of peace with our neighbors had left everyone in the city and the surrounding lands as happy and fat and dull as could be. No one bothered to have adventures.

Though, to be fair, almost all of them had more ways to enjoy their leisure time than I did. If I saw one more happy couple kissing in a corner of the courtyard, or emerging from a bedroom all rumpled, I might scream.

"You're going to lose all your teeth before you're thirty," Philippa commented casually. Fuck. How had she heard the faint crunch of my molars? She'd always had ears like a bat, damn her. A rustle of paper and the soft shake of sand suggested she'd finished her letter despite my best efforts. "Perhaps you ought to wear that helmet at night—"

"Shut up, Phil," I snarled, goaded past my patience. I spun around to face her, gripping the window ledge behind me with both hands so hard that my fingers ached. How dare she refer to that contraption the court physician had recommended to help with my habit of clenching my jaw? The moment I'd been forced to try it on, at the sensitive age of fifteen, had perhaps been the most humiliating of my life. "*You* wear the bloody thing."

She blinked up at me, pale green eyes wide and limpidly innocent in a way that only infuriating elder sisters could manage—and all the more irritating for being a mirror image of mine when I decided to be a pain in the ass.

"It's not the most flattering item, I admit," she said. "But as you refuse to take anyone to bed with you, it hardly matt—"

At that, I saw red, an actual, literal wash of crimson in my vision that obliterated Philippa's stupid smug face for a moment. "I don't refuse, I can't! Who would—I can only—don't you dare tell me what matters! If Mama had only pushed me out a little faster or a little slower, it'd only have been an hour's difference either way, then I'd be—" I broke off, panting, knowing that if I tried to spit out the word *normal* my voice would crack.

I could've been either a normal mage or a normal man with no magic at all, but either would've been infinitely preferable to being born a cursed oddity.

Outside the window the snick of a pair of clippers carried on the soft breeze, a gardener tending the already perfect flowers. Gods, the peaceful beauty of my home would be the death of me through sheer boredom. Usually I didn't care. Most days, I simply drifted. But my mother's decision to take away the very last bit of my independence had somehow brought the rest of it into glaring focus.

"You know damn well a woman can't simply decide when to push a baby out," Philippa said, her words falling into the stretching silence and pinging off of my overstrained nerves one by one. She sat back in her chair and sighed. "Niko, love, it's no one's fault. And there's nothing wrong with you. You are what you are. That's reality. You need to work within it, not against it."

I let go of the windowsill at last, bringing my numbed hands to my face and scrubbing them up and down. It didn't help.

Philippa loved me at least as much as I loved her, damn her—and I adored her. It was so hard to stay angry in the face of her open affection. If I didn't at least try, though, I might cry—tall, grown man though I might be.

"As if you know," I mumbled through my hands. "You haven't had any babies."

"Not only do I have the body parts to do it eventually, which you don't, I'm a trained midwife, and just because you can theoretically heal with a thought and a touch doesn't give you the right to minimize the skills and knowledge I had to work for!"

Oh, for fuck's sake. That *theoretically* had been a hit below the belt, but perhaps I deserved it. I lowered my hands and met her flashing eyes.

"You know I didn't mean that, get off your high horse. Phil, it may not be Mama's fault, but I'm broken, I can't take anyone to bed while I'm using the potion, and I don't want to be another man's helpless dependent if I stop. Who and when I—that's the only aspect of my life I'm apparently allowed to choose for myself, do you understand?" She nodded grudgingly. Of course she understood. The crown princess had even less freedom in some ways. If I eventually married, I'd be expected to pick someone suitable, but she might not get a choice at all. "I can't hand that power over to someone else. So that's that." She opened her mouth, no doubt to keep arguing, and so I cut her off at the pass with, "And I wouldn't wear that horrid helmet even if no one but me could see it. Anyway, I burned the fucking thing years ago."

That earned me the reluctant laugh I'd hoped for, and a shake of her head, along with yet another deep sigh of the kind she reserved for me and our two younger siblings.

"And I don't need a nursemaid," I repeated, bringing us back to the point, damn it all. "I've been riding out in the countryside alone for years, and I won't have it. I simply won't."

Philippa shrugged and leaned forward, setting aside her finished letter and taking up a new sheet of paper and her pen.

"Only because no one had noticed and everyone assumed you were taking a guard with you as you knew you ought to. Go and argue with Mama and leave me alone, Niko. I need to work."

Her small smile indicated that she knew precisely how far that would get me—and also that she knew I'd already tried and failed before coming to her. My efforts to change Mama's mind had resulted in a withering glare and a hint that if I didn't want a guard, she'd assign me a noble husband instead.

I'd run like hell.

Anyway, how dare Philippa mock me. I humphed, fidgeted, was completely ignored, and stalked out of her study in high dudgeon, determined not to give in so easily.

Gods, it simply wasn't fair—and I knew how sulky and childish I sounded even in the privacy of my own head: childish enough to need that nursemaid after all.

But I'd never been allowed to be truly alone, except for those long rides. Royal children had an entourage of nurses and tutors and governesses, not to mention my parents and three siblings, and once puberty brought on the first displays of my magic, I'd acquired mages and physicians to add to the mix. And then there were courtiers and servants…all of them with that expression in their eyes when they looked at me.

Dawn mage. Twilight mage. Those were the official descriptions for what I was.

Cursed, useless, damaged, *dangerous.* Those were the words everyone actually used.

Of course, we were mostly only dangerous to ourselves, aside from the danger anyone possessing magic could present in the abstract— although modern mages were quite weak, compared to the legends of our ancestors who'd received the god Dromos's mixed blessing directly. Most could only set a broken limb or start a campfire. But our relative harmlessness didn't matter to the superstitious, who believed twilight mages were disfavored by the gods and brought bad luck. Very few of those bothered to harass a mage, though. They just avoided us. And in my case, also, I had the shelter of my royal title and royal family and royal guards—much as I didn't always want them hovering, I appreciated their existence most of the time.

But in the end, contempt and distaste, even when it didn't come with a side dish of anything resembling persecution or injury, started to wear on a person after a while.

Riding out alone, in the peace and quiet of the woods around the city, had been my only escape. No one staring at me. No pity or whispers, no veiled disgust.

At least my use of the potion kept me from being a laughingstock. If I'd been using the only other available method to control my faulty magic…well. That would've made me the target of every prurient joke from the palace kitchens to the grimiest dockside tavern.

Down the corridor from Philippa's rooms, I reached a crossroads, both literal and metaphorical: to the left lay my own apartments, my luxurious bedroom and bath, a sitting room and small library, a broad balcony overhung with flowering vines and equipped with a cushioned day bed and a view of the gardens. My opulent prison. Confinement and obedience and safety.

To the right, I could go down a set of stairs and slip out a side door and make my way to the stables. Try for one last moment of freedom from expectations and unwanted attention.

Gods, it wasn't like the surrounding forest and countryside held any dangers, anyway. We hadn't had bandits in our woods or on our roads for decades. The people were too well fed and comfortable to turn to robbery and violence to survive, and our soldiery dealt with the occasional real criminal quickly enough. And politically speaking…no one loyal to my mother would want to hurt me, and no one who hated her, if you could even find someone who fit that description, would bother with me. As a mage, I had no place in the line of succession, a law that had been in place in Surbino for centuries. As a mage who couldn't use his magic, and thank you Philippa for putting it so bluntly, no one had a use for me at all, for good or ill.

Fuck it. I wouldn't go too far, just north of the city along the river to the sea, and then back in through the dockside city gate. I'd clear my head, shake off my temper, and prepare to discuss the issue with my mother in a more rational frame of mind.

On my way to the stables I met a couple of passing servants: a maid carrying a stack of towels, a footman with a letter in his hand. But none of my family and none of the guards, thank the gods. I stepped out through a discreet side door, crossed a small walled courtyard that held a splashing fountain, made my way along the side of the stables, and then ducked into the stable building through another little side door.

My heart pounded absurdly, although I'd made this same short journey hundreds of times before.

What was it about being forbidden that made even the smallest, most insignificant actions take on such absurd significance?

I eased my way around the corner from the tack room I'd entered through and into the stable proper. Hmm. Silent, that was odd for the daytime. Well, no stable was ever *silent*. Horses stamped and whuffed to themselves, hay rustled as a mouse or two skittered around, and a cat leapt down from the hayloft with a soft thump in pursuit of the mice.

But human-silent. No voices. No sounds of work.

What a stroke of luck that the grooms had all had business elsewhere, out in the yard training a particularly recalcitrant horse, or cleaning the carriages, or who knew what. It was enough that they weren't here to question me. My mother might very well have already thought to order them to keep me from riding out alone.

I tiptoed down the row of stalls, whispering a few words to any of the horses who stuck their noses over the doors as I passed, and taking a moment to pat Mr. Nose, my little sister's mare, who'd been named before Amara understood what made a foal a boy horse.

The next stall held Fluffy, my black stallion. And yes, Amara had named him too.

He eyed me balefully, flicking his ear and baring his teeth. His personality didn't match his name, but he did love me. He simply didn't like to wear his heart on his sleeve.

"Don't give me that," I hissed at him. "I know you're just looking for a treat."

"Are you talking to him or to me?" said a deep, pleasant voice.

The fuck—I staggered back a step, all my limbs going cold for a second from the shock along my nerves, as a man's head popped up over the stall door beside Fluffy's. And up. And up even more. His shoulders matched his height: broad and clad in black with a hint of chain mail peeking out at the neck. A muscular neck, and above that, a strong-featured, tanned and freckled face as plain as his tunic, topped with a mercilessly short-cropped mess of dark red hair. He looked to be about my age, perhaps a year or two older. I'd never seen him before, I didn't think. Perhaps a vague familiarity? But I couldn't place him.

Who the hell…? Fluffy didn't let anyone in his stall except for me and the grooms, who'd learned how to deal with him. Could he be an assassin? But no one wanted to kill me, I wasn't worth it. Had this fellow drugged my horse?

He propped his folded arms on the top of the stall door and favored me with a bland, neutral smile that didn't reach his eyes. "Prince Nikola," he said. "I'm Andreas, your personal guard. I thought I might find you here. If you'd like to go for a ride, I'm at your service."

Chapter Two

Well, fuck. My heart, which had barely recovered from the stuttering shock of this man—my guard's—appearance, dropped all the way down to my toes.

I would've preferred an assassin, honestly. At least I could've gotten away with hitting one of those.

It took me a moment to catch up to the rest of what he'd said along with announcing himself as my nursemaid for the foreseeable future: *If you'd like to go for a ride, I'm at your service.*

Could he be mocking me? Those words, and that smile, and the fact that everyone in Surbino knew perfectly well that I had to take a potion to suppress my twilight magic—and the potion's side effects were common knowledge too. He'd be well aware of my limitations, including…going for a ride. My cock hadn't so much as stirred in six years, since the last time I missed a dose of my potion.

Of course, if that had been mockery, I had to give him points for keeping his tone as bland as his smile. He'd ruffled my feathers, but he'd given me no grounds to demand *how dare he?*

We stared at each other in silence for a long moment. His stupid smile didn't falter—even under the scrutiny of a prince, damn him.

"I don't have a personal guard," I finally managed. Of course, that wasn't up to me, but perhaps I could bluff him into believing otherwise. "You have no right to be in Fluffy's stall without my permission. Go at once."

"Fluffy," he said, sounding a little choked, eyes widening. What color were his eyes? Muddy. Maybe some variety of dark hazel. "Your, ah, royal stallion is named Fluffy?"

"My royal sister named him," I snapped, lifting my chin. "Out! If I have to repeat myself again, I'll have words with your superior officer."

"Ah," he said, and removed his arms from the top of the door in order to push it open. I had to step back so it didn't whack into me. "I'm afraid I was appointed directly by the queen, Your Highness. I don't have a commanding officer at present, unless you count Her Majesty."

The door creaked the rest of the way open, revealing…the rest of Andreas, which matched what I'd seen so far. Black tunic. Black trousers. Black boots. And a very long sword at his hip, with a muscular, long-fingered hand resting on the hilt. The fact that the scabbard didn't drag on the ground was a testament to how tall he was.

With incredibly long legs. Like tree trunks. And even the layers of tunic and trousers couldn't quite conceal the hint of another very long sword between them.

"Your Highness?"

I tore my gaze up to his face, feeling my own flood with heat. He raised an eyebrow at me and took a step closer. A little too close, so that I had to tip my head back. I really was tall. Taller than at least half of the men of Surbino, anyway. Mathematically tall.

He made me feel small.

"If you wish to have words with the queen, then I certainly won't come anywhere near," he went on, grimacing in an expressive way that almost, *almost* made me laugh despite myself. "But otherwise, I'm afraid you're stuck with me. The queen was very specific about my duties."

Of course she had been. Of course.

And he clearly knew as well as I did how confronting Mama about appointing a personal guard for me would go.

"Where did you even come from?" I asked without thinking. "And how did you—I didn't tell anyone I meant to go to the stables. Fluffy doesn't like anyone getting so close to him. You ought to have waited to be presented!"

Andreas's smile did light up his eyes this time, and they gleamed in a way mud decidedly didn't. He wasn't a handsome man. Not at all. But that wicked grin…

"To you, or to Fluffy?"

"What—you—" I sputtered, at a loss for words.

"I was joking, Your Highness. I absolutely did present myself to Fluffy. But I didn't think you'd be won over by a sugared apple."

Oh, for the love of the gods. At least that explained Fluffy's acceptance of him, because the beast might be a bitey asshole but he rolled over like a whore for a bit of sugar.

"Yes, obviously," I gritted out. Damn it, couldn't my mother have at least chosen someone dull and stolid and quiet, someone I could ignore? "How stupid do you think I am? Answer my questions, if you please. I don't have patience for nonsense today."

The grin faded away, his brows drawing together, and he straightened himself from his casual, hip-slung stance, hands clasped behind him, suddenly the picture of a soldier at parade rest.

"Forgive me, Your Highness," he said crisply. "In order of how you asked me: I transferred from Bossale last week." That explained why I didn't think I recognized him. We had quite a few troops stationed at the mountain fortresses on our eastern border, including Bossale. Those soldiers tended to rotate through the city now and again so that all of them had the opportunity for lighter duty and a bit of pleasure. I'd visited Bossale once a couple of years ago, but it'd been brief. "I presume 'how did you' refers to finding you here. Her Majesty mentioned that you enjoyed riding out. I extrapolated."

That made my jaw tighten into a painful clench. Extrapolated? He meant he'd taken my mother's hint that I'd probably try to sneak out. And he'd come here to catch me like a naughty schoolboy, the utter bastard. And succeeded. More than that, complaining about it would make *me* look the fool, not him.

What had Mama told him? To treat me like a child, because I acted like one? It certainly seemed so. Her instructions weren't his fault, but how he acted on them was entirely his responsibility. Apparently he'd chosen to participate in my humiliation rather than minimize it. And I didn't appreciate it.

"Fine," I said, with poor grace. "We'll ride out." I needed the fresh air more than ever, and stomping off to my rooms without even going out, when I'd clearly intended to, would be the act of a sulky brat.

"Don't you want the answer to your last question, Your Highness?"

My last question. What had I…and then I realized. Would he really dare? Only one way to find out.

"Go ahead," I said.

He'd been gazing out at some distant point over the top of my head in true soldier-approved fashion, but as I gave my permission, his eyes snapped down to mine. "I understand you're a scholar, Your Highness, and I expect you're far more intelligent than I am. I don't think you're stupid at all. But you need to believe me when I tell you: neither am I. I've sworn an oath to my queen to protect you with my life, which includes sticking to you like glue, no matter what. And only a very, very stupid man would disobey Queen Melena."

Well, message received: if I tried to sneak off, he wouldn't let me get away with it. And much as I wished to, I could hardly argue with his desire to stay on my mother's good side. He'd shown sufficient tact that I couldn't really bite his head off, either.

That said…

I raised an eyebrow of my own. Mine were peaked and quite dark against my pale skin. He couldn't out-eyebrow *me*, the fucker.

"Which is it, then? Since you're only here because I disobey Queen

Melena on the regular. Am I stupid? Or not?"

A brick-red flush flooded Andreas's tanned cheeks, and he bit his lip.

Suddenly, he looked years younger. Gods, how old *was* he? A soldier's life could age a man, I supposed, but sheepish and shifty like this, Andreas could've been five years younger than I was rather than slightly older.

"You're Her Majesty's son," he said at last. "The same rules don't apply to you. I assume she doesn't have you sent off to guard one of the royal gold mines in the mountains when you don't do as she says."

I couldn't help laughing this time, little as I wanted to unbend. But I tended to have a time limit on my temper. That might owe more to resignation than to natural calm, but I'd learned, since my magic manifested at thirteen and then started trying to kill me at fifteen, that it didn't do a lot of good to shake your fists at the sky, my moment of rebellion in Philippa's study earlier notwithstanding.

Allowing myself to be amused by this insolent fellow didn't mean I liked him.

"No, she doesn't," I agreed. "Instead, she's chosen to saddle me with you."

The corner of Andreas's lips twitched, and his eyes gleamed. "She does seem to favor punishing those *not* in her favor by putting us—I mean them, of course—in company they wouldn't choose."

That—actually hurt, a little twinge beneath my breastbone. Twilight mages, with our reputation as the gods' least favored children, weren't anyone's favorite choice of company. That didn't make it more pleasant to have it rubbed in.

"Touché," I muttered, and turned away. "Speaking of saddling, get your horse ready, Andreas. I'd like to be back before dinnertime."

"Your Highness, I didn't mean—"

"Now, if you please," I said, in a tone that anyone who served royalty would recognize as an absolute command.

"As you wish, Your Highness," he said quietly.

We didn't speak another word the entire ride. When we returned, he escorted me silently to the doors of my suite, bowed, and disappeared down the corridor.

He didn't need to say anything. I knew he wouldn't be going far or giving me any breathing room. My mother had made sure of that.

"Your new guard's not very friendly, is he?" Amara whispered, bumping her shoulder against mine. "Not hard on the eyes, though."

"Are you—your eyes must be broken," I hissed in reply, and then quickly spun around and put my very stiff back to the parapet of my suite's terrace as Andreas started to walk along the path below us. His tall, dark, nearly silent figure was distinguishable mainly by the breadth of his shoulders. You couldn't even pick him out of the night by moonlight glinting off of his weapons or armor; he had his sword hilt wrapped in leather and wore his chain mail under a black tunic with black trousers and black boots. The all-black ensemble wasn't just for guard duty, either. I'd never seen him in anything else.

Very practical. And while I preferred function over form too, that didn't make his aggressively competent midnight prowling under my windows any less irritating. "Shut up, will you?" I growled at Amara. "*His* eyes and ears work just fine."

Amara sighed, shook her head, and leaned over the edge. Framed by the vines that grew all over the pillars and hung down from the roof, she looked like something out of a tale: a girl waiting for her lover to climb up for a kiss.

Ugh. Perhaps I ought to trade rooms with her. This terrace, with its potential for romance, was entirely wasted on me.

"We can talk," she said after a moment, leaning back up again and propping her hip on the parapet to face me. "He's gone. Doing his rounds again. Does he sleep? He knows Surbino hasn't been attacked in fifty years, doesn't he? And that there are guards on the walls of the palace in any case? And that if someone did want to sneak in and murder someone, they'd go after Mama or Phil, not you?"

"Yes, he does know all that, and it doesn't seem to stop him, and if our hypothetical assassins had sense or good taste, they'd go after you and save us all some annoyance."

Amara kicked my ankle and stuck out her tongue. Well, she could get away with it. She'd only just turned seventeen, and our mother, bless her, didn't feel the need to force young ladyship on her daughters before they grew out of their childishness on their own. It made my chest ache anyway, that she'd gotten so big—both she and Franco, our brother, who at fifteen had started growing a dreadful little mustache and writing poetry, gods help us all. I missed the toddlers who'd followed me around and squeaked at me when I was an adolescent myself. I missed my father, who'd died when Amara was only four, with a deep ache that hadn't faded much in the thirteen years since.

Perhaps I mostly missed being uncomplicatedly happy.

"*Is* he unfriendly?" Amara pressed, her mature and thoughtful tone very much at odds with the evidence of my bruised foot. "Or did you do something to make him that way? Mama didn't give him any choice in the matter, either. If he could choose his own assignment, I doubt he'd choose you. This isn't precisely an exciting job, walking around the garden all night and watching you read all day."

She sounded so much like Philippa. Superficially, with her lighter brown hair, softer features, and more buxom figure, she didn't resemble her much—except in her expressions, the way she glared when chastising an idiot brother. In that, they were clearly sisters.

I quickly turned back to the garden, lifting my goblet for a deep swig of wine. Even in the limited light of a half-moon and the balcony's brazier, she'd see my irritation and hurt if I gave her the chance—because also like Philippa, young or not, she was too damn perceptive.

No, he wouldn't have chosen to guard me, the most boring duty he could possibly have been given. I did read most of the day. How else would I find another solution to the problem of my magic than through research? And given that my dull, constricted life stemmed from my misfortune, would it have killed him to be at least a little sympathetic, rather than laughing at me in his sleeve? Even his intense devotion to his very undemanding duty read as backhanded rather than sincere. Either he meant to demonstrate his dedication to my mother and get a promotion to something else, or he wanted to rub it in that I was stuck with him, like it or not.

"You're not answering my question, which is as good as an answer," Amara said. "You were rude, weren't you?"

No, I didn't think I'd been rude, but a twinge of guilt at my brusque treatment of him didn't improve my mood.

"He was the rude one! He was—Amara, he was laughing at me. Not enough for me to chastise him for it, but—enough. He obviously knows what I am. What I have to do to live." Another gulp of wine emptied the goblet, and I scowled down at it. If I'd been able to use my own thrice-damned fucking magic, I'd have been able to summon the wine right into my glass from the bottle I'd left inside in my sitting room. My power felt like a faint itch just beyond my fingertips, almost tangible but totally inaccessible. A teasing torment. "And he thinks it's funny, apparently. Half of what he said to me when we met had a double meaning. He—you would've had to be there. And he's so gods-damned young!"

"He doesn't look that young to me," Amara said dubiously. "And I'm not sure why that matters, anyway. If he really did speak to you that way, then you should tell Mama and have him removed, no matter how old he is. Nothing about your situation is funny, Niko. You probably were rude, though," she added.

Ah, little sisters. No one could be so loyal or so bitchy at the same damn time.

Before I could snap at her, she took my empty goblet out of my hand and replaced it with hers, still half full.

"Of course he doesn't look that young to you," I said, a little bit mollified. "But I think he can't be more than twenty-five, now that I've had the chance to observe him a bit. And it does matter. It matters a lot."

I'd given this quite a bit of thought in the week since I'd acquired my very own looming shadow. His youth had immediately rubbed me the wrong way. It'd taken some introspection to get to the bottom of it—and, in the process, the bottom of several bottles of a very fine southern red.

"He's his own master, don't you understand? And probably has been for—gods, nearly a decade. Yes, he answers to his officers or to our mother, but not to his own mother, the way I have to. What do you think he thinks of me for that? And if I had someone older watching me, at least he'd be naturally expected to have more experience. But having someone allowed to constrain what I do, where I go, when he's both younger than I am and also so much more experienced, in every possible way? It's humiliating, Amara. Can't you see?"

Amara sighed and tapped her fingers on the parapet thoughtfully. "I suppose if Franco were to tell me what it was and wasn't safe for me to do, I'd be annoyed," she said at last. "Not that he doesn't. But he doesn't know anything, and I don't have to listen to him, either."

"No, you don't. Lucky you." I polished off the wine in her goblet, letting it flow freely down my tight throat and go, contrary to all the laws of nature, straight up to my head. Everything had started going a bit fuzzy around the edges, thank the gods. "I'm not much of a man to begin with," I muttered. "Having someone who's practically a boy chiding me for trying to ride my own horse doesn't help."

"Oh, shut up," Amara said, and kicked me again.

"Cut it out! I'm tired of—no, hitting me isn't better than kicking me!"

"Then stop talking nonsense, Niko. First of all, you're not that much older, and you sound stupid calling him a boy. And second, I don't know why all men are so obsessed with the function of their cocks—oh, don't look at me like that, do you really think I'm a little child anymore? You're as much of a man as anyone else. You're a prince, and you have a guard, and you ought to be grateful that he's all young and tall and—and—you know the way he walks."

I peered at her through the gloom. She'd turned her head down to stare at where she was picking at a bit of moss on the stone parapet. And was she *blushing*? Oh, by the fucking gods' fucking balls. *That* was what I needed in my life: a lovestruck little sister causing a scandal by pursuing my completely unsuitable personal guard.

"I haven't paid the slightest attention to the way he walks, and neither should you," I gritted out. The way he *walked*? Yes, he had a way of moving that resembled a big cat, and he did have a certain kind of… fluidity in his hips that made me wonder how he'd look using his sword. But he had such a plain face. Too angular, too rawboned and strongly made. No elegance at all in him. "I'm not grateful for having a guard who walks some certain way, Amara. For fuck's sake."

"Well, at least you're not stuck with Tommaso," she said, sounding less like Phil now and more like a sulky little girl who shouldn't know what a cock was. "He's not at all appealing to look at, and he only talks about the way his husband's still looking for a physician who can help with his back pain."

My chest clenched, and I had to close my eyes against a wave of teeth-gritting nausea and regret. Such a small and offhand remark, but it underlined my uselessness in a way that no mockery ever could. Reminded me of my own selfishness. Healing was more complicated than other uses of magic, because the structure and function of a living thing was so much more complex than anything else in existence. A rock? You could duplicate the pattern of a rock. Any inanimate object, really, because it didn't keep moving around and constantly changing itself. Twilight mages, who often had more strength and control than other mages, frequently made the best healers.

When and if we could use our powers at all, of course.

"If I had my magic, I might be able to help."

"And if you had your magic, it'd kill you," she said, patting my hand. Back to practical and mature in the blink of an eye. Fuck, I did not miss being her age, halfway between childhood and adulthood and wearing both awkwardly.

"I could take a—a lover, and then I'd be able to use my birthright to do some good in the world." Except that then I'd have to be a needy, dependent slut, a burden on any man who took me on, if I was lucky, and begging to be fucked and filled, entirely at his mercy, if I wasn't. "Damn it, Amara, I don't want to talk to you about this!"

"No!" Her ferocity took me by surprise, so much that I jerked back. She didn't want to talk to me about it either? What— "You don't owe anyone anything! If you don't want to be—to be—" Even in the faint light I could see her blush had deepened. I couldn't blame her. Talking to your much older brother about how he did or didn't want to get fucked had to be embarrassing—for me, too, which was why I hadn't wanted to talk about it in the first place. But she looked me in the eyes, her own blazing. "If you don't want to give yourself to someone that way, and there's no one you trust enough, then you shouldn't. I don't care if every husband in Surbino has a broken back!"

Oh, by both of the bastard sky gods.

Embarrassing or not, weirdly enamored of my guard or not, Amara was a better sister than I deserved. I wrapped my arm around her and pulled her into my side, resting my burning cheek on her soft hair.

"Thank you," I whispered.

She hugged me hard, squeezing me tightly enough to make my ribs creak.

At least I had the best family in the world. That made me lucky no matter what.

Chapter Three

I was a damned unlucky bastard, and my family could go jump in a lake. Preferably that gorgeous sapphire-blue one a thousand feet up the mountain from Surbino that froze your toes off even at the height of summer.

"Mama's right," Philippa said, not even pausing in pouring herself another cup of tea as she joined our mother in shattering my hopes. "Gennaro says it's going to snow all the way down into the foothills, and then the rain and mudslides will last for weeks. The other side of the mountains will be worse. The journey's simply too dangerous."

"Gennaro also said you shouldn't drink so much tea because it's bad for your digestion," I snapped. "But apparently you only listen to him when it's convenient."

Gennaro, my mother's ancient—and in my opinion, doddering—court mage, claimed to have a special connection to the weather, something no human mage, to my knowledge, could affect. If producing hot air counted as being a weather mage, perhaps Gennaro could be classed as such, but otherwise he seemed to be right far less often than the average farmer.

As if reading my mind, my mother put down the letter she'd been frowning at and turned away from her desk to face me, saying, "The agricultural guild's representative had the same opinion. He believes the rest of the winter, and the spring, will be unusually cold and wet. It's truly not safe to go over the pass, Niko."

In this case, apparently the average farmer agreed with Gennaro. Well, fuck me.

I wished I'd chosen a better moment to have this conversation. If I'd waited for supper, I'd have had Amara as my ally, at least, and she had a way of winding Mama around her finger that the rest of us couldn't begin to equal. But I hadn't realized it'd be a debate, and I'd innocently mentioned my upcoming journey while having afternoon tea with Phil and our mother in the latter's private study. Mama had been sipping and reading her correspondence, and had unbent enough to slip off her shoes and rest her toes in the plush carpet under her desk. We had a fire going, and Phil and I had each lounged on one of the comfortable sofas set across from one another with a table laden with sandwiches and cakes in between.

The rather excessive number of each that I'd scarfed down sat like lead in my stomach. Phil primly took another sip of tea, heedless of Gennaro's dictates. As the crown princess, apparently she didn't have to listen.

"I won't be traveling in a hurry," I said, forcing my voice to remain even and calm. My mother, like a shark, could scent blood in the water. Any sign of weakness and I'd stand no chance at all. "I'll be on horseback with a small entourage. No carriages or wagons to break down or get stuck. I can spend a few extra days at any inn I stop at and wait out the weather. And you know how important this is. The scholars at the conclave can help me—"

A knock at the door forced me into silence, and my mother called out, "Enter!"

Damn it, *damn* it, right when I'd seen a little bit of softening in her expression!

Ser Marko, her private secretary, stuck his bespectacled and bewhiskered head around the door. "Your Majesty, forgive me, but Ambassador Garzole returned, and he's still in a tizzy about those tariffs. Can you see him? He's departing for home tomorrow morning. We have one more opportunity to calm him down."

"Of course," she said, pushing her feet into her shoes and rising, already striding for the door before I'd managed to open my mouth again. "Niko, I'm sorry, but the risk is too great. You can go next time. Your potion is still working well enough, Gennaro says, and there's plenty of time to discuss alternatives."

And with that, she rustled out of the room in an elegant sweep of red silk and pearls, leaving me gaping at her retreating back and the coif of her bejeweled hair, graying but the same color as Amara's beneath.

Phil and I had both inherited our coloring, and more of our features, from our father. My resemblance to him, I realized belatedly, had probably put me in this position. Knowing my mother and her everlasting grief for the man she'd loved, I should've seen it coming.

I slumped back into the sofa, stomach now churning with sick fear and misery, temples starting to throb.

Gennaro says. And that was enough for my mother, no matter what I might say about my own magic, my own health, my own life.

Scholars of magic from a dozen kingdoms would be at the conclave in a month: scientists, philosophers, physicians, mages. The greatest assembly of knowledge about magic in general and twilight mages specifically that you could find on the entire continent. Other places had their own ways of helping, or controlling, their dawn and dusk mages, ranging from the gentle and humane to the downright horrific. One city-state island off the eastern coast supposedly had a whole temple dedicated to helping mages find their "harmonious completion," a silly-sounding term for a legend about each mage having a perfect match, a lover whose natural life-force would complement the mage's and make them exponentially stronger. Nonsense, of course. But intriguing nonsense.

And to the southeast, far enough that we didn't even trade with the kingdoms there, they had another version of the potion that created a bond between twilight mages and mundane men who served as anchors for their magic. I'd heard rumors that the bonding process was dreadfully misused and abused—as were the mages subjected to it.

But that didn't mean there couldn't be some germ of information that scholars from that part of the world would know that I didn't, and which could be turned to good. Some of them would be in attendance, too.

Gennaro hadn't even rated an invitation, and yet he thought he knew everything.

He didn't. Because on a more practical and less speculative note, no matter what Gennaro said, my potion had slowly but noticeably started to become less efficient at suppressing my symptoms. The time between doses had reduced over the last couple of years—only by an hour total, which didn't sound like much unless you knew how precisely the dosage was calculated. And I knew in my bones that eventually it'd stop working. Not now. Not soon—probably. Or it could fail tomorrow, a thought that kept me awake in the middle of the night several times a week.

The extensive notes I'd spent years preparing, and the essay I'd been scheduled to present after supper on the second night, all related to my situation, and I hoped to all the gods that one of the physicians or academics in attendance would have some idea of what I ought to do next.

If they didn't, no one in the world would.

The prospect of staying home, of missing this chance to escape the curse of my tainted magic, and because of the fucking *weather* of all things…I might go mad. They'd scheduled the conclave for the winter and in its specific location to cater to one of the founders of it, who'd grown so old and frail he might not last to the spring and certainly couldn't travel. When I'd received the letter informing me of this, I'd shrugged at the mild inconvenience, unable to even imagine that the time of year would matter to me.

Next time I wouldn't underestimate my mother and sister's abilities to make my life hell.

"If I looked less like him, do you think she'd be less strict? No don't answer that," I said bitterly. "You're on her side. But it's irrational. You know that, even if you won't admit it. Phil, you have to help me change her mind. I need to go. My future depends on it."

She sniffed and sipped her tea, eyeing me over the rim of her cup. "Father did die while he was away from home, I admit," she said after a moment. "And perhaps that has some small influence on Mama's—"

"Horseshit, Phil! Utter rot. It has all the influence on her decision, and she can't keep us all locked up here like treasures in a cabinet forever! Don't tell me you don't still regret it that she didn't allow you to go to the university hospital in Antua instead of studying here."

A crimson stain spread along her cheekbones, and she set her teacup down with a clatter. "That's not the same! I couldn't go because of my responsibilities here. It would've been perfectly safe. But this wouldn't be, and you know it. The last one of these meetings you went to was only a quick sea voyage away through friendly waters. You've never gone so far from home and you're not an experienced traveler, and more than that— Niko, she doesn't trust you." Philippa lifted her chin and stared me down levelly, giving me her heir-to-the-crown look that meant business. "You've proven to her again and again that you won't follow her rules for your safety unless you think you'll get caught. As soon as you're out of sight and in charge, who knows what you'll do."

That hit hard, a blow to the sternum that had me gasping like a landed fish.

Unfair. Completely, horribly unfair.

But no matter how unfair it might be, I'd brought it on myself. Those rides alone along the river…if I'd known the consequence would be missing this twice-in-a-decade opportunity to have some real help with my condition? I'd have taken a guard. A dozen guards. I'd have stayed home in my room. I'd have done anything, no matter how it chafed.

But it had never occurred to me that my mother would deny me this. Not when it might be the key to my future.

"Phil," I choked out, sitting up, holding out a hand to her. "I give you my word I'd—"

"It's too late for that," she said, not unkindly, but with finality. And she stood, shaking out her petticoats and slipping out from behind the table. "Mama won't listen to you on this subject. And I won't get in the middle of it. Besides, I'm sorry to say I don't trust you on this either. You'd give your word to be careful, but 'careful' is subjective. If the road became truly unsafe, I don't believe you'd turn back rather than convince yourself you could make it through and that 'care' could be exercised along the way without breaking your promise. I need to join her with the ambassador now, Niko, excuse me."

A moment later I was alone in the ringing silence left by her shutting the door behind her.

Just me and the remnants of the cakes on a silver tray, with the fire crackling softly in the background. A still-hot half pot of tea. Silk damask upholstery beneath my rigid, clawing fingertips and a soft carpet cushioning my feet.

Luxury.

And I thought I might scream, flip the tea tray and send it flying to splatter jam all over the sofa opposite and the richly embroidered velvet window curtains beyond, smash the table to smithereens and run shrieking down the corridor.

Comfort and safety mattered to me, and I appreciated them.

But some things were more important.

Stiffly, moving slowly to keep myself under control—and because my vision had gone gray and blotchy—I got up, opened the door, went down the hall and up the stairs. If I passed anyone, I didn't see them or respond to any greetings they might have offered. There was no sign of Andreas. Perhaps he'd considered the queen's own study to be safe enough for his charge. But he wouldn't be far away, and he seemed to have some kind of magic of his own: he could always find me, and on the two occasions I'd tried to give him the slip he'd popped up out of nowhere, smiling and unruffled.

Damn him, damn him to hell, because if it hadn't been for him I'd have mounted Fluffy and set out for the conclave now, disappearing into the hills and taking back roads, making a run for it. Maybe they'd have found me and dragged me home, but at least I'd have had a chance.

I shut and locked the door to my suite, opened a bottle of wine, and went out to the terrace, not even bothering with a goblet. A deep swig, and I collapsed onto the chaise lounge I kept out here so that I could watch the moon and the stars through the trellised arches over the parapet at night, or enjoy the breeze during the day. The weather had finally turned wintry this week, and even though the sun shone pale and bright, an icy wind nipped at my fingers and reddened my cheeks.

Who the hell cared.

I drank deeply, and the chill receded—but the cold unhappiness in my chest and belly didn't melt in the slightest.

Brisk footsteps on the stairs up to my terrace from the garden attracted my attention, but I didn't bother turning my head, simply lying there still and silent. I hadn't been sleeping. That would've been too much of an escape. Instead I'd been motionless for hours, watching the shadows lengthen and the birds chirp and flutter their way to bed, mentally composing a letter to the organizers of the conclave informing them that I wouldn't be attending.

Masochistic, yes, but at least it kept me from mentally shouting at my mother, my only other viable option for wallowing in despair.

I'd finished the bottle and a second one, but hadn't bothered to fetch a third, so I wasn't all that drunk anymore, I didn't think. Merely… numb. Mama didn't usually change her mind once she'd made it up, and if Philippa agreed with her, the case was completely hopeless.

The footsteps got louder and closer and then Andreas appeared, standing at the foot of my chaise and frowning, holding up a lantern that nearly blinded me. The last of the twilight had faded out of the sky a while ago.

"You missed supper and didn't answer your door," he said abruptly, and then belatedly added, "Your Highness. I'm glad to find you alive. And equally glad I'm not interrupting an assignation. That would've been awkward for everyone."

I stared at him for a moment before I burst into laughter—and not because of his pathetic attempt at a joke. The spasms made me sick, bubbling up from a place that felt more like weeping. "An assignation," I choked out. "Of course. I can't even get it up, Andreas!"

Well, shit. Maybe I was still a bit drunk. More than a bit.

His eyes widened, and there he went, looking impossibly young again. He made me feel aged.

"How old are you?" I demanded, only slurring a tiny bit. "I bet you can get it up."

Oh, thank the gods I hadn't had the motivation to open a third bottle after all. This could've been even worse if I had, although I had trouble imagining how.

Andreas's already tanned complexion had darkened to something resembling the burgundy of our house's heraldry, and he didn't move a muscle, gone rigid like a statue.

All over? Probably not, even if he was capable. A drunk, disheveled, sprawled-out prince he didn't like much wouldn't be particularly arousing.

"Your Highness, I think you need—"

"I think you need to answer my fucking questions." I blinked up at him and resisted the urge to stick out my tongue like Amara would have. Of course, she probably would have been trying to seduce him.

Except that hadn't I just asked him about his cock? She'd be so jealous.

I started to laugh again, interrupted by hiccups.

"You only asked me one question, Your Highness," he said, very low, "and I'll answer it. I'm twenty-four. And you need water and something to eat."

"I asked you two, you—oh wait," I said, as I muzzily ran back through what had actually come out of my mouth. "Don't mince words with me. I'll ask it now. Can you get—"

"Water and something to eat!" Andreas said loudly enough to make me wince, completely drowning out my mumbled, "it up or not." He moved at last, setting the lantern on the tiles by his feet and coming around the side of the chaise to reach down and grasp my bicep.

Long ago, between when my magic started to flow and when it built enough strength to rack me with agony and begin destroying my body from the inside, I'd set off a spark, something like lightning only much smaller, from me into a fireplace poker and then into my other hand.

My hair had stood on end and I'd jumped a foot in the air.

Andreas's touch struck me the same way that had, a sudden and searing awareness of every hair on my arm and every cell of my skin beneath the heat of his huge hand wrapped around me.

It felt like magic. And the touch of magic had become anathema to me, a sign of my failure and of pain to come.

I jerked my left arm out of his grasp and struck out with my right, my wrist connecting with his forearm hard, the shock traveling up into my shoulder.

"Ow, fuck, that hurt—shit, I wouldn't actually hurt you," I gasped, gripping my throbbing wrist. He'd pulled away from me, taking a step back and staring, opening and closing his hand as if it had gone numb from the brief contact with me.

"No, you definitely wouldn't," he said after a moment.

"Good, I'm glad you—wait, hang on." The quirk of his mouth and the gleam in those coffee-colored eyes had finally registered, and I gritted my teeth, both hands clenching into fists. "Fuck you! I may not be able to—able to, but I'm still a man—"

"Will you stop—of course you are, fucking gods, stop it!" Andreas caught both of my flailing arms, and I toppled down onto my back again, the world spinning crazily around me. I landed hard with my arms pressed against my chest, Andreas's weight pinning them there as he leaned down, one knee braced on the chaise.

I went limp, panting and simply *done*. The burst of activity, hopeless and pointless as it was, had drained what little strength I had left after two bottles of wine and no supper.

Besides, I simply didn't care: about the bruises I probably had forming on my arms, about the insulting ease with which Andreas had overmastered me—although perhaps I shouldn't feel too bad about losing a tussle with a professional soldier while drunk—or even about the way I'd started the fight, by trying to insist that he tell me if his cock got hard.

In the morning I might seek the nearest hole in the ground and bury myself alive rather than look him in the face again.

Tonight, nothing mattered except that I'd be here forever, with no lover and no friends besides my siblings and nothing in my life but endless, fruitless research. If the potion stopped working, it might be even worse than that.

And I couldn't even get myself off to pass the time, damn it all.

The sound of my own miserable mumble and the horrified look on Andreas's face told me I'd said that out loud.

Perhaps I ought to go and find that hole in the garden *right now*, on second thoughts, because the embarrassment of that penetrated even the fog of wine in my head.

Andreas stared down at me, brow furrowed, lips parted as if he was really thinking about it. About me, not being able to get myself off. Fucking gods.

The warmth of his body permeated the air around me, pushing away the damp chill of the night. His hands on my wrists, and the press of his leg against mine where he knelt on the chaise…and simply his nearness. His fingers flexed. Ten points of contact, each one distracting individually, and together almost unbearable. I tried to suck in a full breath, but it wouldn't quite come.

"There's other ways to enjoy your own touch. Or someone else's. Without, um." He chewed on his lip, gaze going all shifty, his grip tightening even more. Had he leaned closer? Or had my depth perception gone the way of my common sense and my coordination? He looked me in the eyes again, his own mesmerizingly dark and intent. "The ladies I've talked to about it prefer a mouth much of the time, anyway, so it's not like you couldn't make one happy," he said, voice going all deep and rough. It gave me an odd shiver along all my limbs. "And—you know, men do too. Not to mention the other, um, possibilities. Your Highness."

I tipped my head back on the cushion and gazed up at him, completely at a loss for words. Probably for the best, given what I'd said so far. But…I ought to have been offended, probably, by being given such patronizing, unsolicited, and entirely useless advice—I mean, really. As if I hadn't thought of all of that on my own. My two attempts to put it into practice had left me shamed, hating myself to such a degree that I'd never been able to try again. And neither encounter had left me with what you'd call sexual experience. My inability to perform had ended things before I could gain any.

But it seemed I'd lost the capacity for offense along with all my other useful functions. Besides. Andreas sounded so…sincere. And no one but Amara had bothered to give a damn about my intimate life, or lack thereof, well—ever.

His grip had started to feel anchoring rather than restrictive. Pleasant. Gods, the warmth and texture of his skin. Calluses, and the subtle vibration of his heartbeat.

More than pleasant. No one but my family and my valet had touched me in so long. How would it feel to have those powerful arms around me?

He hadn't looked away from me.

"You can let me go," I whispered. I really wished he wouldn't.

Andreas hesitated, but just when I thought he might not after all, he released me and stepped back.

Cold, fog-laced air rushed in to fill the gap, my skin instantly clammy. I shivered, suddenly fucking freezing, and lightheaded, and beginning to be hung over, and starving, and utterly, hopelessly miserable. I closed my eyes and wrapped my own arms around my ribs. It didn't come near to what I'd imagined a moment ago. He needed to leave. Being seen like this made me want to cry or hit something. But I didn't know if I could even stand up on my own, find the will to stagger inside and get warm, ring the bell for something to eat. Unlock the door to let the servants in. Take a bath.

Gods.

"Your Highness, please tell me what's wrong," Andreas said abruptly into the heavy silence. "It's not—what we were talking about. It's something else. What's happened? I can't, ah, take care of you if I don't know what the threats are."

The threats. I started to laugh again, and this time it really did come out as a hitching sob.

"The only threats are in my mother's mind," I said. "She won't let me go. It's been—five years. The potion's not working as well as it used to. I need to go. And she says I'll, she doesn't trust me. Not to do something stupid once I'm out of her sight." I dropped my hands and met his steady, serious gaze. I'd wanted his sympathy, and now I had his pity. Lucky me. "I'm twenty-eight fucking years old, Andreas! And my mother doesn't trust me to lead a few guards and servants over a mountain pass that hasn't had a bandit on it in decades. Because it's going to be *raining*," I spat. "Because I used to ride out without a guard and I didn't listen to her, and now she's punishing me like a naughty schoolboy. It's pathetic. I'm fucking pathetic. Just go."

A muscle ticked in Andreas's jaw, and after a moment he nodded and walked away.

Well, I'd asked for it.

I rolled over and buried my face in the cushion, a wave of sadness and loss and maudlin drunken loneliness overwhelming me.

But Andreas hadn't left. He'd gone inside instead. I heard voices inside my rooms, Andreas and—Benetto, my valet. "…needs some supper," Andreas said. "His Highness isn't feeling well. A sick headache, I think."

That made me smile into the cushion even through another hiccup. His attempt to tactfully gloss over the state I was in would fail, because Benetto would not only see the bottles but see me. Still. He'd tried.

I closed my eyes and waited for Benetto to come and fetch me, trying to savor the last bit of numbness from the wine. All too soon, I'd be sobered up, and then I'd have to face what a fool I'd made of myself.

Not to mention the utter shambles of my life.

Chapter Four

As I'd expected and feared, the following morning brought an entirely unwelcome clarity. Benetto startled me awake by pulling back the drapes from my bedroom windows with a horrifying scrape and clatter of curtain rings on rods. I rolled over with a moan, and instantly remembered asking Andreas if he could get it up.

And I remembered his expression when I asked, too: horror and disbelief.

As soon as I felt better, I needed that hole in the ground to crawl into, but for now, my bed would do.

"Benetto, not yet," I whispered. "Thank you. But later."

"Forgive me, Your Highness," he said quietly—but not quietly enough. My temples pulsed. "The queen's sent for you. It's a few minutes after eleven, and she requires your attendance before her meeting at noon."

I squeezed my eyes shut and flopped onto my back again, blinking up at the pale green velvet canopy above. It matched the curtains Benetto had left open to the unforgiving sunlight currently filling the room and burrowing into my brain.

When I'd been a hopeful adolescent, I'd wanted to change the color scheme of my room, thinking that potential lovers might find the pretty shade unmanly and laugh at me. Black, perhaps. Silver and dark blue.

Well, the green hadn't really made much of a difference, had it? I'd stopped worrying about it once I realized no one would be seeing it after all.

No lovers.

No conclave.

My mother had sent my valet to fetch me rather than waiting for me to run into her sometime during the course of the day, which probably meant a lecture, most likely an expansion on her reasons for keeping me home.

And I'd asked Andreas if his cock got hard.

Fuck, at least I'd given most of the morning a miss. What the bastard gods would've done with a few more hours to torment me, I didn't even want to know.

"Your Highness?" Benetto said. "I have coffee for you."

I yielded to the inevitable and rolled out of bed, groaning.

It took twenty minutes of sipping coffee, Benetto fussing around me and getting my clothes in order, and splashing cold water on my face and neck before I managed to leave my rooms and make my wobbly way to my mother's study.

I tapped lightly, opened the door without waiting for her to answer—one advantage of being the queen's royal son—and walked in to find her dictating a letter to Marko while she paced in front of the hearth, a cup of tea in one hand and the other holding her skirts, red damask today, away from the fire.

"…forward to greeting your representative in the spring. Niko, there you are at last." She fixed her sharp blue eyes on me—and then narrowed them. "Which hedge did you go through backwards, and what kind of bottle were you holding?"

Indignation nearly choked me. Did she really expect me to stay sober after our conversation yesterday? I glanced at Marko, who'd bent over the desk in an apparent effort to make himself invisible. His ears would be flapping, though, damn it.

"Wine," I said succinctly, not trusting myself to say more.

She shook her head and sighed in a way only mothers could, the gesture and the sound enough to send shame for every one of my past misdeeds, real and imagined, slithering down my spine.

"I hope you don't make me regret what I'm about to say to you," she said in a tone that suggested she already did. "I have," and she drew a deep breath, nose in the air as if she smelled something sour, "changed my mind. I will allow you to attend this conclave of yours under certain conditions, which will be enforced without any room for argument or disobedience."

For a long moment, that didn't even penetrate my aching head.

She'd allow me to attend? She'd…changed her mind? What could possibly have…?

"Do you mean it? What chan—I mean, you'll truly allow me to go?" I knew I sounded like a child being offered an unexpected treat. But I couldn't help it. Disbelief and tentative hope and joy trickled down all my nerves like some kind of hangover-destroying magic, my fingers and toes tingling.

My mother offered me a quick smile, though it didn't quite get to her eyes. "I will. But Niko—you have to understand. You will not be in command of your expedition. Andreas will. You will obey him as you would me, and he will have the final say over whether you proceed or return home if travel becomes unwise. If you don't agree to this, you won't go at all. And he'll have my leave to tie you over a horse and drag you home if he must. Don't think you'll overawe him with your rank if it comes to it. He's accustomed to command and he's not easily swayed, young as he is."

That I believed. He certainly hadn't seemed overawed by me in any way so far, not that I'd given him much of a reason to be.

A week ago I'd have been horrified and furious if my mother appointed Andreas not only my nursemaid but my commanding officer on this journey of mine.

Today, after yesterday's despair? It came as such a reprieve I could hardly believe it.

Only what the hell had brought this about? I opened my mouth to ask and then immediately snapped my jaw shut.

No, I needed to get the fuck out of the queen's presence before she changed her royal mind yet again.

"Thank you, Mama," I said. "You know how important this is to me."

"I do," she replied, with a slight softening around the edges of her expression. Gods. She loved me so much. That didn't make her overbearing mothering any less difficult, but I supposed that was what you got when you were born to a queen. "That's why I'm letting you go. Don't disappoint me."

And with that, she turned back to Marko.

I scurried out as she started to dictate again. As soon as I'd shut the door behind me, I slumped against the wall beside it, closing my eyes and sucking in air.

I could go. She was letting me go.

Of course, that meant weeks of being in the closest possible quarters with Andreas…whose cock I'd voiced an entirely inappropriate interest in last night. Not that I'd been actually interested, obviously, but I'd probably made him think so. I'd be lucky if he agreed to go and didn't request a reassignment.

Ugh, I couldn't think about that right now, not with my stomach already churning.

Coffee. I needed much, much more coffee, and something to eat in a bit, and a bath—and to organize my notes! We'd be leaving within a week, gods, I still had so much to do that it made my head spin.

That might've been partly the wine, of course.

I shoved off the wall and down the corridor, detouring at the foot of the stairs to avoid a pair of footmen carrying a large chair down, and going around toward the garden. The fresh air wouldn't do me any harm.

Of course, the fresh air hit me like a slap in the face when I opened the side door, icy cold and bearing a hint of the snow that idiot Gennaro had predicted. The thin linen shirt and light coat Benetto had chosen for me didn't quite cut it, but it didn't matter. I turned my face up to the watery sunlight and smiled, the skin of my face stretching almost painfully.

Coffee.

A quick jaunt around the corner of the east wing of the palace brought me to a small gate that led to the royal family's private gardens, and the guard there murmured a greeting and bowed me through. A few more steps took me to my own terrace stairs.

By the time I got to the top my vision had gone a little sparkly, the exertion of walking up making me lightheaded. I so rarely drank that much wine, and I'd forgotten how miserable the mornings after could be, especially when I didn't have any breakfast.

At the top, I stopped and leaned one hand against the wall, head hanging down. I used the other hand to shield my eyes from the glaring reflection of the sun off of the pale terracotta floor tiles. Who'd glazed and polished them to that ungodly sheen? Fuck.

"Wine gives me a hell of a headache the next day, too," said a deep voice. Andreas's voice.

My brain and spine did their damnedest to leap sideways out of my skin, and I yelped and rocked on my heels and blinked my eyes against the sun—and one of my feet met empty air, and my arms windmilled—

"Fuck," Andreas said, and then an arm like an iron bar clamped around my midsection and yanked me back.

Instead of pinwheeling down the stairs, I slammed into a hard chest and stopped moving, my face mashed into his shoulder. It knocked the wind out of me for a second, and I sucked in a deep breath—of Andreas, richly spicy and faintly like coffee and leather and metal, soothing and warm. My eyes rolled back in my head as all my muscles relaxed. Gods, I needed to lay off the wine next time if it left me this weak.

Andreas turned us, moving me a few stumbling steps until my back met the wall. He didn't let me go, though his fingers flexed against my waist. Damn it, I'd found the perfect spot on his shoulder, that bit of a divot between the bone and a ridge of muscle. It fit my throbbing forehead so nicely.

With great regret, I lifted my head and let it lean back against the much less comfortable wall, looking up into Andreas's tight-lipped face. That jaw muscle of his stuck out again. Apparently I had that effect on him. I resisted the urge to reach up and rub at it. Why hadn't he taken his arm from around me? Did he think I'd tumble right down the stairs again, and then my mother would have him hanged? She wouldn't. Probably.

His face was only inches from mine. At this distance his eyes weren't muddy at all, and they weren't really as dark as I'd thought, either. More of a brandy color shot with copper. Tawny, like his hair and his tanned skin. Stubble gleamed reddish against the column of his throat and the angular line of his jaw.

"Where," I gasped, and cleared my throat. "Where the hell did you come from?"

"The stairs," he said, his voice rumbling through my torso where it pressed against his. "Your Highness."

The vein in the side of my neck pulsed.

"Would it kill you," I ground out, "to answer the question you damn well know I'm actually asking you rather than taking everything so literally?"

His slow, innocent-looking blink, and the way he'd pressed his lips together to keep from smiling, didn't fool me in the slightest.

I quickly tore my eyes away from his lips and met his again.

"Forgive me, Your Highness. I'm a simple soldier. Literal is my specialty."

"Only someone who didn't take anything literally would be able to pretend to as much as you do."

All at once, I couldn't take his nearness, his touch, for one more gods-damned instant, the constriction of being surrounded and hemmed in by Andreas's bigger body making me break out in prickles of sweat down my shoulder blades and a hot flush from my hairline to my chest.

He opened his mouth to reply, but I cut him off with, "Move, will you? I'm not going to fall. I need to sit down."

Slightly contradictory statements, but after a moment's hesitation he slid his arm out from behind me and took a step back, waving his hand out in invitation. I glanced up at his face as I squeezed by. How had he learned to hide his thoughts so well? Especially when he had a very expressive face when he let his feelings show. I couldn't read anything from those steady eyes.

I staggered past him and stopped dead, swallowing hard.

My chaise, where I'd planned to collapse and rest for a bit, looked as inviting as ever: soft, out of the sun, with a table for the coffee Benetto would bring me at my elbow.

Except that I could practically see myself sprawled out across those blue silk cushions, all drunk and sloppy, with Andreas's lean, powerful body bent over me and holding me down.

Right after I asked him if he could get it up.

Heat pooled in my belly, the fiery burn of complete, utter mortification.

What must he think of me? Not that I'd made a habit of giving a damn what the servants and guards thought of me, in large part because I already knew most of them thought I was odd and pitiable and best avoided.

But I found that I cared now.

It had to be because my mother might very well change her mind again if he went to her and told her he wouldn't be able to accompany me to the conclave. If he showed sufficient tact, she probably wouldn't even punish him for it. She'd readily believe I'd pushed a tolerant man past the limits of his patience.

"Something the matter, Your Highness?" His tone gave away as little as his face had.

Yes. Yes, lots of things were the matter, from my insistent memories of my absurd behavior last night, to needing Andreas to agree to go with me to the conclave, and ending with having just been in his arms.

I spun on my heel and nearly tripped over my own feet. "I'm fine!" I said quickly, as he made to lunge forward again. Gods, I wouldn't survive another crushing embrace intended to protect me from my own clumsiness. The embarrassment would kill me. "But—my mother changed her mind. I mean, the queen," I blurted out, and felt my cheeks get even hotter. For fuck's sake, of course he knew who I meant by *my mother*. "I'll be traveling to the conclave after all. The one I mentioned last night, and I'm sure you've heard me speaking about it before."

I paused, trying to gather my wits enough to say what needed to be said. Andreas would have to be informed of his authority over the expedition, and I'd prefer it to come from me rather than from my mother; at least that way, I could frame it as graciously delegating the planning of the journey to someone I considered competent, rather than as my mother putting her untrustworthy adult child under the smothering care of someone *she* considered competent.

The right words didn't come. I'd meant to have another pot of coffee before I even thought about broaching this conversation, hadn't I?

But…why did Andreas look as embarrassed as I felt? With his cheeks all red and his hand fiddling with the hilt of his sword?

He drew himself up and squared his shoulders the way he had the day we met. Only this time, it didn't seem mocking or defensive, but respectful.

I froze, bracing myself. That couldn't be a good sign. It meant he felt guilty.

"I know," he said quietly. "I hope you can forgive me, Your Highness. I'd meant to bring it up myself, but you mentioned it first."

Oh, gods. Definitely guilty. My heart skittered and thumped. Had Andreas already seen my mother somehow, between when I'd spoken to her and now? How the hell…? He wouldn't go. Or he'd talked her out of it.

I stared at him wide-eyed, my throat constricting too much for me to ask him any questions.

"By the look on your face, you're horrified, and I apologize, but Your Highness—you were so unhappy last night." Andreas took a step forward, a hand extended as if he meant to touch me, and then he stopped abruptly and clasped both hands behind him. "It was presumptuous of me to interfere. And even more to accept the queen's terms without speaking to you first. I can't believe she listened to me, to be honest with you. I think perhaps she regretted refusing you and was glad of an excuse to change her mind. Although don't repeat that, I beg you," he added in a rush, grimacing. "Speculating about what's in a queen's mind isn't my place."

My own laugh took me by surprise—and Andreas too, by the way his mouth fell open. But relief had hit me too irresistibly for me to control my reaction.

And Andreas's rueful admission of his own impertinence in thinking about how to manipulate the queen, when I knew full well he didn't regret it at all and only wanted not to be caught, simply amused me too much to hide.

Especially since I agreed completely. As long as it didn't actually amount to treason, queens were to be got around and dodged as much as possible.

Perhaps Andreas would…? But no, I dismissed that idea instantly. He might be willing to discuss my mother's motives, something she wouldn't particularly appreciate, but he wouldn't disobey her and agree to allow me to control the journey behind her back. Not when he'd given her his oath. I knew that much, even though he'd only been my guard for a matter of a fortnight.

And anyway…*you were so unhappy last night.* He'd pitied me enough to go to my mother and ask on my behalf. Cared enough—I'd think of it that way for my own self-respect. Anyway, he'd done it out of loyalty to me, and that had to go both ways.

"I won't tell," I said. "And—thank you." Ought I to apologize for the way I'd behaved last night? Yes, but I couldn't. I might spontaneously combust. I could offer him something else, though, as a tacit acknowledgment that I owed him. "I promise I won't be troublesome on the journey."

That earned me the first real smile I thought I'd seen on Andreas's face: not a grin with an edge to it, and not amusement I suspected of being at my expense. A true, friendly smile that lit up his eyes and dimpled his cheeks and made me blink as if the sun had suddenly gotten brighter.

Had he smiled at Amara like that? No wonder she'd developed a girlish partiality.

"You couldn't be troublesome if you tried," Andreas said, and he actually sounded like he meant it. Of course, he might mean it backhandedly, a commentary on how little trouble he thought he'd have controlling me if he needed to. Probably some of both. "It'll be my pleasure to escort you, Your Highness. Do you want to start planning the journey now? Or wait until you're feeling a little more yourself? You know, I drink ale instead of wine to avoid the headache. You might try it next time. If you're not too royal for ale, that is."

I stared at him. Teasing me. He was *teasing* me. And not in a mean-spirited way, either. My own lips tugged into a smile I couldn't have helped with a knife to my throat.

Well, no wonder my mother had given in to his request, if he'd charmed her like this. Buggering gods. Would all the women in my family end up half in love with this fellow? Save me. I had to keep him away from Philippa.

"This evening," I said. "After supper. No ale, though. I want our wits about us as we plan the route."

Andreas bowed. "As you wish, Your Highness."

I stood there for a long few moments after his quick footsteps had faded away on the path below the terrace.

You were so unhappy last night.

Not anymore. My smile hadn't diminished despite the lingering aches in my stomach and head. I turned away and stepped inside to ring for more coffee, whistling as I went.

Chapter Five

The first few days of the journey were easy enough. We rode out of Surbino's eastern gate and made good time through the well-cultivated district nearest the city, a patchwork of deep-green woods and the brown fallow fields that lay in wait for the fresh, pale grass-green that would begin to peek through within a week of the first real winter rains. When we crested the first ridge of the foothills, we had a perfect view of the silvery ribbon of the Surbino River winding through it all to the gleaming sea beyond. And on the coast where river met sea, the city itself sat glowing in the sunlight, all golden sandstone and whitewash and rich red and blue tile.

When I turned back to the road up the mountain my heart lifted and my spine straightened. I did love my home, but thank the gods I could get *out* for a while.

By the time we reached another, higher vantage point where I could've taken a final look at the city, though, clouds had moved in from the north, wrapping everything in an impenetrable blanket of gray. The rain started slowly, a mere drizzle, but it turned to sleet and then snow as we wound our way up and up, making for the pass that would take us through the mountains and into the kingdom of Rabbion, where the conclave would be held.

Each day the weather worsened. Not enough to necessitate extra nights at any of our stops, but enough that we covered fewer miles than I'd hoped. Five days of slow travel and five nights at variously uncomfortable roadside inns found us just on the other side of the pass, riding carefully and in single file between massive jutting rocks piled with white. More snow blew down on the wind that shrieked and howled through the crevices. We stayed that night at yet another small and cramped hostelry perched on a tiny alpine meadow between huge tumbles of granite. At least they had good stew.

The next day brought more snow, just wet enough that it seeped through my thick woolen coat ever so slowly, allowing me to properly experience each damp, miserable minute of it. I kept my head down, grateful for my broad-brimmed hat. The jaunty feathers Benetto had optimistically attached to it had been discarded days ago. He'd have been terribly dismayed if he hadn't remained home, having come down with a cold in the head the night before our departure.

That had left me with an entourage of seven: the six guards under Andreas's command, who rode fanned out, two with us, two ahead, and two trailing a little behind as a rear guard—and Andreas himself. He stayed beside me whenever the path allowed and immediately in front of me when it didn't, as unruffled as always, seeming not to notice the wet or the cold whatsoever.

Of course he'd traveled, and fought, in much less pleasant conditions than these. During our planning and preparations, looking at maps and discussing inns, the care of horses, and what provisions to carry in case of accident, he'd relaxed enough to sit down and drink coffee with me instead of standing and hovering on the other side of my desk.

And he'd started offering stories from his career as a soldier. He'd begun at the age of fifteen in the service of Duke Treviso, late ruler of the duchy to the north of Surbino. They were constantly embroiled in conflict with the warrior tribes on their northern border, and as a result, Andreas had more experience of real fighting than most of my mother's guards combined.

He'd come to Surbino when Treviso died. Andreas didn't like the new duke.

To be fair, no one liked the new duke. I'd met him when he came on a state visit, and he'd been the handsomest, coldest, and least likable asshole I'd ever had the displeasure of trying to make courteous talk with over a meal.

I'd told Andreas that story in turn, and he'd laughed, a low, friendly rumble of a sound that had me smiling in response.

In short, Andreas and I had come to a sort of equilibrium. Young or not, his experience of life eclipsed mine in every possible area, as I'd assumed it would—except maybe in the entertaining, or boring as the case might be, of rude dukes. That had upset me before, but now that I knew him better I had trouble continuing to resent his authority over me. After all, he'd worked so damn hard, and bled so much, to earn it.

On his side, he politely never brought up nor even appeared to remember the "I bet you can get it up" incident. It had me tossing and turning with embarrassment in the middle of the night, of course. But that was my problem.

So aside from my midnight brooding and my perpetually chilled nose and fingers, nothing went wrong until that sixth day of the journey, when I'd begun to think we were in the clear. I'd even started mentally composing a smug, self-righteous letter to my mother, Philippa, and Gennaro, letting them know that their pessimism had been unnecessary and absurd. As she kissed me farewell, Philippa had been muttering about both human and equine broken legs, avalanches that would bury us alive, and hypothermia. It'd be so satisfying to tell her she'd been wrong.

But in the end, she was right.

It was just that the disaster stemmed from something she'd never have anticipated: a broken leather strap on my saddlebags.

Down in the eastern foothills, the slushy snow had begun to melt further into icy rain. The terrain reminded me very much of home; this side of the mountains didn't differ too much from Surbino, which occupied part of the western side of a long isthmus, with a mountain range running down the middle like an exposed spine. On this side, another sea lay only fifty miles or so to the east.

At last the rain slowed, and the clouds thinned, a pale shaft of sunlight peeking through a small gap.

I whipped off my hat and turned my face up into the light, feeling like a potted plant that'd been left to wither in a dim corner of the palace reaching its pitiful vines toward the window.

"Your skin can burn even when it's cold or the sun's barely out, especially at this elevation," Andreas said, reining slightly closer to me.

Not that he ever went far. He'd been constantly within six feet of me, except when I retired for the night—and even then, I suspected he'd spent as much time dozing in the corridor outside my room as sacked out in his own. The only night he'd slept well, I was pretty sure, had been last night, when we'd all had to double up. He'd laid out a blanket on the floor of my room in front of the door and snored softly until dawn.

"Take it from me," he went on. "Redheads know everything about sunburns. That's why I'm so tanned. I had to burn a hundred times first. Made my first couple of campaigns miserable. You'd think it'd be the danger, but no. It's always something like a sunburn on the back of your neck."

"I believe it," I said. "I think I could probably face another man with a sword. But I'd end up deserting if it got too uncomfortable. Maybe I need to toughen up a bit," I said, turning to him with a grin. "I should leave my hat off and see if I can get a little less pale by the time we go home. I look like someone who's never set foot outside a library."

Andreas smiled, the nice one that creased his cheek. "You look perf— pale, yes, but there's nothing wrong with that. You should keep your hat on. If you burn, you'll be uncomfortable for days." He turned back to the road, tapping his reins and going a few feet ahead of me for no apparent reason other than ending the conversation he'd initiated.

Well, all right then. He could be so strange sometimes.

Or maybe he wanted to go single file here, though two could fit abreast. The ground fell away steeply to our right, studded with jutting boulders and brushy plants clinging to the hillside, all of it absolutely soaked and muddy. It looked like it could give way at any moment.

As I nudged Fluffy to the left, my saddle shifted. A moment later, my right-hand saddlebag tore off and fell. I lunged for it, crying out, but my fist clenched on empty air, and the bag went tumbling down the slope and out of sight.

Andreas was at my side in an instant, one hand on my reins and the other holding his sword, already out of the scabbard. "What happened? Are you hurt? You're dead white, not pale. Your Highness? Are you injured?"

His eyes darted from me to our surroundings, clearly torn between looking for the threat and examining me.

"No," I said hoarsely. I squeezed my eyes shut for a moment. There could be a sheer drop just out of sight. A river down in the gorge. Anything. Or my bag could be right there within reach if I simply leaned over the edge. I had to keep it together. "No, I'm not hurt. But my saddlebag fell down the hill."

Andreas relaxed visibly, his shoulders losing their hard tension. "Then there's no problem, is there? You're carrying your notes in your coat, aren't you? We can replace anything else in the next town."

If he'd been right, if the only things in that bag had been clothing and oddments, then I'd have been touched—and a little surprised—by how well he understood me. My notes were terribly important, and things in and of themselves didn't matter that much to me.

But my notes were only the second most important thing I'd brought with me.

"I need the bag, Andreas." My voice came out thin and shaky. The potion, at least in my case—every twilight mage had a different cycle— had to be taken every forty-two hours like clockwork to keep the pain at bay, down from the forty-three hours it'd been a couple of years ago. And it'd been…fuck, it'd been thirty-five hours already, give or take. I'd need to get out my pocket watch to confirm it. I glanced around; the rearguard had ridden up to overtake us and lingered a few feet away.

Leaning down to put my face near Andreas's felt so intimate, but I simply couldn't have any more people than absolutely necessary knowing about this. Andreas leaned in to meet me. "My potion is in that bag," I whispered.

Watching his expression change might've been fascinating if I hadn't been able to feel my heartbeat vibrating in my extremities from the force of my terror and anxiety. Andreas's smile faded, and his brow furrowed, lips pressing together tightly.

"Fuck," he said. "Sorry, Your Highness," he added.

"Don't apologize. 'Fuck' sums it up." I tried to smile and failed.

Andreas nodded, sheathed his sword, and strode away. "I need ropes!" he called out to the guards. "Find a good anchor. Get the horses out of the way for now…"

Andreas's deep, commanding voice washed over me, sanding the rough edges off of my fear. I took a moment to bow my head over Fluffy's neck, breathing deeply, shoving away my incipient panic. The last time I'd forgotten my dose had ensured I'd never forget again. Searing agony, like flame racing along every vein and nerve in my body, my lungs compressed, my throat raw from screaming, every muscle cramping as I curled into myself and thrashed…

Gods, I couldn't go through that again.

And it sounded like I might not need to, because Andreas said, "I can see it. It's on that rock. Give me the end of the rope."

I looked up to find him shrugging out of his coat and then unbuckling his sword, making to tie the rope around his own waist. And I froze, my blood running cold.

"Don't," I said. And then more loudly, "Stop!"

Andreas turned back to me, eyebrows raised. "I can see the bag, Your Highness. I'll have it for you in a moment."

I'd swung my leg over Fluffy before I even realized I was moving, dropping into the thick mud of the road with a squelch and slogging to the edge of the cliff. Andreas dodged in front of me, an arm out to keep me from getting too close. With a twinge of irritation, I craned my neck. Yes, there it was, about five yards down, tauntingly safe on a flat outcropping of stone. It had landed perfectly; two feet to either side and it'd have been gone forever. But to reach it, Andreas would have to scramble down over a truly filthy and slippery stretch of mud, climb around several large rocks, and push his way through a thorny bramble.

Damn it. "If it's not safe for me to stand by the edge, it's hardly safe for you to climb down with that stupid rope around you! The ground looks so saturated those rocks might not hold your weight. And do any of you even know how to tie a decent knot?"

"I do," Carlo, one of the older guards, piped up from behind me. "My whole family are fishermen. Grew up on a boat. I can tie a knot that won't unravel, no-how."

"You sound like the queen," Andreas said to me, his eyes glinting with mischief. "She listed a great many ways we could all die on this journey when I spoke to her."

Well, damn and blast it—*damn* him.

"I do not sound like my mother!"

"You look like her, too, Your Highness. With your nose in the air like that. Very regal. I'm going down the hill, Carlo will tie the knots, and it'll be fine. Besides," he added, pitching his voice low for my ears only, "there's really no choice. And I'm not going to ask one of the men to do something I won't do myself."

"But that's precisely what I'm doing!" I protested. "I ought to be the one to climb down. I'm a lot smaller and lighter than you are, too. Out of all of us, I'm the best—"

"Out of all of us, you're the worst possible choice, for reasons that are glaringly obvious and don't need to be discussed," he said briskly, although he had an odd look in his eyes that didn't quite match his firm tone. "Besides, you're not in command of this expedition, remember? So you're not making anyone do anything, and that logic doesn't apply. Now stand back, Your Highness. If you please."

That wasn't a request, and we both knew it.

And I stepped back, obeying him instantly without any resistance, a strange heat pooling in my belly. Embarrassment? Shame? Both, maybe. But when he spoke like that, without the slightest question that he'd be obeyed, no one could possibly have the will to argue.

He looked as confident as he sounded, standing there all broad-shouldered and sturdy, his black tunic and trousers and tall black riding boots silhouetting his muscular frame against the snow. Carlo tested the knots several times, tying the other end of the rope around a rock on the other side of the road, and two of the guards took hold of it to pay it out as Andreas descended.

The clouds had crowded back in again above us, driven by the icy wind that swept through our group and set me shivering. The horses stamped, their breath making even larger plumes than the humans'.

Perhaps it owed something to the circumstances of my birth, but I'd always been superstitious. Twilight mages had a unique view on the mercurial cruelty of the gods, after all, and we tended to pay more attention to omens and instincts and that prickling sensation on the back of the neck that indicated trouble brewing.

I had it now. Badly. The air practically crackled.

And Andreas was making a joke, disappearing over the edge of the cliff while the guards chuckled.

A drop of water hit my nose. Then two on my scalp. And then the heavens opened up again with a roar, water sluicing down and drenching all of us instantly, icy cold and so thick I could hardly breathe. The guards cursed as their hands slipped on the rope. Andreas had to be blinded by this, his feet sliding out from under him…

"Andreas!" I shouted through the din, barely able to hear myself. Something terrible was about to happen, I could feel it… "Come back up!"

I stumbled forward, the mud sucking at my boots, water sheeting into my eyes, chilled to the bone and shivering.

And then Carlo shouted and dived for the edge of the cliff, his face a white rictus. Something flipped through the air: fuck, a trailing end of rope. The rope had broken. Carlo flung himself onto his belly in the mud and reached—and missed. The rope slid out of sight.

Andreas. He'd fallen. Gone, and all for me, and I could've borne the pain of missing my dose, but he'd given his life for me and I didn't think I could bear the guilt of it—I skidded to a stop beside Carlo and leaned over the side, chest clenched tight with horror.

And I saw him. He'd fallen where my saddlebag had. On top of it, in fact.

As I stared down at him, he pushed himself up on his elbows and grimaced, shaking his head and spitting out water.

The rain slowed as abruptly as it'd come down, the cloudburst over. It still pattered down on us, but quietly enough that I heard him call out, "Next time, let's worry less about the knots and more about the rope, hmm?"

Beside me, Carlo let out a hysterical-sounding whoop of laughter, rubbing a mud-drenched hand over his mud-drenched face. He couldn't have been covered in more of the stuff if he'd tried.

The others came forward in a body, Sergeant Salvius taking charge and organizing them to lower another rope, anchor it firmly, move that rock out of the way, damn you…

My heart galloped so quickly it could've beaten any horse in my mother's racing stables, so much that my vision went gray and I couldn't feel my fingers and toes. I tottered a few steps away and dropped down on a boulder, my face in my hands.

Andreas was alive.

He'd retrieve my potion.

Everything was fine.

But the sensation on the back of my neck, and the chill running down my spine, hadn't abated in the least.

Of course, that could be the freezing rain.

But I didn't think so. The gods weren't done fucking with us yet, I just knew it.

Chapter Six

"You're lucky to have made it here," the landlady said, bustling ahead of us as she led the way upstairs to our rooms. "That last switchback on the way down into town always goes out in this much rain. It won't be passable by morning. They'll have to bring engineers or mages in to clear it. And they say it might snow again tonight, too."

I wasn't paying much attention, barely able to lift my feet from one stair to the next. A combination of cold, wet, exhaustion, and the aftermath of several different shocks had left me with my head swimming and every joint wobbling.

"We're very glad you can put us up for the night, thank you," Andreas said from behind me. "My lord's worn out."

We'd agreed that it'd be better if I traveled incognito. It still sounded very strange to hear myself referred to that way.

"Oh yes, you all look done in," she said, clucking a bit. "I'll have hot water up for you in no time at all. And you may be visiting us for a few nights or more, you know, if you were planning on going east. The river's flooding."

She finally stopped nearly at the very end of the narrow corridor, and

I almost crashed into her. The gloomy shade of dark green on the walls made it impossible to see where I was going, even with the few lamps along the corridor.

"Here's your room, your lordship," she said, bobbing a curtsey and letting the door swing open. "Best in the house."

"It's very nice," I said, though I hadn't seen it yet and couldn't care less. "Thank you."

I staggered through the doorway. A maid or someone had already lit a fire and a lamp, and I immediately collapsed into a chair next to the hearth. My wet clothes would need to come off, and the quicker the better, but I simply didn't have the strength. Damn Benetto for catching cold, anyway. My clothes instantly started to steam, and it made matters even worse.

Heavy footsteps and a couple of soft thumps sounded from my right: Andreas bringing my bags.

"You need to get dry, Your Hi—my lord," he said, clearly mindful of the open door. Good for him. I didn't have the energy to remember my own name, let alone someone else's fake title. "Do you need—" He stopped abruptly. "I'll be next door. I'll be back to look in on you in a few minutes."

The flames crackled and spat merrily, and the door clicked as Andreas left.

Do you need probably referred to helping me get undressed. Fuck. I shook my head, shoved myself up out of the chair, and creakily bent to open my bags. Nothing could possibly be more motivating than the prospect of Andreas, all big and silent, tugging off my boots, running his hands down my legs to strip my stockings…I'd die of awkwardness.

The room boasted a decent-sized dressing table by the window, so I hoisted one bag up there and then went back for the other, the one that had fallen.

As I set it on the table, I caught a whiff of mint and vervain.

My cheeks went burning hot and my whole body flushed. Damn it, damn it, please no…

Fumbling, moving too hastily for any kind of speed, I tore at the bag's fastenings, cutting my finger on the buckle and cursing. The waxed leather saddlebags had been carefully crafted to be waterproof and to seal tightly. That had kept the smell mostly inside.

But as I tugged it open at last, the scent rose up so strongly it choked me, and my head went floaty.

I knew what I'd see when I set the lamp on the windowsill above and looked closely in the depths of the bag, but it still sent another shock through me. When I pulled out the stack of shirts on top, I saw that the velvet-lined steel case holding my potion bottles had torn in half at the hinges, the lid hanging askew—probably, I realized, from Andreas falling on top of the bag rather than from the original drop off the cliff. And all three of the bottles were broken. Two had shattered completely, and the third had cracked.

Oh gods, perhaps, perhaps—and yes, most of that third bottle had leaked out, soaking the velvet and my clothes. But a few tablespoons remained in the bottom, less than half a dose. It'd keep me sane until tomorrow night, probably.

And then…

The bastard gods definitely hadn't been done with me today.

I didn't know how long I stood there staring into the bag, shivering with cold in my wet clothing, and seeing and noticing nothing around me—but that was how Andreas found me. His pounding on the door and calling out for me had vaguely registered, but not as anything important. It wasn't until he took me by the shoulders and tugged me around to face him that I snapped out of it a little bit, blinked, and focused on his intent, serious eyes and worried frown.

Those big hands on my shoulders transmitted heat even through my clothes, the only two points of anything but frozen chill on my body.

"Your Highness, you need to change, you need to get warm," he said. "What the hell have you been—"

His impertinent scolding didn't even matter at this point. "The bottles broke, Andreas." My tone came out so flat and dull that I sounded like I was commenting on the wallpaper.

"—doing in here—they *what?*" He probably didn't even notice the way his hands tightened on my shoulders, tightened until his grip hurt. "The bottles. Your potion. Those bottles?"

"Yes," I said, through lips almost too numb to form the word. All of me felt that way, down to my gods-cursed soul. "Those bottles. Of course those bottles!"

With a wrench, I pulled myself out of his grasp and turned away, planting my fists on the table and letting my head hang down, because it was either that or collapse into his chest and sob like a baby.

Andreas had risked his life to retrieve the potion for me. He'd almost died. For a moment, I'd thought he had.

And it hadn't made any difference at all.

But I couldn't give up, damn it. We'd made it to a decent-sized town, at least; Perona serviced all of the trade that went over the pass. Other routes might be more popular, but this one still had its share of caravans and travelers, not to mention a respectable population.

There might be an apothecary here capable of making more.

"Do you think—" I began, at the same moment Andreas said, "Your Highness, I think—"

We both stopped. The weight of his gaze prickled the back of my neck, and the heat of him spread down my back. He stood so close behind me that he could've shifted his weight and been pressing against me, so close that I almost didn't have room to turn around again.

My breath came faster as I said, "Do you think you could go out and—it'll be a miserable errand, in the dark, in the freezing rain. And probably pointless, too. To look for a mage or an apothecary, someone who might have a stock of what I need?"

"I'll go at once, if you promise me you'll change into dry clothes and get warm while I'm gone. Falling ill with pneumonia won't help the situation. And if there's no one here in town, I swear to you I'll go wherever I need to," he added in a rush, for once sounding less than calm and in control. "I don't care what that woman said about the flooding, my horse and I can swim the river. I won't sleep until I find someone and bring back what you need. Please don't worry, Your Highness."

Oh, for—he didn't understand a fucking thing about it, and yet he'd be willing to risk his life, again, on a fool's errand. Didn't he have any common sense at all? Something warm ignited just below my breastbone. Annoyance, or gratitude? Both?

I turned, forgetting how close he was, and glared at him. Andreas actually rocked back on his heels. Well, I'd learned my glare from my mother the queen. He ought to.

He was still only inches from me. I had to brace my hands on the edge of the table behind me and tip my chin up to meet his dark, troubled gaze.

"You don't think that you trying to swim a horse through a flooded fucking river would worry me, Andreas? You wouldn't send a man to do what you wouldn't do yourself. Now it's my turn. I won't allow it, and I don't give a fuck who's nominally in charge of this expedition."

A smile lit his eyes and teased at the corners of his mouth. He leaned down, a shuffle of his boots bringing him impossibly closer. "Nominally," he repeated. "No. Your Highness. I'm factually in charge, and if I want to swim a flooded fucking river I damn well will, especially if it—if it's for you. Are we clear? I—gave my oath to the queen, that I'd bring you home safely."

"Oh," I gasped, as all the air left my lungs in a rush. His oath. To my mother. For a moment, I'd almost thought—but of course that was why he'd gone down the cliff, and of course that was why he'd swim a river. I closed my eyes for a moment and gathered my wits, opening them to say, "I'll write home when the road's clear. To suggest you receive a commendation."

For a moment he went very still. And then, at last, he stepped back, clasping his hands behind him. "I'd be honored, Your Highness," he said. "In the meantime, I need to earn it. I'll ask our landlady first, and I'll go and make other inquiries here first, of course. But I'll go farther afield in the morning if I must."

Andreas wouldn't be swayed by attempts to pull rank on him, obviously. And so long as he considered himself honor-bound to die for me in order to keep his vow to my mother, asking him to reconsider wouldn't work either.

But I couldn't allow it.

Which meant I had to tell him the degrading truth, no matter how it scraped my throat raw to choke it out.

"No," I said. "You shouldn't take the risk. Because it wouldn't do any good anyway. Days before you return, if you return at all, I'll either be dead of an apoplexy from the strain of my symptoms or I'll be climbing onto a stranger's cock." Andreas's mouth dropped open. He shut it again. I smiled sourly, the twist of my lips feeling like the precursor to tears. "Unless there's someone with the necessary skills and ingredients here, I'm—" *Fucked*. I swallowed the word down along with a mouthful of bile, my esophagus spasming painfully. It applied both figuratively and all too literally.

Andreas's face had set into hard lines, a granite carving of a soldier rather than the man who'd smiled and joked with me all the way over the mountains.

"Then I'd best be about it," he said. "Please, I hate to belabor the point, but will you please care for yourself in the meantime? Get warm. Eat. Rest, Your Highness. Promise me."

"I'm fine," I protested—and then shuddered with cold, a full-body tremor.

"Obviously," he said dryly. "Promise. Or I'll—I'll send that landlady up here with instructions to chivvy you into bed with a hot brick."

That startled a laugh out of me despite everything. "Gods forbid. I promise, Andreas. Just chivvy her into getting me that hot water. And— thank you. You need to warm up and eat and rest too, you know."

"Plenty of time for that when you're safe," he said offhandedly as he turned for the door. He opened it, stepped through, and then paused. "Don't drink any wine, please."

Before I could do more than gasp in indignation, he was gone.

And with his confident, bracing presence went any of the hope that I'd tried to nurture. I looked around the tidy little room, taking in the simple table and chair, the narrow rope-frame bed with its mattress full of straw, the rag rug on the plank floor. Andreas had traveled this way before, and he'd led us to this inn specifically, saying that it was the best of the four in town.

Which didn't really give me a lot of faith that specialized potions for mages who made up only a small percentage of magically-born people, not to mention the population at large, would be easily available.

Or available at all.

Gennaro and my mother's court physician made my potion together, from rare components sourced from all over the place. It wasn't an easy thing to compound even if you knew how and had everything to hand.

A knock at the door spurred me into action, but no amount of hustle and bustle of maids and the landlady, of food and tea laid on the table and hot water poured into a basin, of that heated brick Andreas had joked about being put into my bed, could distract me from the clock ticking away in the back of my mind.

One hour until I was due for my regular dose. I had half of that. If I waited a little, took it late…but that wouldn't help me either. Some dawn mages had a much more gradual onset of symptoms when they neglected our gods-inflicted necessity, either to "receive the proxy of the god Ennolu's blessing and possession," as the ancient text the priests used so inaccurately described it, or to take the potion that stunted our magic and prevented it from attacking us from the inside. They might have hours, or even a few days, from the beginning of their pains to a point of complete incapacitation.

For me, it took minutes, half an hour at most. And I cycled more quickly than most, too. My research had spanned every written account of twilight mages and their lives I could get my hands on, and as far as I could tell, the range was anywhere from a day and a half to ten days or so. I barely made it over the minimum.

I tossed my wet clothes out the door into the hall, where a maid called out her assurance that they'd be clean and dry in the morning, and stood before the fire to scrub myself down.

The potion would be best taken with my supper. Forty-two hours with a normal dose. Twenty-one, perhaps, with this. By early evening tomorrow I'd be in agony.

I'd be begging someone, anyone, to fuck me and come inside me and end the pain.

Fresh clothes and a glass of wine, with a mental not-terribly-polite salute to Andreas, didn't help much. My supper stuck in my throat like sawdust and the wine was thin. The potion tasted like it always did, heavily herbal and with a bitter tang that set my teeth on edge. I tipped my head back and held the bottle over my mouth for ages, letting every last possible drop slide onto my tongue.

And then I had nothing to do but wait, watching the fire dance and listening to the rain pattering steadily on the roof. A few stray drops made their way down the chimney and hissed in the flames like tiny snakes. Someone laughed in the corridor, and a door slammed in the distance.

And I waited. Twenty hours to go. And then nineteen. And then…I poured another glass of wine, put another log on the fire, and settled in for the night.

Andreas might have told me to rest, but I knew I wouldn't close my eyes for a moment until he returned.

Chapter Seven

Something startled me out of a shallow slumber, and I sat bolt upright in the chair with a grunt of surprise. Riddled with nerves or not, it seemed I hadn't been a match for my exhaustion. The fire had burned down to embers. I glanced to the window, a faint gray square in the gloom, the edges all patterned with frost.

Dawn, or close. Ironic, maybe—or very sensible and understandable, take your pick—but I hated the early morning.

A soft tap sounded on the door. Or another one, probably.

I sprang up, or tried to, but my stiff knees made it more of a stagger. The latch stuck, because nothing ever worked in the morning, but after a moment of cursing I pulled the door open.

Andreas, as I'd expected, and he looked very much the worse for wear: pale, with grooves around his mouth and purple shadows under his eyes, his auburn hair a damp and spiky mess and the shoulders of his coat dusted with snow.

"Come in, come on, I'll stir the fire," I rasped, cleared my throat—gods, I hated waking up so early, and I felt like I hadn't slept at all—and stood aside to let him in.

It was a testament to how tired he was that he didn't argue or thank me or demur, but simply nodded and went to the fireplace, propping an elbow on the mantel and slumping there.

But of course, he hadn't gone so far as to sit down. I rolled my eyes at his back. "Andreas, sit down before you fall down."

"There's only one chair, Your Highness," he mumbled into his arm.

"Sit down and tell me what you found, if anything. That's a royal command."

Because he pushed off the mantel and collapsed into the chair as bidden, I chose to ignore his muttered, "Gods forbid I disobey one of those."

I took up the poker and a few sticks from the basket and started to revive the fire. Andreas sighed, shifted in the chair, and then sighed again.

"This poker's going through your forehead if you don't tell me how you spent the night." Fuck, that sounded— "What you found, overnight," I said in a rush. "Did you find an apothecary or not?"

He hesitated so long that I'd gotten the blaze going again and turned around, the poker clutched in my fist, before he spoke.

Andreas looked up at me, expression bleak. "Yes and no, but considering we have a deadline, mostly no," he said heavily. "There is a physician in town who's made the potion before and is perfectly willing to do so again. I rousted him out of bed and listened to a half-hour tirade on inconsiderate assholes with no sense of decency before I could even get him to get to the point, though. Fuck, I'm sorry, Your Highness." He scrubbed a hand over his face. "He's missing some of the herbs he needs. Long story short, there's an herbalist who lives out in the woods, and she'll have it all, but it'll take a day to get it. And then another day at least for him to brew it. We're looking at tomorrow night at the earliest."

Gods, I wished we'd had a second chair after all, because my knees didn't want to hold me up.

That was better news than I'd expected, honestly.

But it wasn't good enough, and my brain buzzed with calculations that it was far too tired to perform adequately. That would be…a full day and night between when my symptoms started and when the physician could deliver the potion. Twenty-four hours of being in unbearable agony, racked with fever and shooting pains in every muscle, my bones feeling like they were melting and shattering all at once.

I hadn't endured it in a long time, but I'd spent years suffering from the pains on and off as my cycle changed and settled, as Gennaro and my team of physicians found the right dosage and the right schedule through unavoidable but torturous experimentation.

There were other combinations of herbs that would put me in a state of such deep unconsciousness that I wouldn't have to bear it; I could simply wait it out and be awoken when the potion was ready for me.

Except that my body would still be suffering the effects of the gods' curse, and I'd be lucky to wake up at all. That apoplexy I'd mentioned to Andreas would be likelier than not.

On the other hand, a theoretical middle ground existed. My research into my condition had encompassed some herbs and medicines, though they weren't my greatest area of expertise, and I knew of mixtures that would slow the heart, cool the body, thin the blood. Perhaps it wouldn't be enough to spare me all of the pain, but that physician might be able to concoct something, while we waited for the components for my potion, to keep me alive and somewhat sane in the meantime.

"Your Highness? Your Highness!" I snapped my gaze back to Andreas—back to the real world in front of me, and away from the horrid visions in my mind. "Are you—please tell me it's not starting now."

"No," I said, and choked on a bubble of hysterical laughter. "No, I took what was left in the last bottle to buy some time. And believe me, you'll know." I dropped the poker to the hearth with a clatter, too exhausted to bend over and put it down quietly, and made myself jump. Fucking hell. "I don't think you understand what's going to happen to me in about twelve hours. What you'll be dealing with when it does, if you mean to watch over me."

"Of course I mean to watch over you, you don't have a chance in hell of getting rid of me, and you need to explain it to me. And will you—I can't sit down while you stand there looking like you're about to fall over."

Andreas stood up so abruptly I didn't have time to move, and since I'd pulled the chair near to the fireplace, he was suddenly *right there,* so close we were nearly touching. The strong column of his throat filled my vision. I blinked, swayed, and put a hand up to steady myself without thinking. It landed on his chest, my fingers digging into the body-warm, snow-damp wool of his tunic.

"Your Highness," he said softly, very close to my ear. As if he'd bent down a little to speak to me. His breath ruffled my hair. "Please. Tell me how to help you."

"You've already done as much as anyone could do. More. You need to—" *Put your arms around me, pat me on the back, and tell me it'll be all right. Pour me more wine until I pass out.* "—go and get some sleep. I'm going to—to catch a few hours too. And then we'll go and see that physhin, I mean, doctor, because I want to ask him for something to help me through the next day. All right?"

Every word had started to feel thick and heavy on my tongue, harder and harder to push out of my mouth. My eyelids drooped. From the knees down, my legs were useless lumps.

"All right," Andreas said softly. His voice dipped into an even deeper register as he added, "Let me help you to bed, if nothing else, Your Highness."

Any protest was beyond me. I nodded, more of a droop against his chest than anything. He shuffled me across the room and more or less just let me tip over onto the bed, the ropes creaking beneath me and the mattress leaping up to catch me. My cheek hit the pillow, and I sank down and down.

I was out before I even heard him leave the room.

Andreas and I returned to the inn around teatime, just as more freezing rain began to patter down. He'd woken me a little bit past noon by sending a maid to my room with coffee and pastries, a choice I thoroughly approved in every possible way.

We hadn't bothered taking out the horses, simply walking the ten minutes to Doctor Serrano's practice, and the visit had been short. The doctor himself had been out attending a birth. I'd asked his young assistant for advice and had been referred to a magical apothecary a few streets over; fifteen minutes later, Andreas and I were on our way back, and I had a small paper-wrapped packet of bottles, each one a different type of mild sedative or reliever of pain.

I could only pray one or more of them would be enough to get me through. Though I'd read about them, I'd never used drugs to dull the effects before. I'd always taken a suppressing potion instead. And when my caretakers had been learning how to dose me appropriately with that, they couldn't risk mixing it with anything else. Besides which, strong drugs like these could kill a man if used too frequently or in great quantities. In all ways, this would be a new kind of experiment. Oh, what joy.

The wet and cold had the advantage of being at least a little bracing, the wind whipping some sensation into my face and the walk making blood flow through my stiff limbs.

I had about three hours, probably, before I collapsed into a sweaty, moaning mess.

Denial had hit me hard, though. In the light of day, with the bustle of a busy town all around me, my situation didn't seem real. As we turned into the inn's small courtyard, one of the stable boys jogged past us, whistling and smiling despite how cold and damp he looked. He called out a friendly greeting to someone passing by driving a mule and a wagon. The shops across the street had their doors closed against the weather, but their windows were lit and bells jangled as people went in and out.

All of them had normal lives, daily activities, errands to run. They'd be going home shortly, shaking out their coats and stamping off their boots and stirring up the fire, settling down for a quiet evening.

At that moment I could almost feel like one of them, stepping into the inn with my parcel under my arm and anticipating a hot cup of tea.

That sensation of pleasant normality sat uneasily on top of the tight knot in the pit of my stomach, and it dissipated completely once the door of my room shut behind us and Andreas said, without preamble, "How long do you have? And what's going to happen, exactly? I need to know, Your Highness. No more avoiding the question."

Andreas leaned back against the door, one ankle propped against the other and arms crossed. That particular pose cast his tall, lean body, wide shoulders, and heavy biceps into sharp relief. Did he do it on purpose? Or could he possibly be unaware of how he looked? Had he intended to block my only means of escape from a conversation I desperately didn't want to have?

To delay just a few moments longer, I busied myself with setting the package on the table, undoing the string, and taking out the bottles, lining them up neatly in a row.

When I looked up I found Andreas's eyes fixed on me and his jaw set. He hadn't so much as twitched, and he had the air of a man who could maintain his current position for the foreseeable future, outwaiting any stalling tactics I might attempt to employ.

Well, he'd done a lot of guard duty. He probably could.

Damn it.

I swallowed hard around the lump in my throat.

No choice. "I assume you already know that my magic's cursed. That without the potion, or, or other means, it eats me alive from the inside."

"I know what everyone knows, and I've also read anything I could find in the palace library," he said. The expression on my face must have told him what I thought clearly enough, because he quirked a half-smile and said, "Yes, I spend time reading, and yes, I take my job seriously. I didn't think I could protect you unless I knew what I was dealing with. So I'm aware your magic will kill you if it's left uncontrolled, and I know it hurts like hell. But I'm not sure about the timing or the details. The Temple texts were all about Ennolu and Dromos squabbling over who's more powerful, and everything else was incredibly vague."

"Most of the really useful books on the topic are in my rooms, actually, not the main library. You should've asked me." My voice came out all soft and husky. He'd truly researched my condition. No one outside of my family, or those whose occupation it was to know, like mages and physicians, had ever bothered to try to understand. No friends. No lovers. No one but Andreas.

His cheek dimpled as his smile widened. "So you could've stonewalled me like you're doing now, Your Highness? I'm sure that would've been extremely helpful."

"You—fuck you," I sputtered, and Andreas laughed, head tipped back against the door, eyes half-lidded and still intently focused on my face. An amused predator. I shivered a little.

Damn it to hell, didn't he understand how incredibly difficult this was for me? That this shame, this weakness, had shaped my entire life, made me the lonely and frankly unhappy man I was?

"I'm not stonewalling you. I'm—fuck it." I closed my eyes for a moment, gathering my strength. Seriously, fuck it. He wanted to know? I'd damn well tell him. "All right. Fine. In an hour, maybe a little more, I'll double over in agony when all my muscles start to cramp. I'll get shooting pains along every one of my bones, and my veins will pulse. My body will heat up. And I'll get this ache—"

That was it. No more words were coming out. My tongue simply wouldn't move.

"Tell me," Andreas said.. And he used that voice of his, the one he brought out when he had to direct his subordinates, when an emergency situation required absolute command. "Whatever it is, say it, Your Highness."

His eyes gleamed coppery in the pale light through the window behind me. I couldn't look away from them.

And I couldn't resist him, either.

"Inside me," I whispered. "Inside, where—I need it. Someone. Need to be—you know what dawn mages need if they don't have a potion for it, Andreas!"

Everyone knew what dawn mages needed, because it was the most salacious detail in the Temple texts. All human magic had been gifted to us by Dromos, god of the night, as a way to gain more followers and increase his own power compared to Ennolu, ruler of the daytime sky. Ennolu had been less than pleased, and he took his revenge by cursing mages born at the times of transition between his power and Dromos's. All mages were born at night, but those born just at dawn, as Dromos yielded, were doomed to yield themselves, and their magic, in order to survive. And those born at dusk could only control their magic through accepting the surrender of another.

When I'd been younger, I'd wished with all my heart that if I couldn't have been born a normal mage or without any magic at all, I could at least have been a dusk mage. With maturity had come the realization that it might be even worse in some ways.

In the end, all of us were Ennolu's cursed playthings.

And anyone literate, devout, interested in sex, or any combination knew all about it. The Temple published their doctrines widely. Besides, almost everyone was interested in sex.

"Yes," Andreas said, still unblinking, still unmoving, still implacably focused on me. His voice dipped to a deep, rumbling register that spread through every part of me. "I've read everything the Temple's published about it, and I've heard all the rumors." Hopefully they weren't rumors specifically about me. "I wasn't sure if that—if you felt it like that, and I didn't want to assume. Now I know. But that's not all, is it? Tell me the rest."

It was not all, and I couldn't possibly look him in the eyes while I told him. I stared down at the table, tracing the grain of the wood with a finger. He had to know. His job, generally speaking, was to protect me from anyone else who might want to hurt me.

Tonight, and until the potion arrived, his job would be to protect me from myself.

Gods, the thought of Andreas seeing me like that, of what he'd have to do, made my flesh try to crawl off my bones and jump out the window. How much would he despise me?

"You don't have to do this," I blurted out, meeting his eyes at last.

"This is going to be horrible. For both of us. I wouldn't blame you if you wanted nothing to do with it. With me." I sucked in a deep breath and dug my fingertips into the table to brace myself. There wasn't any way to say this but bluntly. "It's an irresistible compulsion, to try to have someone relieve the pain. If you stay, I'll beg you to fuck me. When you refuse, then I'll try to get out of the room and go find someone who will. You'll need to restrain me. You'll probably need to gag me, too, because I'll be screaming the house down."

Andreas frowned and pushed off the door, uncrossing his arms and advancing on me, a slow prowl that nearly had all of me trying to leap out the window. He stopped a foot away, head cocked, examining my face. The metallic glint in his eyes mesmerized me.

"Your Highness," he said at last, after the sound of my own rough breaths had started to drive me mad, "there's no power on this earth or above it that could make me abandon you. Do you understand?" He leaned down a little, and said, almost roughly, "I'm sworn to protect you and I fucking will. And—I promised the queen, but she's not the one who matters right now. So I'm promising you. I'm yours. I'll take care of you no matter what. You have my word."

I gazed up into his eyes. The rest of the world, outside of Andreas, faded away. His breath warmed my face and his body's nearness warmed mine all the way down.

I'm yours. There's no power on this earth or above it that could make me abandon you. No one could doubt his sincerity. And no one had ever spoken to me like that. I could almost believe it had more to do with me, Nikola, a mage and a man, than with my title or my mother's authority.

Besieged by that earnest promise, my defenses crumbled into dust.

"You'll be so disgusted, Andreas," I whispered. "You'll hate me. And then I'd—"

"Never," he said, without any hesitation, saving me from whatever folly might have tripped off my tongue next.

"But—"

"Never," he repeated. "No, shut your mouth—with all respect,

Your Highness. Enough. You can't get rid of me. Now I'm going to go downstairs and send up a maid with a tea tray and another chair, if you don't mind, and I'm going to clear as many guests out of this wing of the building as I can with persuasion, intimidation, and bribery. All right? And then I'll be back. And I'll take care of you."

I opened my mouth, and Andreas added, "If you're not about to say, 'Yes, Andreas, I'll drink my tea and calm down until you come back,' don't say anything at all."

The hot tightness in my chest and my belly almost didn't allow me to say anything at all, but I managed, "Yes, Andreas."

He nodded. "Good. I'll be back soon."

When he'd left, I stood staring at the empty air where he'd been a moment ago. My mind seemed to have gone blank; it had so much to do that it'd stopped working entirely.

At last I shook my head and took out my watch. Four o'clock. By my best estimate, I had barely an hour until the potion wore off completely.

Too soon.

Chapter Eight

I't'd occurred to me once or twice, in particularly morbid moods, to wonder how a condemned prisoner felt in those last few minutes before the axe fell: kneeling on the scaffold, each breath too fast and too slow all at once, the anticipation possibly worse than the event.

This couldn't compare, of course. I knew, logically, that sitting across a tray of sandwiches and a pot of tea from Andreas and waiting for my body and mind to betray me couldn't be as bad as anticipating a violent death.

But tell that to my galloping heart, my clammy palms, and my roiling nausea.

Fear or the beginning of my symptoms? I couldn't tell, and that made me sicker still.

Andreas picked up another sandwich and took a giant bite, more than half of it disappearing into his mouth. Fuck. It wasn't fair at all, but I wanted to shove it down his throat until he choked on it. Despite my own hunger, I couldn't eat a single bite. I drank more tea instead, the cup clattering betrayingly against the saucer as I set it down again.

And then it cracked, a sound like a branch breaking, as my arm spasmed and my fingers clenched convulsively.

Now I could tell, and how I'd thought my mere nerves a moment ago were my cursed magic, I didn't know.

Scorching pain swirled in my abdomen and radiated out, sending tendrils like fiery worms into my hips and my ribs, up to my shoulders and down into my groin. I doubled over, panting against the urge to scream.

"Your Highness! Your Highness, fuck, look at me, tell me what's happening..." Andreas's voice washed over me for a moment, but his hands on my shoulders grounded me enough that I could focus on them, return my awareness to his voice. "...which one to try first? Your Highness!"

I lifted my head from my knees, assisted by his grip on me. Andreas had knelt down beside me and bent to try to look into my face.

"What?" I gasped. It took a second to remember, and pain shot down my right arm so suddenly that I yelped. "Try...you mean the drugs. The... labeled for palpi, pitations."

He released me and I slumped over again, gritting my teeth, trying to force my muscles to relax. My heart hammered. A headache built behind my eyes, sizzling bolts striking my skull at random.

Andreas pushed me up again, tipping me against the back of my chair. "How much?" He tugged the cork out of the bottle. "I don't want you to take too—"

Desperation gave me more speed and strength than usual, and I snatched it out of his hand and took a deep slug of it. As soon as it left my lips, Andreas seized it and took it back, muttering something under his breath that sounded like, "irresponsible." Well, it sounded like "reckless idiot," but I preferred my more polite translation.

And I could have a coherent thought because...the pain had simmered down enough that I could focus on something other than the fire ripping through my body.

"It's working," I said, only a little slurred. My lungs expanded all the way as I sucked in air, and it felt glorious. "It's better."

Andreas tilted the bottle toward the lamp and frowned, squinting at the label. "That fellow has the most ridiculous handwriting—there are sixteen doses in this bottle, meant to be taken two hours apart," he said, and looked up at me. "Sixteen, Your Highness. I estimate you just took four of them. Possibly more."

"It doesn't feel like too much. My heart's almost beating normally." I let my head fall back against the chair. My racing heart being reined in to a more reasonable pace had reduced all of my symptoms, as the physician's assistant had speculated it might. He deserved a higher wage.

Only…not quite all of them.

My eyes popped open as something throbbed deep inside me. I'd always associated this particular sensation with pain, since they'd always been bound up together. But it didn't actually hurt, not on its own. Between my navel and my hips and my balls, I'd gone molten: hot and swirling and somehow achingly empty. Needy. Demanding.

Fuck, *very* demanding. I forced myself to be still rather than squirming in the chair, spreading my legs, arching my back, trying to ease the sensation by opening myself up as much as I could. The effort of keeping my body in check had sweat breaking out on my hairline and starting to bead on my spine.

"Your Highness?" Andreas leaned down, lines of anxiety bracketing his mouth. "You said you were feeling better."

"I am, it doesn't hurt so much as it—"

"You were whimpering."

I stared up at him in horror. I absolutely had not been…whimpering. "That's not a sound that I make, Andreas," I said, as confidently as I could.

His frown deepened. "It wasn't an insult. Are you in pain or not?"

"Not exactly," I hedged, and then another spasm hit, this one very clearly centered behind my balls, a piercing twist of heat. "Oh gods," I— whimpered. I couldn't even deny it. My grip on the arms of the chair went so tight my knuckles popped. Any second now, I'd— "Andreas," I gasped, bending down again, trying to curl around it, but it didn't do a damn bit of good. "Listen to me."

"I'm listening." His voice was so close that it startled me, and I lifted my head to find him crouched down in front of my chair again.

His eyes were extraordinary at this distance, more dark bronze than anything and ringed with a thin black line. And steady. Andreas was steady. He'd never let me down, I knew it in my bones. I could trust him.

"It's not pain, it's the—other thing," I said, almost whispering, as if I had to keep this between us, in this tiny space separating us. "I'll be begging soon. I'm halfway sane right now, but that won't last long. Those drugs won't help with the cravings, just the pain. Andreas, I'm so sorry, please forgive me—"

The words caught in my throat as he reached up and—laid his hand over my mouth. My lips, against the callused skin of his swordsman's hand. The heat of him.

And perhaps I should have, but I hadn't expected the skin-to-skin touch of another man to make me collapse again, moaning, *needing*, my balls drawn up and my hole tightening around nothing.

"Please," I gasped, my lips sliding against his palm. He tugged it away instantly, and it didn't help, it made it *worse* that he'd stopped touching me. "No!" I flailed an arm out to catch him as he stood and walked away—and missed, my hand flopping down.

"One second, Your Highness," he said, his voice flat with tension, and I squeezed my eyes shut and rested my forehead on my knees, panting, trying to center myself. It worked, except that my center had become the place between my legs where another man would force me open, stuff and fuck me, fill me with heat, make me wet.

I moaned pitifully, aware enough to hope he hadn't heard it.

Andreas's hand landed on my shoulder and he pushed me upright again, and another moan burst out, the stretch in my abdomen almost unbearable. His face swam in front of me as if I viewed it through shifting water or a poorly made sheet of glass.

"Drink this," he said, and set something against my lips. I drank, this liquid thicker than the first and tasting faintly like caramel. "It says on the label it's to calm the nerves. Tell me when the pain comes back, and I'll give you more of the first one."

Drugs made by apothecaries capable of infusing their creations with magic, like the one we'd bought these from, worked extremely quickly. Like the other, this medicine took effect within seconds: everything slowed down, the air going cool and slippery against my skin. The chill sank in, soothing my desperate need for a moment.

Until it sank in too far, and shivers skittered down my limbs. I shifted in the chair, wrapping my arms around myself, teeth starting to chatter.

And then Andreas was there, pulling me up, arms sliding around me, his body a solid wall of glorious, wondrous heat. I'd gone far beyond the point of having any pride, or self-respect, or even consciousness of anything but my own misery.

"Cold," I muttered, voice shaking, and buried my face in his shoulder. Mmm. He'd taken off his chain mail while he was gone, must have, because I wasn't resting against the texture of metal rings beneath his tunic, but of lovely firm muscle and the ridge of his collarbone.

Bliss: the scent of him, and the strength of his arms as they wound around me, one at my waist and the other cradling my shoulders, and the way my knees started to give out but I didn't fall, because Andreas could hold me up, and he would.

"I could tell," he said, and then we were moving. "Come closer to the fire, you'll—"

"Bed," I managed. My head swam. No more standing up. Besides, he felt so much better than any fire could. "Lie down with me and keep me warm."

We stopped moving. "That's a very bad idea, Your Highness," he said, his voice low and tight.

Even in my state of near-incoherence I knew I was being unfair when I nuzzled into his shoulder and murmured, "You promised you'd take care of me."

"Gods," Andreas choked, and his arms tightened until I struggled to breathe. "Buggering fucking gods. Your Highness—damn it."

I smiled into his chest as he finally started walking, half-dragging me the other direction, toward the bed. He got me sitting down and then crouched and pulled off my boots, the tugging motion sending me toppling backward. The shivers started again instantly, goosebumps covering every inch of my skin and making it unbearably sensitive. I tried to curl in on myself, panting, as the heaviness in my lower abdomen built and built, a horrible counterpoint to the crawling cold on my outer parts. At last Andreas's boots hit the floor with a pair of thuds. More rustling and the clink of a buckle suggested he'd removed his sword belt.

By the time Andreas climbed onto the bed with me, I'd gotten myself into a ball like one of those little bugs in my mother's rose garden that would roll up when they were frightened, and I'd burrowed into the quilts, hiding my face in soft fabric that still felt too rough against my burning cheeks.

The straw mattress crunched and rustled, and then blessed warmth enveloped me. Andreas wrapped his arms around my back and tugged me in close, letting me nestle into his chest and tuck my knees against his legs.

The first dose of medicine had maybe begun to wear off, my heartbeat speeding up. But as I listened to his, it evened out again, matching itself to the steady thump against my ear.

The strung-tight tension in my muscles loosened, and I let out a long, helpless sigh of relief.

As if in response, my gut clenched into a twisted knot again.

I gasped, writhing, all my limbs pulling in.

One of Andreas's hands stroked my back, a soft sweep from my waist to my nape and then down again. The other clamped onto my hip.

Oh, gods, I needed that first hand lower, cupping my ass, sliding fingers between my cheeks, and the other holding on even harder, holding me down.

But I couldn't have that, could I? I closed my eyes, holding them shut tightly until I saw stars, and then I opened them, staring into the black fabric of Andreas's tunic. No. No, I couldn't have that. I wasn't going to have that. I didn't want Andreas. And even more to the point, he didn't want me.

My guard, paid by my mother. That was all. Protecting me until I could get my potion.

The idea of the potion seemed so far off, like something glimpsed in a dream. This was real. Andreas's body, the emptiness inside me, the pain starting to gnaw at me again and filter down along my veins and into my arms and legs. All real.

Red-tinged and cloudy and all the more real for it.

I stretched out my legs, wriggling closer to Andreas, taking hold of his tunic in my fists and pulling myself up until our hips aligned.

"Your Highness, what are you do—fuck, don't, you don't want this," he protested, as I shoved myself against him, throwing a leg over his hip.

He tried to pull back but I clung to him, moaning, and gods, I needed him between my legs, I *needed* him.

And I could feel him.

I stopped.

Because…I could feel him.

And that, more than anything else could've, broke through my fugue of curse-fueled desperation.

"Andreas," I breathed, and shifted my hips slightly, because I couldn't quite believe it. But unless he'd stuffed several rolled-up pairs of stockings into his trousers…I could feel him. He'd gone stiff all over, not just in that one crucial area, his arms like steel bands around me. He was barely breathing. I started to laugh, hitching almost-sobs that shook me down to my core and had me rubbing against him almost frantically. "It looks like you can definitely get it up."

"And so can you," he snapped. "You didn't tell me you'd—stop. Please, Your Highness. Stop."

But I couldn't stop, because I could *feel it*. His cock, pressing between my legs, thick against my thigh and against my own cock, which was—it was hard, for the first time in years. Hard and eager for Andreas to impale me with his.

With strength I'd never have had without all the magic coursing through me, I shoved at his shoulders, and he rolled onto his back with me on top and straddling his hips.

Andreas gazed up at me, eyes blazing, lips pressed tight, a deep red flush along his cheekbones.

And I couldn't look away. I went still, caught and pinned by the force of his eyes on me.

"You don't want this, Your Highness," he gritted out. "Stop before I have to hold you down."

Hold me down—fuck, he meant that as a deterrent? I moaned and shuddered, and it took a moment for me to come back to myself.

His hands rested on my waist, fingers digging in, belying his words—and the long, thick erection pressing up between my legs didn't help his case, either.

Andreas wanted me.

He *wanted* me.

The last of my scruples evaporated in an instant. If Andreas wanted to fuck me, then I didn't need to feel guilty for begging him to do it. And at that moment, I couldn't remember why I'd been so insistent on maintaining my independence, on never giving another man the power over me he'd have if I predicated my control of my magic, my freedom from pain, my very life, on his willingness to fuck me.

It didn't matter. Nothing mattered but ending this torment, the hollow ache inside me.

I'd simply have to convince Andreas, my guard who'd sworn to protect and respect my royal person, that the best way to accomplish that would be to spread my legs and use me like his whore.

Chapter Nine

"You should hold me down, only you should fuck me," I gasped, grinding down with my hips. Wait, hadn't I meant to say something seductive and persuasive? The ridge of his thick, perfect erection pushed between the cheeks of my ass, teasing my hole, making me burn with helpless want and erasing any other thoughts from my mind. "You can have me if you want. Take me. Use me. Or I'll sit on your cock and do all the work. Please, please—"

Everything went upside down, my stomach flipped, and then suddenly I was flat on my back and blinking up at Andreas's flushed face and tight-lipped grimace. His fingers tightened around my wrists where he'd pinned them over my head. Andreas had landed between my legs, knees spreading my thighs wide around him.

"Please let me have your cock in me," I finished, and Andreas went even redder and let go of one of my wrists. A quick scrabble ensued, me trying to touch him, and him getting me pinned again, this time with only one of his big hands wrapped around both wrists and the other flat across my mouth.

I bucked and fought, trying to rub my cock on him, and fuck, but it was so incredible to be hard, to want, to know I could be satisfied if he'd only give me what I needed—

"Knock it off," Andreas snarled. "Please. Fuck." He closed his eyes, opened them again, and said, "Your Highness, I know you can't help it. But you don't really want this. And I'm going to keep you from doing something you'll regret. You asked me to."

My eyes widened. *Asked* him to? The hell I had! I shook my head frantically, but his hand didn't budge. Finally, in desperation, I licked him, shuddering with desire at the heat and salt of his sword-callused skin.

Andreas yanked his hand away like I'd bitten him instead, clenching it into a fist at his side.

"I never asked you not to fuck me," I said the second I had my mouth free.

"You told me you'd beg, and that I should…" His voice trailed off, and his jaw went all hard and set.

"You see?" I pushed up again with my hips, because I couldn't help it, and the pulsing desire inside me kept building. Licking my dry lips, I tried to blink away the haze in my vision. Nothing helped. "I told you that you *wouldn't* fuck me. Not that you shouldn't. And you should. Please, Andreas? Please!" Nothing. Damn him. What would tempt him? My mind raced and my belly clenched and there was only one card left to play…no matter how much it shamed me that no one had ever wanted me before. But I could phrase it slightly differently, at least. "No one's ever had me before. You could be the first. Show me how it feels to be filled. Please!"

Andreas's hips bucked forward, the bulge in his trousers straining the fabric, and he hung his head down, shoulders like rocks. I cried out as the hand on my wrists clamped down like a vise. The pain stilled me, and I stared up at him, startled and shocked.

At last he lifted his head and met my eyes. His expression had me pressing myself back into the pillows, genuinely afraid of him in a way I'd never have thought I could be. Those metallic eyes. Mostly pupil, and fixed on me the way I'd seen a hawk look at a sparrow.

"I'm going to tie you to the bed," he said, his voice terrifyingly level. "I'm going to gag you, and I'm going to bring—any one of the men. You choose. To watch over you. I'll come in and out and give you doses of your medicines. Your Highness, I'm sorry. I thought I'd be strong enough to do this. But I can't."

Shock turned to horror as that sank in, even as the words *tie you to the bed* arrowed straight down into my balls and made me shudder.

Andreas meant to leave me. "You can't," I stammered. Horribly, tears stung the corners of my eyes and blurred my vision. "You said nothing could make you ab—abandon me. You promised—"

My throat tightened too much for more, and I choked on a sob, and it was all too much, the pain starting to creep back along my limbs and the way I thought I might not be able to breathe if I didn't relieve the straining ache between my legs, my racing heart and my bruised wrists. And now Andreas would leave me.

"No, it's not—don't you understand, I *can't*," and this time he sounded tortured. "I'll do it. If I stay, I'll do all of it. Everything you said. I'll betray your trust in me. You're not yourself, and once it's done you'll hate me for forcing myself on you."

His free hand landed on my hip and slipped under my shirt where it'd ridden up as I thrashed and fought and tried to climb onto his cock. My skin burned where his fingers pressed into me. That heat went all the way through, down into my belly, lower, into my balls and my cock and my hole.

I blinked, dislodging some of the water from my eyelashes. Andreas loomed over me, his big body filling my vision, hiding me away from the rest of the world, sheltering me and keeping me safe. But he was trembling with strain.

And the drugs had really worn off, perhaps burned out of my blood by stress and fear and struggle.

"It hurts," I said simply, and the catch I couldn't keep out of my voice probably told him more than the words. I was trembling too, shaking like an autumn leaf. "Please, Andreas. Make it stop hurting. Please don't leave me. Please—"

"Stop," he said abruptly. "Fuck. Don't. I can't hear one more word from you." The hand on my wrists released, the hand on my hip too, and then—I barely had time to cry out before he'd flipped me over onto my stomach, face mashed into the pillow. "I really will gag you if you keep talking, Your Highness. I'll come before I get a chance to help you if you say another word."

He thought he'd come before he had a chance to…that thought drove every word in the language from my mind, but it made me moan helplessly, rising to a high-pitched cry as Andreas wrapped his hands around the waistband of my trousers, his knuckles pressing into the small of my back—and ripped the trousers down the seam from the waist to my balls.

And then he didn't touch me. Didn't do anything, as I lay there panting into the bedding with my ass exposed to the cold air.

Or…no, he was doing something. Just not to me. The rustling of cloth, followed by harsh, deep breaths, and the unmistakable soft tug of skin against skin.

I tried to twist around, push up to see him, and a big hand landed between my shoulder blades and shoved me unceremoniously flat again. "Fuck, don't look at me," he said, and before I could take offense, added, "If I see your face I'll come on it and I won't get any inside you, fuck."

"But what are you doing? Andreas, I need—"

"You need me to come inside you, and I will. I only need to get the head of my cock in you. You're a—a virgin," and his voice dipped impossibly low. "And I—fuck," he said again, as I shoved my ass up in the air as best I could. "You're trying to kill me."

No, *he* was trying to kill *me*, because my whole body shook, coated with a sheen of perspiration, and I had a horrid cottony mouthful of pillow, and those pathetic little whines were issuing from my dry throat, and I didn't care that he'd ruined my trousers or about anything but that my hole was so empty, I was so empty—

"Almost, almost there," he gasped.

Everything in the world came to a halt as something thick and hot and smooth and not-quite-wet-enough pressed between the cheeks of my ass.

Andreas's cock. I had Andreas's cock against my hole. He grasped my cheeks and pried them apart, one hand fitting perfectly over each, his thumbs stretching my hole open as he thrust forward.

It hurt, but not nearly as much as something that big should've hurt, I didn't think. Andreas must have used saliva to get his cock a bit slick, because it slid in, one nudge at a time, such a bizarre intrusion, wedging me open but not nearly enough, damn it, I'd die of this, or old age, before he fucked me—until I squeezed my eyes shut, braced my hands, and forced myself backward.

He groaned, and I let out a sharp cry, as what felt like all the cock in the universe slid inside me all at once.

"Gods, Your Highness," Andreas said, sounding like he was the one who'd just been stabbed in the guts and not me.

So thick, and deeper than I'd thought I'd feel it, and both cooler than the inside of my body and equally hot, so strange, and I clenched around him and felt the shape of him, the head of his cock and the girth of his shaft.

I felt it when he stiffened even more and started to spend in me, a spurt of blood-hot fluid. The essence of him, filling me and completing me. My magic flared and danced and then settled into a balance so perfect that I could hear and feel its resonance, humming like a struck silver bell inside my soul. For a moment I remembered those priests on the island to the east, the ones who called this a harmonious completion…perhaps they weren't so absurd after all.

And then the thought fled as that throbbing ache in me coalesced into a brilliant, white-hot burst of pain and pleasure, and I turned inside out around him, keening into the pillow as I clenched on him again and again and came in pulse after pulse, my balls twisted into a knot and my cock soaking the quilt.

Most people didn't fully appreciate how much better relief from pain could be than actual pleasure. I hadn't before my magic manifested, but in recent years, I'd have taken the absence of pain over even the most spectacular climax imaginable.

Both at once, it turned out, overloaded my body and mind to the point of near catatonia. Ringing in my ears, and a buzzing in all of my limbs, as if my blood had fizzed into foam in my veins... Vaguely and distantly, I felt Andreas's hands petting my ass, gentling me, and the thick, wet slide of his cock out of my stretched hole.

More caresses, and then a tugging on the fabric of my trousers, as if he thought he could put them back together. That struck me as unbearably funny, and I started to giggle, the bed shaking along with me.

"It's hopeless, and I'm sorry, I probably shouldn't have done that," he said in a rueful rumble, sounding more confused and breathless than anything.

That was what he shouldn't have done? He was kneeling over a royal prince of Surbino, his charge, looking down at the royal and recently-virginal ass all wet and open and dripping with his come, and he probably shouldn't have...ripped my trousers?

I howled with laughter, curling up and quivering, hands over my face. I couldn't fucking help it. Nothing hurt right then, nothing whatsoever, and every cell in my body sparked with magic and pleasure and warmth. And my guard had come inside me and then tried to repair a ruined piece of fabric that couldn't possibly be put back together without...

Magic. *My* magic, which theoretically included such things as the fusing of torn objects that had once been whole. I hadn't had the chance to use it in so many years. Barely even then. Could I make it work without lighting the bed on fire or killing myself?

"Your Highness?" Andreas sounded cautious now, wary. Well, not too surprising. He'd come in my ass and then I'd gone completely hysterical. "Please tell me you're all right, and that wasn't for nothing."

I smiled into my hands. I'd show him *for nothing*, and I'd graciously ignore the implication—obviously false—that neither of us had gotten anything else out of what he'd just done to me besides the cessation of my symptoms.

Focusing on my magic took serious effort—at first. I had to close my eyes again, hold perfectly still, and reach for it cautiously from within, the sensation something like trying to seize a solid handful of a spiderweb, only with a part of my mind that ached and throbbed, a mental phantom limb.

And then it fell into place, viscerally satisfying, like a deck of playing cards shuffling into a perfect stack between my fingers.

Warmth and energy suffused me, focused in a spot under my breastbone and radiating out, much as the pain had done a few minutes ago before Andreas temporarily relieved me of my curse. Everything around me had its own presence in the world of magic, too, so that I could almost see shapes and colors even with my eyes closed.

Andreas shone like a beacon, impossible to ignore. My breath caught as I turned my attention to him directly; he was so beautiful, so alluring, so full of life and strength, drawing me in irresistibly. Even with my back to him, he glowed.

But I had to focus on my torn trousers. I could bask in Andreas once I'd properly impressed him with my abilities.

And once I'd proven to myself that I had them at all after so many years of atrophy and neglect.

First I had to get out of the trousers, though, because the way they clung to my sweaty thighs felt fucking awful and I wouldn't be able to get the edges together like this. I shoved at them, grumbling curses, and after a moment Andreas's hands joined mine, tugging them down and away along with my stockings. I rolled onto my back and sprawled there, looking up at him through my lashes.

Any thoughts of repairing my clothing, of using my magic, or of anything else evaporated into the ether.

Damn it, he'd taken a moment to put his cock away. I forced my eyes up from the bulge in the front of his trousers to the rest of him. He knelt there without moving, my clothes dangling from his hands, staring down at me as if mesmerized, lips parted and brows drawn together. The hem of my shirt didn't cover much. His gaze seemed to be fixed between my legs.

The weight of it made me want to squirm, and I clenched my fingers in the quilt to keep myself still.

Gods. He'd fucked me and come inside me. My magic had been cleansed for the moment. That ache shouldn't be starting all over again, pulsing deep within where I could feel the slick evidence of how he'd filled me.

And then I froze, a cold shudder working its way down my back…

What if it hadn't worked?

My potion had been slowly becoming less effective. What if it wasn't the fault of the potion, and it was *me*? Because this didn't feel like satiation: the heat gathering in my low belly, the renewed sensation of emptiness, of need.

"Your Highness, you look like you've—I'm sorry. Please forgive me. I hurt you, or—staying or going seems equally wrong, so tell me what to do, please."

Fuck, Andreas. When my eyes refocused on him, I found him still kneeling there, but with his knuckles white where he gripped my clothes and his face nearly as pale under his tan.

"You didn't hurt me," I said at once, because I couldn't possibly let him believe that even for a moment, no matter what else might be wrong. "You saved me so much pain. The opposite of hurting me."

Andreas let out a long sigh, his eyes fluttering closed for a second.

They popped open again as I added, "And please don't go anywhere, because I think you need to do it again."

Chapter Ten

Andreas stared, eyes wide, his gaze flicking down between my legs again and then up while his cheeks went from pale to red again in an instant. "You what?" he said blankly.

My chest tightened. That was far from the enthusiasm I'd been hoping for. He'd wanted me—or at least I'd thought so. And that had given me a glorious few moments of confidence. But suddenly, I realized how I must appear to him: sticky and sweaty and flushed and blotchy, my legs akimbo and my torso half-covered with a shirt that hung all askew. And which was also damp with sweat.

Oh, gods. I probably *smelled*.

Perhaps it didn't matter if something was even more wrong with me than I'd thought, and if I needed him again to prevent my magic from killing me—because I couldn't possibly try to seduce him now.

Begging him to fuck me when I'd been in the throes of the worst of my symptoms hadn't felt shameful; I hadn't had the leisure for shame.

But now my magic had settled enough that I could fully appreciate how humiliating this truly was.

Trying to squirm away from Andreas and tug my shirt down to cover my cock and my ass went against what my body and my magic wanted and needed, but *I* needed to be covered, *I* needed to hide, and the push and pull of two conflicting urges had my head spinning.

"Nothing, it's nothing," I stammered, my face and neck going painfully hot. I couldn't quite get my legs closed, because he still knelt between them, and shoving myself up the bed with my elbows didn't work. It only bounced and rustled the horrid mattress. "The—it doesn't hurt much. Only an ache, nothing terrible. You have no obligation, Andreas. Never mind."

I'd almost managed to turn onto my side, away from him, and gods, that'd put my bare ass right in front of him again, fuck, I had nowhere to go—

And then warmth enveloped me as Andreas leaned down, covering me with his body, his knees pressing into my inner thighs and his elbows braced on either side of my shoulders.

"Your Highness," he whispered against my ear. "Look at me, please."

No, I couldn't. I couldn't possibly.

But of course I would, because he'd told me to, and that *please* had been a meaningless formality. I turned my head and opened my eyes, and I found his face an inch from mine, lips a breath away.

"Obligation. Are you suggesting that's what you pay me for? Because I'm not that kind of man, Your Highness," he said, with a glint in his eyes that meant trouble. "Of course there's no gods-damned obligation. Although I suppose you could increase my wage on general principle. But that's not why I'm here. You should already know that."

"My mother pays you, not me," I said without thinking—and then I thought about it. Fucking gods. "Andreas, I didn't mean she pays you for—"

"Enough," he said firmly, and leaned in that final inch between us and caught my lower lip between his teeth.

The shock of it went all the way down to my toes, my legs stiffening and the hair rising on my arms and the back of my neck. "Mmph," I said, and Andreas bit down, making me squeak and squirm, my hands flying up to land against his chest. He sucked on my lip, hard, and then let it go with a pop.

"What was that?" I gasped, my mouth throbbing and tingling far out of proportion to the cause. I couldn't see anything but his face, couldn't feel anything but the heat of his body surrounding me, couldn't hear anything but my panting breaths—and his, a rough counterpoint.

"No one needs to pay me to touch you, that's the point," he said, very low, eyes so dark and intent he could've pinned me in place with just his gaze, no manhandling needed. "If anything, I think I'm paid partly not to do that. And I don't know how you got the idea that no one would want you. But I'm very close to stripping every remaining thread of clothing off of you and showing you how completely fucking wrong you are. If you ask me again to fuck you, you'll find out how fucking close, even though I'm pretty sure you don't mean it. Are we clear? Your Highness."

Oh, gods. That swooping sensation in the pit of my stomach owed nothing at all to magic gone awry and everything to the way his deep voice made every cell in my body tremble, the way each one of his words hit me harder than the last. How had my cock gone stiff again so quickly, tenting the hem of my shirt and pulling all the blood away from my brain—and clearly it had, or I wouldn't have gone so lightheaded and fuzzy, would I?

My eyelids drooped, my breath coming faster. *Your Highness.* When had those words started to sound like the punctuation to a command rather than a sign of respect? They made me want to spread my legs again. But I didn't have any leverage, squished down into the bed beneath him the way I was.

Instead, I slid my hands up his arms, squeezing the powerful muscles, tracing the bulges of his shoulders, savoring the way he tensed under my touch as if I affected him as much as he did me.

His mouth was so close to mine. When I spoke, he'd feel my breath, caught in the tiny space between us that somehow managed to eclipse the rest of the world.

"We're clear," I whispered. *If you ask me again to fuck you, you'll find out how fucking close.* I could only hope. "I'm asking again. Kiss me, and then fuck me. You already fucked me once. What difference does it make?"

Andreas bit his lip and made a sound like I'd punched him in the sternum. "What difference does it—you have no idea what you're asking for," he said after a moment. The bed jostled as he lifted one hand and set it across my throat—carefully, gently, but without any hesitation, broad palm and long fingers wrapping all the way from side to side. He didn't hold me too tightly, didn't hamper my breath. But he pushed on me, tilting my chin up, forcing me to put my lips even closer to his. His voice dipped to a rasp. "I'm going to give it to you anyway."

Andreas's mouth met mine with the same unwavering surety he always had in everything he did, warm and firm and in complete control. I opened for him, because his tongue pushed in, tasting me, showing me how to move my own to twine with his and kiss him back, how to please and obey him.

The spark of that kiss ignited a fire deep down, where I was empty and wanting.

His hand moved from my throat to my chest, stroking and petting, goosebumps rising on my skin wherever he touched me. I arched up into him, my own fingers clawing into his shoulders.

Gods, too much and not enough, the soft friction of my shirt on my cock maddening, Andreas's mouth and hands an unbearable tease. It'd been years since I'd kissed anyone at all, and I'd never been kissed like this, with focused intent, as if owning my mouth was a goal in and of itself and not a steppingstone to more.

When he broke the kiss I fell back, dizzy and short of breath. His hand reached the hem of my shirt and slid beneath to spread across my stomach, and his hot mouth closed on the side of my throat and sucked hard, making me cry out and try again to arch up. But he had me pinned. And then it became a blur of sensation I couldn't begin to parse: the sudden rending rip of my shirt as he bared my chest, letting out another startled cry and twitch as he bit my nipple and then soothed it with a swipe of his tongue, the weight of him above me and the way I was pressed into the mattress beneath, my mind echoing, too hot and sweaty and overwhelmed and with my balls drawn up painfully tight, my head thrashing on the pillow.

Andreas kissed me everywhere, my nipples and down my chest, back up and along my collarbones, stinging nips to my ribs and my waist, a tongue flicking ticklishly in my navel and making me jump.

Somehow he'd moved down the bed without my noticing, and when my hands slipped off his shoulders and flailed in the empty air, I propped myself up on my elbows and blinked down at him.

On a solitary ride through the hills years ago, I'd encountered a mountain panther, gazing down at me with gleaming eyes and bared fangs from his perch on a rock above the path. That had been the one occasion on which I'd wished to the gods I'd brought someone else with me. Fluffy and I had gotten the hell out of there on the double, and I'd been looking over my shoulder for two miles.

Andreas looked just like that huge cat, all coiled strength and bunched muscles, crouched between my legs with his eyes glittering and his cock a heavy bulge in the straining front of his trousers. He slid his hands down to the backs of my knees and wrenched me open, spreading my legs obscenely wide to display everything I had.

The force of it tipped me back again and I collapsed with a gasp, digging my fingers into the bedding to try to catch my balance.

My hips ached, forced into such an unnatural angle, and I couldn't do a gods-damned thing but wait for Andreas to…I couldn't begin to guess, because I'd have thought he'd have been inside me by now.

"Are you trying to make me beg again?" I demanded, voice embarrassingly thin and peevish and strained. Fuck, a lie was beyond me right now. "Because I absolutely will."

"I was looking to make sure I hadn't hurt you. And you can beg if you want to," he said, tone unusually rough, and cleared his throat. He dropped my legs, sticking a hand into his pocket. "But I'm going to do precisely the same things whether you beg or not."

Something glinted in his fist: a small bottle much like the ones my medicines had come in. Andreas had been speaking to the apothecary at the counter for a minute while I'd been browsing, hadn't he? That sneaky bastard. He popped out the cork and poured something into his hand, his intention quite clear. The cork and bottle went on the nightstand, and he took hold of my leg again, lifting it and opening me.

For a moment, indignation left me speechless. He'd made me beg, when all along—!

"You," I sputtered. "You—I can't believe you. You acted like you weren't going to—"

"And I wasn't," he snapped. "But if it came to this, I had to be prepared. What did you think, that I'd fuck you dry and hurt you?"

"You already did fuck me dry, and I was fine! Why didn't you use this then?"

Andreas's fingers tightened around my thigh, and his jaw set. "I didn't have time to get you wetter, you were in too much pain. And I didn't fuck you, despite your best efforts. That was just the tip plus a bit."

"Just the—the hell it was!" Just the tip? Was he out of his mind? Plus his whole cock! "The tip of yours isn't bigger than my entire cock, Andreas." He glared at me, let go of my leg again, and started to tug at the buttons on his trousers. "You're delusional if you think—oh." The placket of his trousers fell away and he grunted, probably in relief as his erection escaped the constriction of a piece of fabric meant for something much smaller. "Oh," I said again, as my mind went entirely blank. "Oh, fucking gods."

That was…to be fair, I hadn't seen a lot of pricks. Mine. Glimpses of guards' and servants' equipment when I was traveling and all the men went aside to wash in a stream or a pond. I'd seen precisely one up close, right before the man it belonged to put his hand in my trousers and found me limp and unresponsive and then broke off the encounter on the spot.

It was possible most of them were that size. I doubted it. The majority of the world's women and a fair number of the men would be bowlegged.

I tore my eyes away and looked up at his face. Andreas bared his teeth at me in something like a grin, except that he seemed more likely to bite me than be friendly.

My gaze flicked back down again as he wrapped his oil-coated hand around his shaft.

His very large, long-fingered hand.

Which only covered a little more than half of his length, with his rosy-purple cockhead sticking out of his fist.

Andreas stroked down about two inches, leaving that and the monstrously thick head exposed.

"That's all I had inside you," he said. "Even after your little stunt." He ran his thumb over the head, leaving it gleaming with oil. I gazed at it, transfixed. "You still think you've been fucked, Your Highness? That one more time won't make any difference?"

If by *make any difference* he meant *might not survive the experience*, then…no.

The clicking sound of my hard swallow carried clearly in the nearly silent room. The fire popped along softly in the background, but otherwise…Andreas really had cleared out this part of the inn, because I couldn't hear a single sound of human occupancy. And it was dark as well as silent, the sun having gone down some time ago without my really paying attention, leaving the low-burning fire and the branch of candles on the dressing table the only illumination in the bedroom. Golden flickers danced on the ceiling and cast Andreas into stark relief.

I was afraid to glance over at the wall. The shadow thrown by his cock had to be terrifying. Like something out of a comic-erotic pantomime.

But terrified or not, chastened by the correction of my horribly naïve assumptions or not, I still had the same clenching heat in my stomach. My breathless longing had only intensified, my cock as stiff as Andreas's and my body feeling horribly empty again. I tightened the muscles of my ass experimentally. Some of his come trickled out of me, and I shuddered with something between disgust and unbearable desire.

Maybe I needed him to fuck me as well as fill me. Another man's spend, with or without a lengthy encounter to produce it, had always been the cure for the symptoms of cursed dawn magic, as far as I knew. Perhaps this was another way in which I was…special, needing more than that. Lucky me.

Andreas made an impatient sound, let go of his cock, and yanked his tunic up and off, tossing it to the floor. His singlet followed a moment later.

He leaned down, somehow prowling like that predatory forest cat without doing more than shifting his weight on the bed. Broad shoulders and a lean, muscled torso, the sharp V of his hips leading to that massive cock, even more spellbinding now that it stuck out on its own without a hand to hide any of it…

Lucky me indeed. I swallowed again, my throat horribly dry, and dared to look up and meet his eyes.

Steady as always, but with that gleam in them that promised more than I'd bargained for. Everything about him, from the short, soldierly brush of his auburn hair to the faint silvery scars along his ribs to the firm set of his jaw intimidated me, left me off-balance. He had from the moment we met.

Andreas cupped my face in his hand, thankfully the not-oily one, stroking my lower lip with his thumb, pushing it into the corner of my mouth and rubbing the pad of it over the tip of my tongue, thrusting lightly. He tasted like salt and steel. I whimpered helplessly as every muscle in my body went tight.

"I won't," he said softly, something flashing through his eyes and then gone again. "You should save that for someone you choose."

Before I could even begin to formulate an answer, possibly that I'd choose him, or that I wasn't quite sure what he meant but wanted very much to find out, he'd slipped his thumb out of my mouth and bent down the rest of the way, cutting off any possible words with his kiss.

Chapter Eleven

My impression of how it went getting fucked in the ass had been formed mostly on the several illustrated works I'd found in the palace library tucked behind a very weighty, and dust-coated, treatise on political theory. In those, all by the same author, bending over and then immediate insertion had been typical. It didn't take long, anyway, either before or after penetration.

Andreas clearly hadn't read those books.

He kissed me breathless, kissed me lightheaded, kissed me until I didn't know which direction was up, until the occasional searing brush of his cock against mine had me crying out in something more like agony than when I'd been in real pain earlier.

And then he lowered himself down and thrust, cock sliding against mine, his hard muscles rubbing all over me and pushing me into the mattress, overwhelming the few senses I still had functioning. The warm spice and musk of him surrounded me, his lips ravaged mine, his tongue fucked my mouth. He thrust again, this time catching the ridge of my glans with his own cock.

My body tensed like a bowstring and everything went all swirly. Hot wetness spread between us, drenching my cock and his, as I spent like a lad.

That high, desperate cry that echoed off the ceiling had come from me, apparently.

I subsided, limp and damp and shaking, the whole world tilting gently sideways at an angle.

Andreas's groaned curses barely registered, or the loss of his heat on the front of my body—the cool air against my sweaty skin felt incredible, even though I wanted him back.

But my eyes popped open again when his fingers, slick with oil, pressed between my cheeks and stroked over my hole. Andreas had his head bent down to peer between my legs, making me reflexively try to pull them closed.

He wrapped his other hand around the back of my knee and shoved it up almost to my face—which went blisteringly hot.

"You can't possibly want to look at—"

"Oh, believe me, I want to do a lot more than look," Andreas said, glancing up at me with such a glow in his eyes that I couldn't possibly doubt it. "Like this."

Two fingers pushed inside, crooking to tease me, making it impossible to ignore the fact that he could feel me too, just like I could feel him. The inside of me, at his mercy and available for his appreciation—or not.

"Andreas, please—" His fingernail gently scored the most sensitive part of my flesh, not enough to hurt, but more than enough to have me falling back on the pillows with sweat beading my hairline and my hands clenched in the quilt.

"That's right," he said, and if he sounded almost unpardonably smug, he also sounded almost as breathless as I felt, so I could forgive him for it. "I'll make you come a third time, Your Highness. At my leisure."

I gazed up at the ceiling unseeingly, breath hitching with every motion of his fingers. Everything in the world had narrowed down to their thick pressure, the way they were stretching me to fit.

"That sounds mildly treasonous," I gasped.

Andreas laughed and twisted his fingers, and I cried out. "Well worth being hanged for."

"I can't believe that. No one would—" The words had slipped out without my permission, and I bit my lip to stop their flow, hard enough that I tasted iron.

Andreas moved too quickly up the bed for me to follow, thrusting his hand at the same time. I blinked and twitched, and when I opened my eyes again his frowning face filled my view. He'd leaned down over me, eyes almost too close for me to meet his gaze.

"I told you I'd show you how wrong you are," he said, and pushed deeper, knuckles stretching me, and I choked and squirmed and felt my cock stirring again, my third erection in the last two hours and in the last five years, take your pick. "I don't give a fuck who—look at me, Your Highness," and he clamped the fingers of his other hand around my jaw and pinned me in place. His eyes blazed. I couldn't have moved a single muscle of my body if my life depended on it. The tip of his hard cock was against my stomach again, and I could feel it burning all the way through me. "Whoever didn't want to fuck you the way you deserve, forget him. You're in bed with me. Only me. And you have no idea what I want to do to your incredibly beautiful ass. All of it treasonous. Understand?"

With the heat and strength of his body all around me and half his hand buried inside me, I didn't have a lot of choice, did I?

But...he had half his hand buried inside me, and I couldn't get past that.

"You can't possibly tell me you're enjoying that," I whispered, a little slurred because of his grip on me. "You don't have to."

Those incredible eyes softened, and a little smile teased the corners of his mouth. My breath caught. No one, but no one had ever looked at me like that before.

"Enjoying it," he repeated, and bent down even more, brushing his lips over mine. I opened for him, my skin tingling and my eyes sliding shut, but he didn't really kiss me, the fucking tease. Instead he kissed my cheek, the hinge of my jaw, still holding me in place. "Mmm." He wiggled his fingers, the most bizarre sensation that still managed to make my balls tighten almost painfully, the pit of my stomach twisting. Hot lips touched the side of my neck. "You're very soft inside. And wet from my come." He thrust his fingers in, and the squelching sound managed to be even more obscene than his words.

"You have a texture," he went on, murmuring into my collarbone and punctuating himself with another kiss. "It isn't quite like skin on the outside. I want to feel it with whatever I can fit in you."

Oh, gods, every bit of that skin on the outside had gone painfully hot, and when I moaned and tightened convulsively around him, he only laughed and licked my nipple and thrust his fingers deeper.

Whatever he could fit in me…his cock might or might not qualify. Andreas pulled back, and added a third finger, and he pushed and turned, and he could feel my texture, inside…

The thudding and rushing of my own blood echoed in my ears, the world was nothing but glimpses of a shadowy ceiling through tear-glazed eyes, and everything came to me in bits and pieces: his voice, telling me to be still and he'd give me everything in a moment, and the pressure of his hips against my thighs, the tease of his cock behind my balls, slippery and thick.

He hadn't even turned me over, though, so how could he—but then his cock pressed into me, not just the head but more and more, irresistible, deeper and deeper.

My breath caught in my chest and my hands flailed and landed on his shoulders, fingers digging in. Andreas knelt between my legs, my ass practically in his lap, and when I craned my neck to look, I could see his thatch of auburn hair around the thick base of his cock, with inches more still pushing in.

"It's too big," I gasped. "I need to—Andreas, don't I need to be on my knees? Men don't do it like this!"

He looked up sharply, lips parted, cheeks flushed. "I beg your par— where the hell did you get your information from? We absolutely fucking do. And it's not too big." Andreas swooped down and pressed his lips to mine, swallowing my protests. I whimpered into his mouth as he sank in another inch, the inside of me strained to the limit, it had to be. There wasn't room for him, how could anyone take this much stuffing without ripping apart, I'd—and oh, gods, he'd stopped at last, hips pressed firmly against my ass and the very thickest part of his cock wrenching my hole open.

A tentative squirm around the massive intrusion earned me a groan from Andreas and a thrust that had me making a sound I hadn't known I could make, a helpless, pitiful whine.

Andreas lifted his head, with one last nip to my lower lip that left it throbbing. He gazed down at me, wild-eyed and flushed.

"Listen to me," he said, low and tight. "This," and he thrust, and I clutched his shoulders and cried out, but I couldn't look away from those eyes, "would be worth," another thrust, so deep it punched the air from my lungs, and I felt the tears gathering at the corner of my eyes, "any form of royal punishment you could think of."

He leaned down again and softly kissed the corner of my mouth. Under my death grip, his shoulders felt like hot stones, so tense and rigid. Restraining himself? Gods, because of me, because he wanted to please *me*…

"I was fairly certain being assigned as my personal guard was already your punishment," I gasped, arching up to try to ease the weighty ache in my lower body.

Andreas laughed against my cheek. "Then I ought to commit much more treason on your lovely royal person. Am I hurting you?"

"No, it's—a little bit." He'd stopped moving, letting me get used to him, and it didn't really hurt, it more…made my head spin, left me confused and needing something I couldn't define, edgy and needy and impaled. "I don't know what I want," I finished miserably.

"Mmm. I do. You want this." He pulled back, the slide of his heavy cock halfway out of me horribly strange and slick and wrong-feeling. "Tell me when it feels good."

I opened my mouth to tell him it wouldn't, that I was terrified and stuffed and too hot and sweaty and still utterly bewildered—and then he thrust, a long smooth glide that rubbed every inch of him over some sensitive places within me that I'd never known about until he touched them, and every nerve in my body lit up at once like a chain of fireworks.

"Oh gods," I moaned, and clenched around him, and it happened *again*.

"No, just me," Andreas growled in my ear.

He wrapped an arm under my waist, scooped me up like I weighed nothing at all, and slammed into me, over and over, the most delicious friction on every inch of me on the inside, until I teetered between coming again and crying out from the pain of how tightly he'd wound me.

Andreas lifted me higher and pressed me against his body, and now he wasn't withdrawing between strokes so much as forcing himself deeper with every motion of his hips. It trapped my cock between the rough trail of hair down the center of his abdomen and my own sweat-slick skin. Almost, almost but not quite—

"Fuck, Niko—Your High—fuck," Andreas groaned, and his whole body stiffened, the hand at my waist clamping down bruisingly hard. His hips juddered to a halt. The head of his cock twitched inside me, and he finished like that, pressing me to his heart with his face buried in my hair.

So close, even closer with the heat of his seed flooding me, and I squirmed there, pinned and helpless and almost sobbing in frustration.

"Fuck, I'm sorry," he gasped, and dropped me to the bed. I bounced, yelped, tried to get my bearings, and then cried out in shock as he pulled out of me all at once, heavy and thick, leaving me jarringly empty.

I managed to push up on my elbows just in time to see him bend over me and put his mouth around the head of my cock. The sudden wet heat had me curling in, breathless, my limbs gone rigid.

And then he tightened his lips, slid down, and sucked.

Dromos and Ennolu could've manifested in unison and danced a jig at the foot of the bed and I wouldn't have noticed. Everything in the world grayed out into a haze except for the exquisite, unbearable perfection of Andreas's beautiful mouth.

A choked-off moan was all the warning I gave him before I spent down his throat, feeling him swallow around me, his tongue flicking my oversensitive glans until I writhed and tried to push him off, fingers slipping through his too-short hair.

At last he had some mercy, letting my cock slide out of his mouth and rest limp against my hip, the cool air on my wet flesh sending a momentary shudder up and down my spine.

I let myself drift for a while after that, my mind light and floaty, my body humming with more satisfaction than it'd known for…ever.

No, nothing had ever or probably could ever equal this bliss. More than anything, I'd always feared the loss of control that my flawed magic would inflict on me if I went without my potion. But instead of agonizing, the night had been more wonderful than I could've imagined.

And now I feared it more than ever. I could easily come to crave being drenched in pleasure, fizzing with contentment, savoring the warmth and intimacy of a lover's touch.

But if that lover grew bored with me? If he turned against me, didn't want me anymore, or worse, wanted to punish me for some fault or other? He could keep me suspended in agony for as long as he chose to draw it out simply by refusing to take me. I could find another man, but not easily, not while I was incapacitated with the effects of my magic—and not at all if my lover, someone stronger and more physically capable than I was, chose to prevent it. Being a royal prince meant nothing at all when you reduced a relationship to its crudest essentials: who was the stronger, who the more ruthless.

That would probably never be me.

And so now I knew what I'd been missing, and every time I lifted my potion to my mouth I'd think of this night, of Andreas's arms around me, his cock buried deep in me, his hands and lips drawing out all my closely kept secrets. I'd wonder if I ought to throw the potion away and find someone to love me.

No one could ever love me enough, I didn't think, for me to trust him implicitly with my life and my dignity and my body.

But that had to be for later. Right now, I had an idiotic little smile on my lips and faint tremors, aftershocks of ecstasy, running down all my limbs. The bed rose up to support me like a warm, fuzzy cloud rather than the hay bale wrapped in cheap linen I knew it to be.

    And so I gave in to it.

    For now, I could stop fighting and simply be.

Chapter Twelve

The outside world filtered back in slowly, one sense at a time. First hearing: the soft susurrus of my own breath, the gentle crackle of the fire, and the tapping of rain—or possibly snow, and I couldn't be bothered to open my eyes and find out—against the window.

Scent next, the fireplace's smoke and the sharp bite of icy air trickling in around the window frame, and the salty, sweet, and bitterly delicious aroma of Andreas and of my own pleasure.

All of that might've soothed me into a nap if it weren't for the awareness of my own body which came next. More specifically, the heavy weight of Andreas's head on my hip. Shaving apparently hadn't been a priority for him in the last couple of days, and thick stubble prickled my thigh.

Of course, that paled in comparison to the sensation of his hand between my legs, his thumb teasing behind and under my balls and rubbing over the tender, slick rim of my hole.

Extremely slick. Slippery, in fact, with the bed under me all wet.

Oh, that was *disgusting.*

My eyelids popped open as my whole body went tense. So much for the way I'd been floating in complete contentment. I tried to shift my position, but Andreas had me pinned. Peeking down my body, I found him looking up at me, gaze steady and serious. Another idle circle of his thumb over my well-used flesh had my face and neck burning.

A helpless, involuntary squirm accomplished precisely nothing. Andreas pressed against me a little more firmly and blinked at me.

"I wondered if you were asleep. Don't try to get away from me, Your Highness. It won't work," he said mildly. "I've decided I may as well be hanged for a lot of treason as a little, so you're not going anywhere tonight. And neither am I."

"It's not about hanging you," I sputtered. "How can you want to—I'm all wet and—and—stretched, and—"

"Mmm," Andreas said, and leaned in a few inches to press a kiss to my balls. His hot lips on that incredibly sensitive skin stopped me dead in my tracks. The way he glanced up at me through his lashes as he… oh, gods, he *licked* me, tongue laving the side of my balls and his thumb pressing into me slightly—I fell back, gasping, little tremors flickering through every one of my overwrought nerves. "Wet and stretched," he whispered against my skin. "I did that to you. And I like admiring my handiwork. Your Highness."

"You kissed my testicles," was all I could manage. "You—I can't believe you!" I broke off in a moan as he licked me again and then laughed, the vibrations burrowing down into the center of me where he still had the tip of his thumb buried in my body.

Gods, the pleasure of it transcended the physical. The tenderness of it, the playfulness…a few poorly written erotic books hadn't prepared me for the idea that sharing a bed, sharing my body, could be filthy and sweet at the same time. It was almost more of a revelation than learning how it felt to be thoroughly fucked.

"I told you, you have no idea," he breathed, and lifted his head a bit, moving across to the crease between my groin and the opposite hip and brushing his lips over my skin. "I'm going to kiss—you know what, I think I'll show you."

Before I could blink, he shoved himself up, clambering over my leg and bouncing off the bed with more energy than I thought it right or just for anyone to have after so much exertion and strain. I was only four years older than he was, for fuck's sake. Then again, I'd come three times to his two. That had to count for something.

With a hop on one foot and a muttered curse, Andreas shoved his trousers down the rest of the way, stepping out of them and toeing off his stockings at the same time.

He should've looked ridiculous. I would have.

But he managed it with such insouciance. And I'd never seen anything more mouthwatering than his completely nude body. I could only gape at him, mouth hanging open, as he crossed to the dressing table and started to pour fresh wash water into the basin the maid had left there hours ago. Limned by firelight and candlelight, all the shallow curves and sharp angles of his soldiering-honed body gleamed honey-gold. Perhaps I understood, a little, why one would want to lick a lover. That ridged V of muscle just inside his hips begged for a worshipful mouth. And the curves of his biceps.

Andreas turned halfway toward me, pausing to wring out a cloth.

Mmm. Fucking gods. His hips and his biceps weren't all that tempted me to kiss and lick and taste: even limp, his heavy cock hung thick over his large balls. I licked my lips in lieu of something better. Although I might wait until he'd had a thorough bath, considering where his cock had been.

Too bad we didn't have a tub in here, and I didn't want to try to send for one, with all the hustle and bustle. On the other hand…I might be able to do something about it myself. My magic hummed along contentedly, already rewoven into the fabric of my mind and soul. Sparks flickered just behind the tips of my fingers, an oddly pleasant itch. I hadn't gotten around to mending my trousers yet, so this would do for a demonstration.

"What were you planning to wash with that?" I said. "I might be able to offer an alternative."

I'd have to try it on myself first, though. Testing one's long-dormant and possibly flawed magic on someone else's cock seemed rude at best.

Andreas glanced up and smiled, and I went dizzy all over again. Fuck, I'd forgotten how disorienting it was to stop using my potion, and I'd obviously never actually switched from that to the more traditional method of controlling my twilight magic. If my personal guard, naked and smiling at me, was enough to make me lightheaded and short of breath, then obviously this wasn't an experiment I ought to repeat. What would happen if I lived like this all the time? I'd be horribly needy. A slave to my own body's desires, helpless to stand up to whichever lover had me in his power.

Living like that, subject to my mother's control in every other aspect of my life and a lover or husband's in this one, would be hell on earth.

But that didn't matter at the moment. Because Andreas was sauntering toward me, giant cock swinging hypnotically and the rest of him, smooth expanses of muscle and freckled long limbs and a perfect dusting of dark red hair, on full display. I'd get my potion tomorrow.

For tonight…

"You," he said, reminding me that I'd asked him a question before I got lost again in mentally tracing every line of him. "You seemed uncomfortable. And more to the point, I have plans for you. What's your alternative? If it doesn't involve my plans, I may have to overrule you, Your Highness. I am in charge of this expedition, you may recall."

Oh, gods. As if I'd had the chance to forget.

And as for his plans, well. That could be negotiated.

Clenching the muscles of my ass didn't…hurt, precisely, but it didn't feel wonderful, either. More of his come trickled out of me. The bed really had been, if not ruined, then put into a less-than-ideal state. Ugh. And I could say the same for my body. Another deep, hard fuck, Andreas's thick cock pounding me into jelly, his heavy body pinning me, all of him showing me how in charge he was…well, all right, maybe I'd manage despite the soreness between my legs. That hot, swirling sensation had returned, making my lower abdomen heavy and tight.

"I don't know what your plans are," I said hoarsely. This would be so revealing, too revealing, in more than one way. If I failed it might be the most humiliating thing that'd ever happened to me—and possibly the most injurious, too, depending on how badly I failed. Using magic on one's own ass might be more polite, but it certainly carried its own set of risks.

Although if I succeeded, Andreas might finally see that I had some value beyond my royal title.

I might see it too, for that matter.

"You won't need that cloth, though," I added, and propped myself up on my elbows, drawing up my knees with my feet flat on the bed. "Watch."

That instruction appeared to have been redundant. Andreas had stopped dead, the cloth dripping unheeded onto the floor, with his eyes fixed on me avidly.

His cock stirred and went from soft to half-roused within seconds. I'd been uncertain a moment ago, embarrassed by my wantonness. But Andreas's reaction gave me confidence I'd never have believed I could possess.

I shifted my weight, spreading my legs a little more, and reached between my legs, lifting my balls out of the way and massaging them as I did simply because it felt so incredibly good, exposing myself to him completely.

Andreas's chest rose and fell sharply, his fist clenching around the cloth. In a moment he'd be fully hard again. My focus wavered.

No, I had to do this—but I obviously couldn't look at Andreas's erection while I did. Forcing myself to close my eyes, I sank into my other senses. It didn't help much. My eyelids were no barrier to my magic and how it helped me see the world. Andreas still stood out to me just as he had before, golden and glowing and seductive in a way that had nothing whatsoever to do with his body or the pleasure I knew he could give me. Gods, he was even more beautiful like this than he was physically. There were places in the world where mages' impressions of a person's nature were used as part of the criminal justice system, a way to determine the contents of a soul. We didn't employ mages that way in Surbino. It was too subjective a process. And I'd always thought, bluntly, that it was bullshit to begin with.

Now I knew differently. Andreas *shone*, his honesty gleaming and his honor glowing.

And something else…arousal. Fuck, I could see it as clearly as I'd seen his erection with my physical eyes, a thread of shimmering crimson through his being, a warmth that strained toward me.

All of the texts I'd read by mages about the actual practical usage of magic—and the few that I'd been able to find were maddeningly vague and glossed over most of what you'd really need to know—emphasized the critical importance of concentration, of keeping the mind focused on the task at hand. The careful manipulation of the forces inherent in objects took great care. The one thing all mages seemed to agree on was the principle that destruction and chaos were far easier to bring about than orderly creation.

But my magic disagreed vehemently on the subject of control and focus. The sparking heat of my magic-infused being yearned irresistibly toward his glow. It felt right.

And so…I took a leap of faith. Instead of sticking to the scientific precepts of magic, such as they were, I followed my instincts.

Somehow, like I'd reached out with a physical limb—only I knew I hadn't moved, I could feel the stillness of my body too, superimposed on the motion of my mind—I shifted toward Andreas. My questing spark seeking his steady, luminous presence.

Below the range of my physical ears, a steady, low buzzing began to build, as if I'd stirred up a hive of magical bees. It grew louder the closer I came to Andreas. And it hurt, a stinging behind my teeth and an ache in my temples, akin to the sensation of being too close to a lightning strike in the midst of a storm.

I pulled back. Maybe it made me a coward, and I couldn't shake the sense that I'd been close to something incredible, but the relief was also instantaneous.

I was stronger now, though. I could feel it. Had I somehow harvested some of the brilliant energy that poured from him, the radiance of his soul? That had to be impossible, didn't it? Only mages had magic. If you had magic, you were a mage. That was the definition of it. He didn't have magic to harvest.

Gods, it didn't matter. Power thrummed in my blood and tingled in my fingertips. It strained at the leash, begging to be set free.

Examining my skin and the small particles of matter that composed it, the oil and come that coated it, and the layer where one stopped and the other began, I began to disassemble the mess and detach it from my body. Making an object cease to exist was impossible, but anything could be altered into anything else if you could hold the target shape in your mind. Most people wouldn't know it, but even air had a texture, a pattern, a substance. Matching that took less effort than I'd thought, my natural abilities taking over. And once I had the shape of it, pushing energy through the slick on and inside me to tear it apart and reform it into a pattern like the air took a fraction of a second, a blink, a shimmering twist in the fabric of the universe and a sensation deep inside me not unlike the moment before an orgasm when everything in my body was poised and ready to fall.

My eyes opened as I fell back on the bed, panting, staring up at the flickers of candlelight on the smoke-blackened beam that crossed the ceiling, at the faint flutter of a cobweb, all of it thrown into sparklingly bright relief by the wash of residual magic across my mind.

"Your Highness?" Andreas's voice reverberated as if I'd heard it through a drum. Everything spun around me. "Your Highness, are you all right?"

Through numb lips, I managed, "I'm fine. I told you to watch. Did you watch? I used my magic. I'm all clean." I wanted to tell him that next, if he allowed it, I'd use it on him, clean him up and then lick him everywhere.

But before I could muster the right words, he'd climbed back onto the bed and leaned over me.

Those eyes, all coppery and dark at once. And that hair, catching red glints from the fire. The set of his jaw. The faintly sweat-sheened gleam of his freckled shoulders. The glow of his perfect Andreas-ness around him, like the corona of the solar eclipse I'd seen years ago, so bright it'd damage your eyes without a shade to block some of it out. The lingering effects of using my magic had left everything brighter, sharper, more beautiful—although Andreas had looked almost that perfect to me before, too.

"That was magic?" he said. "It only took a second." His fingers brushed over the inner curve of my ass, one finger delicately slipping between my cheeks. "You're not wet anymore. Huh. Magic. Impressive, Your Highness. It probably takes more skill to do something careful like that than to do something that looks all big and fancy, doesn't it?" He smiled, the corners of his eyes crinkling. Gods. If I hadn't already been lying naked under him, I'd have flung myself down with my ass in the air when he looked at me like that—and praised me like that. "And you read my mind." He circled my hole with his finger, teasing, making me shiver. "I was going to do that with a cloth. Although now I'll need to start all over again with filling you up, won't I? Will the pain start again if you don't have some of me inside you?"

I hadn't even thought about that. Would one of the scholars at the conclave have an answer for that? Maybe, maybe not, but I doubted I'd have the courage to ask anyone.

Perhaps it might be best to simply test it myself, in the interests of science.

"Let's not risk it," I said faintly. "Just in case."

Of course, actually testing it would involve waiting to see if the pain came back *before* letting him fuck me again.

Oh well. Magical science would probably manage without me for now.

"Mmm," Andreas hummed, and moved—down, not up, bending to kiss my stomach, grasping my thighs and pushing them further open. As if he meant to fuck me, but how could he, positioned like that? "Agreed. Just in case. But first I need to make sure you're ready for me."

Ah, so he meant to use his fingers, and he wanted to see what he was doing.

See very closely, it seemed. Did he have poor vision in low light? Because he'd used one hand to lift my balls out of the way, rolling them in his palm in an incredibly distracting way, and why did it feel so much better when he did it than when I did…he kissed my inner thigh, his breath hot in the cleft of my ass.

And then he leaned in even more, and he wasn't *looking* at me, was he? Gods, he was—my shaky moan rose up to the rafters as he swiped the flat of his tongue over my hole, wetting me from the top of the crease all the way to the little strip of skin behind my balls.

"Andreas," I choked, "I don't think you can—oh gods, that's—you shouldn't, should you?" So wet and strange, and he licked me again and again, up and down, like my body was a canvas and he was painting me thoroughly, laving me, sloppy and filthy, the ring of muscle at my opening clenching and releasing under his assault. "You shouldn't do that!"

"Oh, I definitely should," he said, muffled by my flesh, and licked again, making me yelp and squirm. "Speaking of magic. You taste like it. Open for me, Your Highness. I want to lick the inside of you."

He wanted to…I lifted my head enough to peer down at his dark auburn one buried between my legs, bobbing up and down as he pushed his tongue—oh gods, inside me like he'd said, penetrating me in a slick, mobile way his cock couldn't have done, moving so agilely. And thrusting. And then he groaned, and I felt it inside, and everything went blurry.

Andreas licked and sucked and nibbled and held me open, growling into me, soaking me and opening me, and I buried my fingers in his hair and clung on for dear life. I bucked and thrashed, and he pinned me down. He brought me so close to spending again, my cock so hard it pushed up to throb against my belly.

By the time he lifted his head, grinned down at me, and wiped off his face with his forearm, I was sobbing for breath, eyes glazed, throat raspy.

"I think that ought to do it," he said, and wrapped his hands around my hips.

When he flipped me to my front, I didn't even try to move. I knew he'd position us both however he wanted to take me. And he did, kneeling between my legs, stroking my back, leaning down to nuzzle my shoulder and my neck, whispering words of encouragement as he pushed my knees up.

The cool air on my very wet hole felt incredibly wrong, the kiss of the head of his slick cock a relief. I squeezed my eyes shut and listened to the rush of my breath echoing against the pillow and held perfectly still, letting all my muscles relax as he slid his massive shaft into me with no resistance at all from my body. He filled me easily this time, as if he'd already claimed a space inside me and now only needed to use it at will.

He moved slowly, too. Almost carelessly. There wasn't any urgency this time, after all; my magic had never been more contented, and we'd both spent enough to be able to take our time.

I tilted my ass up a little further, stretching my thighs, making room for his cock. Andreas made an approving sound and palmed one cheek of my ass, rubbing a proprietary hand over me, pulling me open.

The straw mattress rustled, the ropes creaked, the frame started to thump gently against the wall. Andreas fucked me harder, fingers digging into my skin, balls slapping into mine and making them swing, the tug of the motion pulling me tighter and tighter, between that and the unending friction of his cock on that sweet, swollen spot in me…

The rush of his come inside me and the flood of my own felt like one release, one tensing and then softening. His cock slid out of me. I moaned, and Andreas ran his thumb over my hole, dipping in, soothing the emptiness.

I sank onto the bed as he released my hips at last and gentled me down. Big hands petted my ass and thighs, straightened my legs, massaged my calves. I shivered, and a blanket settled over me an instant later.

Oblivion settled over me a moment after that.

Chapter Thirteen

Losing one's virginity, it turned out, encompassed far more than simply fucking for the first time.

Had I ever imagined how it'd feel to wake up in another man's arms? Yes, if I were being honest: often, tossing and turning and hugging a pillow. But I'd never have been able to imagine how the arm clamped around my back would be a little sweaty, a little too hot, or how my leg thrown over him would nestle my cock and balls against his hip and make me want to squirm, or how chest hair would stick to my cheek.

Or how the heavy, steady beat of Andreas's heart under my ear, under my hand, would be almost more intimate than having him coming inside me. I blinked. Andreas must have put out the candles, because only the faintest reddish glow from the remains of the fire lit the room. But it was enough to show me my hand, his shoulder, the edge of the quilt across his ribs.

I didn't even remember him settling down into bed with me. He might just as easily have slept in his own room, or knowing him, in a chair or on the floor—and I found myself pitifully grateful that he'd chosen to join me instead. Another chance at this kind of intimacy might never come my way. Feeling Andreas pressed against me so closely, from head to toe, was a kind of magic not even the most skilled practitioner could create.

His hand tightened on my waist, and then he let go, tracing over my hip, along the curve of my ass, teasing into the very top of the crease with a finger.

"I know you're awake," he said. "Your breathing changed."

Well, that was…under other circumstances, I'd have thought it alarming to be observed quite so closely. On the other hand, I couldn't possibly be closer to him. And he cared enough to pay attention to how I breathed.

My heart gave a stupid little flutter.

Gods, could I be any more pathetic?

"I slept too," he went on. "But it's getting close to dawn. I always wake up right before the sun. I've been staying still to try not to disturb you." He turned his head and nuzzled into my hair. And that might have been a kiss to the top of my head.

With any luck he'd stopped listening so carefully, because the flutter became a vibrato, and my breathing sped up.

Yes, yes I could be more pathetic, as it happened.

"I slept well." I cleared my throat, hoping to rid myself of that soft, fond tone along with the slight roughness of sleep. "You kept me warm. Perhaps I should pay you more after all, if you're willing to tolerate my weight on you all night."

Damn it. That hadn't worked at all. I couldn't have sounded needier and more desperate if I'd tried, practically begging for reassurance that he'd tolerate me even if he weren't paid to do so.

A short silence fell. Had his heart sped up too, or was that simply my imagination?

"It was my honor, Your Highness," he said at last, his tone rather stiff. "All of it."

All of it. His honor? He felt…*honored* by having fucked me in the ass with his cock and his fingers and his tongue, and his cock again? Honored. I couldn't help the way my nails dug into his chest, the way I went tense against him. That answered that question, anyway. He might like me well enough. In fact, I was sure he did. He'd been genuinely friendly since we started preparing for the journey. And he hadn't been faking how much he wanted me, either. But apparently he wouldn't be lying here in bed with me, caressing me, comforting me, acting like a lover, unless he felt it was his duty to do so. After all, you couldn't fuck the virgin and then walk away, could you? That wouldn't be gentlemanly even if he hadn't been paid to take care of me.

My pulse pounded in my temples. With an effort, I forced my fingers to unclench, and I rolled away from him, turning partially onto my back. That trapped his arm under me. Fuck. And the blankets had slipped down as I moved. My chest and stomach and cock felt cold and bereft, the chilly air of the bedroom hitting me like a slap on skin that had been cozily pressed to Andreas for hours.

I cleared my throat again, since now it had a horrid lump in it.

"I'm very grateful," I said, summoning all of my training, extensive and from birth, in the art of remaining formal and polite even when you were screaming inside. "You probably saved my life, Andreas. I'll never forget it. And I couldn't ask for a more faithful guard."

My voice wavered on the last two words, but hopefully he wouldn't notice.

He tugged his arm out from under me, letting me drop down to the mattress, and I shivered as he sat up and took the last of his body's heat with him. I tried to keep my eyes fixed on the ceiling: that same cobweb from the night before drifting in the draft, the faint gray of dawn through the window beginning to cast the corners in gloomy light. But I couldn't help tracking Andreas out of the corner of my eye. He rolled out of bed and stretched, the muscles in his shoulders and back shifting and bulging mesmerizingly, and then bent over to pick up his clothes. The swing of his cock and balls between his legs almost had me begging him to come back.

Instead I tugged the covers up to my neck, trying to capture some of his residual warmth. It didn't work. I was chilled down to the bone, and it had nothing to do with the temperature of the room.

When I finally dared to look up, he'd made himself surprisingly presentable given how we'd spent the night and how carelessly his clothing had been removed. His tunic hung a bit crooked, and he held his sword with the belt wrapped around it.

But he'd put on his boots and looked more or less ready for his day. My last little shred of hope that he might get back in bed with me, take me in his arms, and kiss me senseless laid down and died.

Our eyes met and held. Gods, his face really didn't give much away. Washed out under his tan, and a bit pinched, but who wouldn't be after such a late night, and all the excitement? Besides, an overcast dawn flattered no one. I probably looked like death warmed over.

"You ought to go back to sleep, Your Highness," he said abruptly. "We're not going anywhere today, obviously. And you need your rest after—" Andreas stopped even more abruptly, his cheeks going from pale to brick red—as if even speaking about it embarrassed him now that we weren't in the throes of arousal and magic.

Gods fucking damn it all. Shame hit me directly in the solar plexus, and I might've doubled over if I hadn't been lying down.

He'd spent the night with me. First caring for me as I became ill, and then fucking me because I needed it to survive, and then holding me while I slept and watching over me—even if he'd wished he could be elsewhere, he'd stayed. And he truly had saved my life in the process.

Andreas hadn't chosen any of it. We'd joked about his committing "treason," and I believed him when he said he didn't feel obligated by his position as my guard, but in the end…he truly did receive a wage. From my *mother*. The *queen*.

The least I could do to thank him would be to summon rather more of that deeply ingrained royal courtesy I knew I possessed and allow him to withdraw in good order.

Preferably without flinging myself on the floor, wrapping my arms around his booted legs, and forcing him to drag me across the room as I pleaded with him to stay. To give me a few more hours to pretend that I had a lover, a life, someone who desired me and cared for me.

"I am still very tired," I said, and half-faked a yawn that became real after a moment. The flash of relief that passed across his face made my chest hurt, but at least I knew I was doing the right thing. That could comfort me in my cold, lonely hay bale of a bed, couldn't it? "You should rest more too. I give you my word of honor I'll send for you if I need anything at all."

Andreas nodded and turned for the door, opening it halfway and glancing out as if to make certain no one would see him. Gods, I hadn't even had the chance to worry about that; what would the men think of this, if they knew? It'd be incredibly awkward for everyone.

And then he paused, shoulders tense, head bowed, and drew in a breath deep enough that I saw his torso expand with it even across the room.

"Are you quite certain you're not going to experience any more of— any more. Symptoms, of your magic. Will you need me again before your potion's ready, do you think?"

He'd kept his tone perfectly neutral in a way that would've done any wily courtier proud. Did he hope I'd say yes? Hope to the gods I'd say no? Without being able to see his face—which might have been equally carefully blank, anyway, as I knew he could make it when he chose—I had no way to tell.

"I doubt it," I said truthfully, and with regret. "If the potion's ready tonight as promised, I ought to be fine. With leeway, even. I wouldn't expect to feel anything untoward until tomorrow evening."

"Then I bid you a good rest, Your Highness. You know I'll be nearby if you need—anything."

And with that, he slipped out the door and shut it softly behind him, leaving me alone with my thoughts.

I'd had better company. Beginning with Andreas, in fact.

Despite my exhaustion, it took me a long time to go back to sleep.

Andreas didn't come near me all day. I woke and rang for food and tea and fresh wash water halfway through the morning, and he didn't appear even when that was brought and the landlady came to check on me. I sat stiffly with my head bent over my breakfast and my back to the bed as the maids took away the linens and replaced them. Concern about someone else seeing my sheets had never even crossed my mind before now. Did other people with servants, who actually had spouses and lovers, feel embarrassed like this every morning? Ugh.

But the maids didn't say anything about it, thankfully.

And other than the servants, I didn't see anyone but Carlo, who sat on a stool in the corridor outside my room in lieu of Andreas's usual hovering. He didn't comment either. If he or the others had noticed anything last night, he was tactful enough to hide it.

Just past noon, I ventured out to take the air, going as far as the stables to pet Fluffy. The snow had stopped and it'd warmed up a bit, enough that the inn yard had turned to churned-up slush and the sky had taken on the unpleasant glare of the sun trying to push its way through pale clouds. On the whole, unappealing.

Despite the reek of damp horse, I lingered in the stable and petted Fluffy's nose, not-so-subtly waiting for Andreas to find me.

He didn't. Or maybe he'd been watching me all along, hidden behind a hay bale. I wouldn't have put it past him. And I had a prickle in the back of my neck that could've been from being observed. I knew it wasn't Carlo. He'd stuck his head into the stable as I entered, nodded, and then vanished back outside again, clearly satisfied that I'd be safe enough.

Andreas wouldn't have been so casual about it. When had I stopped wishing I could be left alone and grown to expect and enjoy having a six-foot-something shadow?

Finally I grew tired of the creeping discomfort, and of trying to pretend I wasn't waiting for Andreas, and went back to my room, too out of sorts to tolerate the noise of the taproom. Besides, most of my guards were gathered there around a table littered with ale flagons—without their commander, of course, because apparently he'd become invisible—and I knew they wouldn't really relax and enjoy themselves with me lurking about, no matter how unobtrusive I tried to be.

The afternoon passed slowly. Wind buffeted the windowpanes and whistled down the chimney, the maids brought me tea and snacks at intervals, and I went over and over my notes for the conclave. I still had a week to get there, and presumably the river would be passable soon enough.

My magic rose and fell within me like the tide, tingling in my fingers and making the hair on my arms stand on end, and then ebbing away temporarily, lulled down to almost nothing. I used it only once, repairing my torn clothing at last. For a moment I lost my focus and relived how they'd been ripped in the first place, and I nearly disintegrated my newly whole trousers into threads, cursing and shaking the sparks from my lightly smoking fingertips.

That discouraged me from trying again. Clearly I'd need more practice, slow and steady, before I could reliably use my powers. And I wouldn't be getting that, because the potion would be here within hours.

The conundrum that posed left me sullenly staring into the fire for the remainder of the afternoon, until the watery light faded out of the window and my eyes burned.

Quick, firm footsteps broke me out of my fugue, and I blinked into what felt like sudden darkness. Andreas. I'd have known his step anywhere, and my heart skipped a beat and then settled into a whirling tempo that had me breathless in seconds.

I shoved out of my chair, biting back a curse as my stiff legs nearly toppled me, and scrabbled for the candelabrum on the dressing table. If he found me sitting here alone in the dark sulking, what would he think I'd been doing?

Worst case, he'd come to the correct conclusion: that I'd been sitting alone in the dark, sulking—and also wondering where the hell he'd been all day.

He rapped out a brisk knock on the door. Fuck, I'd run out of time to light the candles the mundane way. In desperation, I turned my attention to the wicks—all of them at once.

And of course the door opened right as all three candles exploded into flame, sizzling halfway to the ceiling and all but taking my eyebrows with them. I yelped, fumbled the candelabrum and barely caught it, and Andreas dived for me and almost knocked it out of my grip again, wrapping his hand around mine where I held the base of it.

The flames settled down with a hiss and a spit of green and purple sparks. I looked up, breathing hard, to find Andreas's eyes fixed on my face.

His hand tightened, fingers pressing between mine, spreading them apart. Magic shot up my arm and arrowed into my chest and then down.

"Andreas," I whispered, and his eyes widened, going dark and molten.

Somehow we fumbled the candelabrum and the wooden box he'd carried in with him onto the table before his mouth came down on mine, hard and claiming. I stumbled back, his weight slamming me into the dressing table with a rattle and a slosh of the basin, his hands behind my knees to hoist me up onto the top. Andreas's hard cock pushed between my legs, insistent even through several layers of clothing, his hip bones bruising my thighs. I clung to his shoulders, tearing my mouth away so that he could bite at my throat and let me moan.

"I brought the potion," he gasped against my skin. "It's—gods, Your Highness, it's ready. You—your potion, fuck."

Distantly, I knew I ought to care about that. The potion was ready. I'd been waiting for it, hadn't I? Not waiting for Andreas.

This wasn't right. We ought to have been sated. *I* ought to have been sated. My curse *was* sated. And yet the thought of pushing him away, of taking the potion and never touching him again, had my heart pounding and my mind swirling with something terrifyingly close to panic.

And it had nothing to do with my magic.

I wrapped my legs around his waist and tried desperately to align his cock with mine, to feel his length and his hardness and his heat. "Fuck," he repeated, and kissed me again.

My trousers and drawers were in the way. So were his, but he could simply drop them to the floor. I couldn't remove mine without letting him go. And I couldn't bring myself to do it even for a second. It was such an overwhelming relief to have him here, to know that he hadn't left me. Hadn't abandoned me, or decided he never wanted to see me again.

So I funneled my magic again, reckless and past caring, and tore my clothes to shreds.

Andreas jerked back and froze, staring down between us at my suddenly bare lower body, at the drifting strands of what used to be my pants and undergarment, at my straining cock reaching up toward him as if begging to be touched.

Slowly, he lifted his head and looked back up at me. "You told me you wouldn't need me again before the potion was ready." I couldn't read his tone at all. "Did you just use your magic to tear off your own pants? I ripped the last pair. How many do you have, anyway?"

Gods, I had, and I had no excuse for it. I swallowed hard and tightened my legs around him. Damn him, if he tried to get away I'd use my magic to tackle him to the ground.

"Yes? I mean, yes. I did. I'm not sure if I need you." He frowned, and I hastened to add, "I'm not in pain! I don't know if I strictly need anything. For my magic. But I feel—" I stopped, because I had no idea what I felt or why. The pit of my stomach had clenched tight, my balls and my hole ached, my breath wouldn't quite catch and my skin didn't feel right and I simply *needed*, nonspecifically and indefinably. This didn't feel at all like my curse.

It felt like something more. Something I couldn't possibly explain to Andreas even if I could put the words to it in my own mind.

Something that terrified me. Because if it wasn't my curse…

"Maybe I do need you again," I said haltingly, praying that he wouldn't ask any more questions. "I feel so strange."

He leaned in and kissed me, softly, tugging on my lower lip and then pulling back enough to bend his head and look into my eyes. "Seeing you use your magic is—I can't describe it. And you should know, Your

Highness. If you take your clothes off, with or without magic, I'm going to take *you*. Whether you need me or not. You've been warned."

One of his hands slipped between my legs, teasing behind my balls and stroking me, and even though his skin was cold from being outside, heat spread under my skin everywhere he touched me. He reached for the bottle of oil he'd left on the nightstand with his other hand. Thank the gods the room was small and rather cramped. He didn't need to do more than lean a little. I didn't have to let him go.

"Now I know," I said breathlessly, my belly twinging with something hot and almost painful and so wonderful my vision blurred. "But I suppose it's too late this time." I rolled my hips and crossed my ankles behind the small of his back and tugged him closer. "Now you'll have to fuck me. I don't have any choice."

And thank the gods for that. If he made the decision for me, I didn't need to think about why I couldn't stop touching him.

He tugged the cork from the oil bottle with his teeth and spat it onto the floor, and if I hadn't already destroyed my own trousers and spread my legs, I'd have done it at that moment.

"You don't," he confirmed, voice low and dark, his teeth flashing in a wicked grin. "Do you know why?"

He took his hand from between my legs and poured oil on it, and I couldn't tear my eyes away from those long, muscular fingers glistening and ready to open me up again. I knew they'd fit. I knew his cock would fit. That didn't stop me from shivering in disbelief. How many times would he have to fill me before I grew used to it? I'd probably never find out.

"Your Highness?" he prompted me, and I snapped back up, eyes wide and mouth hanging open.

"Oh," I managed. Did I know why... Oh. "Because you're in charge of this expedition," I said obediently.

"That's right." Andreas's hand went between my legs again, his slick fingers pressing unerringly to the center of me, two of them pushing in suddenly enough to make me squirm and gasp, the stretch just this side of deliciously painful. "This expedition includes you," he added. "In case you were wondering."

He leaned down again and brushed his lips over mine.

"That really ought to be treasonous, except that my mother's annoying," I whispered, and he laughed into my mouth as he kissed me.

Even my insistent magic faded away to background music, the faintest thrumming melody beneath the soaring harmony of Andreas's hot mouth, his fingers exploring me, his big body between my legs and in my arms, with the rhythm of his movements guiding both of us. I stroked down over his shoulders, wishing I could feel the muscles of his chest through the chain mail shirt he wore beneath his tunic.

Drowning in his kiss, I didn't even notice him getting his own trousers open or positioning himself until the thick head of his cock nudged against my slick hole.

"Hold on to me," he said, and barely gave me time to wrap my hands around his biceps before he sheathed himself in one hard thrust up and in.

I clung to him, too stretched and full, transfixed, gasping like a landed fish. Andreas leaned back to look at me, but he didn't move below the waist. He simply—stayed inside me, thick and hard, letting me feel the length of him all the way from my ass to somewhere below my ribs.

"How's that?" he asked, and when I let out a soft, helpless whimper, he ground his hips into me and made me moan and wriggle and dig my fingers into his arms hard enough to bruise him. Somehow, I doubted he minded. "Answer me, Your Highness."

"You can't," I choked out, "make me tell you how you—how I—"

He angled his hips back, pulling an inch or two of his shaft out of me, and slammed back in, and I wailed and shuddered and collapsed against his chest. "I think I can make you," he said, and did it again. And again, until my ankles ached with the force of how hard I had to hold on to him, until unbearable pressure built in my cock, straining, so close—

And then he stopped.

My whole body pounded with the force of my heartbeat and his, and my breath rasped painfully.

But Andreas held perfectly still, even though his chest rose and fell quickly against mine, and sweat sheened his temples.

"Tell me how I feel in you," he said, voice a hard, low command. "Tell me or I won't finish. I'll pull out and get myself off."

Oh, gods, I wanted that almost as much, Andreas standing in front of me and stroking his own massive cock, and maybe he'd let me kneel in front of him while he—I used all my strength, lifted myself up on him, and forced myself back down on his cock, the dressing table thumping and banging. He pierced me so deeply that I screamed, and Andreas grunted and cursed, and that was enough.

Sobbing, head pressed to his shoulder, I spent all over the both of us, clenching down and writhing on his cock like a slut. My magic burned in me, blindingly bright, but the sweet warmth that suffused me as my peak faded had nothing to do with my body or my magic. It was all Andreas.

"Fuck," Andreas groaned, and held me closer, thrusting up into me almost desperately, my body jolting.

I pressed my open mouth to the base of his throat and tasted his pulse. Hot and hard, just like his cock in me.

"You feel like you own me," I gasped into his skin.

Andreas's hips stuttered, the arm around my back went tense, digging into me painfully, and he buried his face in my hair.

His body shook as he filled me, almost silently, his breath hitching.

It was my turn to gentle him the way he had me the night before, releasing my death grip on his shoulders to stroke the tense muscles of his arms, nuzzling into his neck, reaching one hand up to trail my fingers through the short hair at the nape of his neck.

Andreas shivered, sighed, and held me closer, tilting his hips to keep his softening cock inside me. I'd be dripping soon. Disgusting, but also… not so much.

But that would be the next moment.

For this one, I had Andreas in my arms and in me, and I felt whole, my magic and my mind and my body calm and at peace. I closed my eyes and breathed him in, letting everything else go.

Chapter Fourteen

The aftermath of sex felt very different when one didn't want to go to sleep immediately—another thing I'd never even imagined when I lay alone night after night, virginal and without any hope of changing that.

And I savored it far more than I could ever have anticipated, the slightly awkward dance of separating our bodies, the sticky sounds and sensations, the way our eyes met for just an instant as he leaned back, how I had to avert mine when my face went hot, my cheeks burning even more as he lifted my hand and kissed my fingertips.

Even the heavy slide of his spent cock disconcerted me less than it had before. Rather than leaving me changed forever, wanting and lonely, his withdrawal felt temporary. I might still be changed forever, true, but he'd fucked me before, and now he'd fucked me again and made it a habit, and my body insisted that Andreas surely wouldn't leave me empty for long.

He stepped back, steadying me as I slid down off the edge of the table. I pressed my thighs together, all slick with his come.

Andreas cleared his throat, tugged his pants up, fastened the button.

He had his head bent down, but his height meant I could see most of his face anyway. It was as flushed as I knew mine had to be.

A wave of tenderness swept over me, leaving horribly betraying and nearly irresistible impulses in its wake: my fingers twitched with the urge to reach out and stroke down his stubbled cheek, and I had to restrain the rest of me from trying to nestle into his arms like a needy idiot.

Of course, I'd already more than proven that I was a needy idiot when it came to Andreas.

Maybe he hadn't noticed yet. And if he hadn't, maybe I ought to keep it that way—for my own self-respect, if nothing else.

A trickle of his spend made its way down the back of my leg, and I shifted my weight, tugging my shirt down so that it hung to the middle of my thighs. The awkwardness had begun to feel rather less sweet and exciting now that Andreas wasn't touching me anymore.

He cleared his throat again and looked up at me, a flash of something in his eyes that made the pit of my stomach clench before it was gone again.

"I'll leave your potion for you, Your Highness," he said quietly, and gestured at the table. "It's there in the box. Two flasks of it, and a note from Doctor Serrano. He said to come by and see him before we leave town if you have any questions."

My heart sank down more with every word out of his mouth.

Right. My potion. Which I didn't need if he meant to keep fucking me…and which he might not be so eager to hand off to me and encourage me to take if he had any intention of doing so.

No, *I'd* been the one who didn't want him to keep fucking me, hadn't I? To keep my independence, such as it was? How many courtiers' marriages and loves had I seen dissolve into mistrust, mutual betrayal, bitterness and cruelty? Even when a man seemed to be of good character and had conducted every other aspect of his life honorably, he could turn into an absolute bastard to a lover. And I wouldn't just want my lover's kindness; I'd depend on it for my life and my sanity.

Fuck.

"Thank you," I managed, realizing the silence had stretched far too long to seem natural. "I appreciate your diligence."

And that had sounded *so* very natural, gods.

Andreas quirked an eyebrow at me and fidgeted with the hem of his tunic, smoothing it down. Would he comment on my stiffness and stupidity?

"You're welcome," he said after a moment. Gods, where was a trapdoor to the cellar when you needed one? "I need to check on the men, Your Highness. I've been out with Dario since after breakfast. I took him with me to reconnoiter since he's from these parts originally, but the others have probably been drinking all day," he went on, and I let out a breath. A change of subject. I could've kissed him, if that wouldn't have made everything even worse. I couldn't kiss him when we weren't actually fucking, could I? The thought left me flustered, hot, licking my lips.

It took a moment, a long one, for me to focus on his words again, rather than the firm, warm lips producing them.

"…and the best place to cross the river. They say the waters won't recede enough for the ford to be usable for weeks. And no boats large enough to carry our horses can cross here safely when it's flooded. Dario found someone who'd come down the northern road a few days ago, and he said the bridge forty miles upstream was passable, as far as he knew. It's far out of our way, but downriver there's nothing safe. So that's our best bet, I'd expect. Unless you'd like to abandon the journey, Your Highness," he added, with an irritating note of hope in his voice.

Irritating and unexpectedly painful. He'd been the one to convince my mother to let me go. Had he been lying to me all along about thinking this was important?

I had to work hard to keep my voice even as I said, "I'd prefer not to. But I realize the decision isn't mine to make, in the end."

A note of bitterness crept in despite my best efforts. Gods, if he didn't mean to take me in his arms again, why couldn't he simply go? I stared down at the floor, trying to hold still as more of his spend dripped out of me, no matter how I clenched my muscles to try to keep it in.

Silence crept over us, choking and thick.

"We'll proceed if you wish," he said at last. "Of course we will. I wouldn't have spent all day out in the sleet looking for a route otherwise. Fuck, I mean, excuse me, Your Highness. I didn't mean to sound as if I were complaining."

Andreas's set jaw and furrowed brow made my heart sink, weighed down by guilt and disappointment. He didn't want to go on. And how could I blame him, after all? He'd nearly died on the pass when the rope broke. And then he'd had to deal with the crisis of my cursed magic. Now, we faced a difficult river crossing, who knew what challenges on the road on the other side, and the entire journey back after the conclave. What if my potion ran out again, or we had another disaster?

The words trembled on my tongue: an acceptance of his authority, a yielding to his judgment.

Damn it all to hell, no, no I would not. A chill coursed along all my limbs. He'd fucked me, and now I'd almost—subjugated myself to him. Thrown myself on the mercy of his will and his whims. Precisely what I'd feared might happen if I gave up my potion, in short.

I lifted my chin and looked him in the eyes, fists so tight my nails dug into my palms, doing my royal best to ignore that I stood before him with goosebumped bare legs, with lips swollen from his kisses, with his spend trickling out of my body.

"You didn't sound as if you were complaining," I said. "Either way, we leave tomorrow. If we're going to detour so far out of our way we'll need to get an early start. As soon as it's light, if you please."

Andreas's mouth pressed into a thin line, and he nodded. "As you wish, Your Highness," he said, bowed, and turned and left the room without another word or a backward glance.

It was possible he shut the door with slightly more force than necessary.

When I moved, his come spread slickly between my cheeks, and I winced. I'd need to bathe as soon as possible—not just that, but pack my things, give orders to the maids for the morning, eat, go to bed, get ready to travel. I didn't want to do any of it. I wanted to chase Andreas down the hall, grab him by the shoulders, and shake him.

After that, my fantasy became a bit hazy.

First things first, though. Before I washed, before I did anything, I'd make sure that I wouldn't behave this way again—that I'd be clear-headed and sane the next time I saw my guard. The ability to use my magic, even temporarily, had been…seductive. But I'd done without it for fifteen years. I could go without it as long as I needed to. It didn't define me, damn it. I had other abilities, other talents, other value. And I'd tell myself that as often as I needed to.

When I flipped open the lid of the box Andreas had brought, there were two glass flasks inside just as he'd said there would be, along with a letter. I skimmed that first, checking Doctor Serrano's dosage instructions as compared to my previous formula, and then took one of the flasks out of its nest of straw.

I didn't need it yet. I wouldn't need it, almost certainly, for another forty-one hours.

But I swallowed the first dose then and there, naked and wet and cold and miserable, with no delay. I had to have control over myself.

And I couldn't, I *wouldn't* need Andreas again.

We rose at dawn to continue our journey, just as I'd demanded—like the idiot I was. Andreas knocked on my door and woke me before the window had even turned gray. Of course this was the time he chose to obey me to the letter, damn him.

"I'll send someone up with coffee and breakfast, Your Highness," he called through the door, sounding disgustingly alert for someone who must've risen at the same time I'd have been going to bed when I was at home.

Rolling over onto my side, I blinked blearily into the darkness, able to see only the faintest line of light around the edge of my door. The fire had burned down to nothing at all. Twisting about in bed tugged on muscles

I'd never known I had. I tightened them, feeling the space Andreas had left in me—or at least it seemed that way. Surely I didn't really have an emptiness within my body in the precise shape of his cock.

"Your Highness?" A note of worry there, and for a long, shameful moment I toyed with the idea of not answering at all, which would force him to open the door and come inside to check on me. If he'd wanted to, he already would have.

"Yes, thank you," I said, my voice rasping. I couldn't possibly have sounded less seductive.

Not that I wanted to seduce him! I didn't need or want him at all. I'd taken my potion the night before.

"Breakfast in five minutes, Your Highness. We'll ride whenever you're ready." His footsteps retreated down the corridor.

Ride.

That really had been my idea, hadn't it? To mount a horse and trot through the rain and sleet along a pitted road, bouncing up and down in a hard, damp saddle. Why hadn't I thought to try to heal myself before I drank the potion the night before?

Because I hadn't been thinking at all, my mind taken over completely by the way Andreas had taken *me*.

I sat up with a shudder, fumbling a blanket around my shoulders to keep the chill off while the servants came to light the fire.

The day, if you could even call it that given the gloom, didn't particularly improve from there. Icy water dripped off the brim of my hat and blew sideways under the collar of my coat. My fingers went too numb to feel the reins, and heavy dark clouds obscured the sun so thoroughly that the sky hadn't brightened at all even after we'd been riding for hours.

We took the northern road, passing through endless expanses of soggy fields and frosty woodlands and exchanging a few words of greeting with other occasional soggy and frosty travelers. Andreas remained remarkably silent, riding beside me with his hat pulled down enough that I couldn't even sneak looks at his face.

Partway through the morning, Andreas reined in and gestured that we'd stop for a rest, leading us under the shelter of a grove of spreading oaks.

As I stiffly swung my leg over, wincing at the tug between my legs, he appeared at my side and slipped a hand under my elbow as I slid down to the ground.

His fingers wrapped around my upper arm, strong and sure. Trapped between Fluffy's bulk and Andreas's tall, broad-shouldered body, I almost felt warm for the first time since I'd crawled out of my bed. The urge to lean into Andreas and close my eyes nearly overwhelmed me. Would he catch me? Wrap an arm around my back and tuck me against his shoulder? Would the men stand in shocked silence, or would they laugh? Would I care?

Heat bloomed in my belly, a tickling ache that I wouldn't have recognized until a couple of days ago—a tight, needy sensation that should've been impossible given that I'd taken a full dose of my potion only sixteen hours before.

My breath hitched as my heart skipped and then thudded into motion again.

"Your Highness?" Andreas asked quietly, bending down toward me, too close, painfully close, close enough that I could've tilted my head into a kiss. "Are you well?"

Was I? Yes, in fact. Despite the heaviness in my balls, the rapid beat of my heart, I was. No pain, no fever, none of the lightning-bolt pains that shot along my veins and nerves when my tainted magic tormented me. And no magic, either. If the potion hadn't been working I'd have had access to my powers, and I couldn't detect so much as a faint flush of usable magic anywhere in me.

"Yes. I'm fine."

That didn't quite amount to a lie. Andreas wanted to know if he needed to take immediate action to solve a specific problem. He hadn't intended a more general inquiry into my state of mind.

When he let go of me, nodded, and strode away, the air between us seemed to stretch like syrup, clinging and sticky, a prickly tug on every inch of my skin that made me lean toward him and catch myself with a fist around Fluffy's reins.

As he got about ten feet away from me it felt like the stretched air between us snapped, and I reeled back, the air whooshing out of my lungs. But my cock stirred, and my balls tightened enough to make me gasp, and that space inside me…

I had to bite my lip to keep in a whimper, squeezing my eyes shut and leaning on Fluffy as my knees turned all watery.

Fuck. What was happening to me? I'd taken the potion. I knew it was working. And when it worked, it made me completely impotent, able to want in the abstract, perhaps, but not able to feel desire in a more visceral way. Certainly not capable of an erection. And while I hadn't gotten even half-hard, anything more than completely limp *shouldn't be possible*.

We were in the saddle again within twenty minutes, the sensations in the lower part of my body still unsettlingly powerful. Every time I shifted in the saddle my fingers twitched on the reins, my whole body going tense. Every time I couldn't stop myself from glancing over at Andreas, it made me ache: desire, deep inside, clawing its way to the surface.

By late afternoon, we still had seven miles to go according to the signpost we'd stopped to examine, and the grisly gray of a wet winter twilight had fully closed in. My cock hadn't gone completely soft since we stopped for our lunch. No matter how hard I tried, I couldn't get a full breath.

Panic hadn't quite set in—but I was working on it. For fuck's sake, I'd done the right thing! I'd taken my potion! But if I didn't get Andreas's cock in me, I felt like I might die—figuratively, if not literally. And if the potion truly didn't work, then literally might be an option too. Andreas would string Doctor Serrano up by his toes after I died, but that didn't comfort me much, especially since my mother would do the same to Andreas.

Gods, the pressure inside me…by the time we stopped for the night, I might go mad.

"…Highness? Are you all right?"

I shook my head, startled, and Fluffy shied as I tugged the reins a bit too hard.

"Yes," I managed, and cleared my throat. "What?"

Andreas had turned his horse to face me, and the rest of our party had clumped together in a circle around us. "There's a village half a mile down that track, according to this," he said, and waved a hand at the signpost. "We'll stop there for the night. Find the bridge in the morning. If it pleases you, Your Highness."

Oh, thank the gods. "Yes," I said, hoping I sounded decisive rather than pleading. "It's too dark to go on." *And I'm too eager to bend over for you and beg.* "Lead the way."

Andreas nodded, turned his horse, and set off down the small side road that led away through the trees. I nudged Fluffy into a trot, biting my lip as my ass bounced up and down.

The way the branches encroached on the path made me wonder if we'd find anything at all besides more trees on this route, but sure enough, another turn brought us onto a village green, with a smithy to the right and the stable yard of an inn on our left. A boy ran out and called to us, taking Andreas's reins and then mine, and a moment later we were all stamping our boots and shaking out our cloaks and coats, the men muttering appreciatively about the smell of stew and ale and oak branches on the two fires in the dining room.

A red-faced fellow with a bald head and an apron bustled up to us—clearly the landlord by his prosperous stomach, and clearly pleased to see a large party of well-heeled travelers by his wide smile.

"Drinks, supper, and rooms for the night?" he asked hopefully, bobbing something between a bow and a nod. "I'm afraid I won't have enough rooms for all of you to have your own, but they're comfortable to share! And there's enough beef in the stew, my word on it!"

"We'll manage," Andreas said. "Your best room for my lord here, and we'll split up the rest. And we'll get cleaned up before supper, if you'd show us to our rooms first."

The landlord started chatting away about the quality of his stew, but I hardly heard a word of it over the frantic pounding of my heart. I couldn't ask Andreas to share a room with me. I could only hope he chose to do so on his own, or that the way they divided meant that he had to.

"We do have only four rooms open," the landlord said as we turned down the corridor at the top of the stairs. "But large enough for three of your men to be comfortable—"

"That won't be necessary," Andreas cut in. "We'll do two to a room. I'll guard his lordship overnight." Oh, thank the gods, and thank Andreas for being overly paranoid about my safety. My eyes fluttered shut in relief for a moment as I sent up a quick and silent prayer of gratitude to Ennolu, Dromos, or whoever else might be listening. They were assholes, but occasionally they came through. "We'll want breakfast before dawn, if you please," Andreas continued. "We'll ride as soon as it's light. Going north, if you have anything you can tell us about the road."

"Making for the pass, then?" the landlord said. The pass? And then I realized he must mean the route across the mountains about another twenty miles north of the bridge.

He stopped at an open door, inside which I glimpsed a maid setting candles and another lighting the fire. Had they used magic to get here before us? Or perhaps they'd simply used another staircase from the kitchen when the innkeeper called out to them. Clearly, I needed sleep. Or coffee. Or…I didn't know what.

"Your room will be ready in one moment, your lordship," the landlord went on. "The road ought to be well enough, if muddy. Regarding the pass, it's likely to be a bit snowed in right now. You'll be waiting at the foot of it for a few days, I expect. Might want to stay here. Our cook's better than at the Three Pines where you'd be stuck if you go that way, if I do say so. And there are some bandits about. Though your party's well armed enough."

"No," Andreas said, "we're going across the river. The ford at Perona's not passable, and won't be for weeks, they say. So we're detouring to the north."

The landlord stepped back to let the maids slip out of the room and down the corridor, and waved a genial hand. "After you, my lord and sir. And I'm sorry to be the one to tell you, but you won't be crossing the river at the bridge, either. The water's three feet over the top of it. Has been since yesterday week."

Andreas stopped and spun on his heel so abruptly that I'd have crashed into him if I hadn't frozen in my tracks.

"What?" he demanded. "The bridge that's seven miles away, by the sign at the crossroads? I had first-hand information that it was in good repair only yesterday."

The landlord frowned and shrugged. "I don't know what to tell you about that, sir. I saw it for myself two days ago when I went to see my mother, whose cottage is only a hop and a skip up the hill from it, and the bridge watchman said as it'd been like that for days already. The bridge is good stone. Stood for a hundred years. It won't wash out, but you can't cross it until it's dry, neither."

My chest tightened painfully.

No ford. No bridge. No way over the river. For a moment I wondered wildly if I could wean myself off the potion again and use magic to get us across somehow.

But no, I'd spent too many years suppressing it, and I had to simply accept that I might never be capable of the magic other mages managed without difficulty. My attempt to light three candles at the same time hadn't been particularly encouraging. I'd get us all killed.

Andreas's troubled gaze flicked to me and lingered for a moment, dark and grim, before he looked back at the landlord. "You're certain. You swear to me that you saw the bridge yourself?"

"On my soul and risking Ennolu's wrath, sir! Couldn't even see the tops of the railings for how high the river's gone. I doubt you'll be able to go that way for near as long as the ford's going to be flooded."

"Damn it," Andreas muttered, and nodded tightly. "I'll speak to you again this evening. Your—my lord? Come in and get warm and dry, will you?"

"Only while we talk about what's to be done," I said, and Andreas nodded again, turning to enter the bedroom.

The landlord retreated down the corridor, bowing and apologizing with all his might, promising to make my men comfortable. I wished I had the wherewithal to reassure him that we weren't the sorts to take out our annoyance at the inconvenience on the hapless messenger, but it was all I could do not to burst into tears like a fool. My guards were waiting to go to their own rooms, all clustered on the stairs behind me and muttering about what we'd just heard, and I couldn't possibly let them see how distressed this news had made me.

It took more effort than it had to ride all day simply to move my feet enough to walk over the threshold and into the room. And then Andreas shut the door behind me, and we were alone at last.

Chapter Fifteen

Leaving Andreas to shut the door, I wobbled my way across the room, stripped my damp coat and dropped it to the floor, and slumped over against the fireplace mantel. Damn it, I'd barely started to believe that maybe the gods would loosen their grip a tiny bit. Did they truly have nothing better to do than torture me? They'd been fucking with me since the moment of my birth.

As if to underscore that, the twisting heat between my legs that'd been simmering all day flared into life again. Andreas stood behind me. I could feel his presence, hear his breath. We had no one observing us. The men had gone down the hall and out of hearing range. And Andreas had locked the door; I'd heard the double click.

I turned and found him still standing near it, one hand clenched around the hilt of his sword and the other raised to massage his temples.

Those fingers. Gods, his fingers, and his hands, and the strength of his arms, those hard muscles…

I swallowed hard around the lump in my suddenly arid throat.

My eyes traveled down.

The way he gripped his sword made my breath catch.

His narrow hips, the muscular columns of his legs, and between his thighs…not even the hem of his tunic and the heavy fabric of his trousers could completely disguise the bulge there.

The world swayed around me as my head went light with an overwhelming combination of despair and frustration and anger, worry about the potion and my magic, and guilt for having dragged Andreas into this futile, dangerous journey at the possible cost of his queen's trust in him and even his own safety. And most of all, confusion at my body's inexplicable betrayal.

"I beg your pardon, Your Highness," Andreas said, "but will you allow me to sit for a moment while we talk? I need to fix my boot, the buckle's loose. And then I'll go down to ask a few more questions. Corroborate that fellow's tale. And order your supper."

I glanced up. Two solid, well-padded armchairs occupied pride of place before the fire. I hadn't even thought to sit in one, simply leaning there in shock. And Andreas had crossed to one of them, eyebrows raised, waiting for me to give him permission to sit in my royal presence while I remained standing.

He'd fucked me three times, kissing me and filling me and making me scream, but he wouldn't sit down unless I gave him leave.

Nothing could possibly have underlined the gulf between us more strongly.

"Of course you can sit. Don't ask me again," I said, with more snap to my tone than I'd intended.

Andreas never took that sort of nonsense from me. He might offer some retort or other, or he'd laugh, or he'd simply raise one eyebrow and give me that *look*, and I'd blush, as thoroughly admonished as if he'd told me off.

This time, he just nodded and sat down with a sigh, tipping his head back and giving no sign of hurrying to deal with his boot.

He'd planted his feet wide, knees splayed, the fabric of his trousers pulling tight across his groin. My eyes ran from his long legs to his sword-belted hips to his broad chest and shoulders, to the strong, lean lines of his arms. Andreas didn't have the bulk of some men, but every angle and curve of his big, loose-limbed body promised power and agility—and I knew from experience those were promises he could keep.

The fire in my lower belly smoldered. Every particle of my body yearned toward him, that same tug I'd felt earlier in the day.

Andreas glanced up at me, eyes dark and intent and fixed on mine. One of his hands flexed: slightly rawboned knuckles, muscled swordsman's fingers, blunt nails. Those fingers had been inside my body.

And that was enough. More than enough.

The smolder burst into wild flame, licking up into my chest, consuming me. My face burned. My limbs shook. Everything between my legs went heavy and thick.

I couldn't have stopped myself from crossing the few feet to him with a dagger to my throat.

Andreas watched me, unmoving except for the way his chest rose and fell faster the closer I came. I leaned over, bracing my hands on the wings of his chair, and straddled him, one leg at a time, wedging my knees between his thighs and the chair arms. Our faces were only inches apart; we breathed the same intoxicating breath. His eyes practically glowed, copper gleaming through shadows. I lowered myself down and gasped as my ass settled into his lap and came to rest on his hardness and heat.

He drew a sharp, rough breath. "I thought you wanted to talk about the bridge. What we do next. Fuck, Your Highness," and his head fell back and his mouth fell open, eyes half-lidded, as I rocked my hips and pressed closer. My cock throbbed, barely erect but desperate for a touch all the same.

"Feel free to talk about the bridge," I said, and rocked forward again.

He'd gotten fully hard, just like that, his cock straining the front of his pants. The ridge of it pressed into my balls. My moan cut off in a yelp as he grasped me by the hips and pinned me down against him.

"I'm serious, Your Highness." Andreas spread his legs a little more, stretching me apart. "Your conclave is in less than—"

"Fuck the conclave," I gasped. At the moment I simply couldn't care less. My hole ached for him, something I'd never even imagined could be possible, and I didn't give a gods-damn about anything else.

I half lunged, half toppled forward and pressed my mouth to his, clumsy and eager, knowing I probably showed every bit of my inexperience in initiating a kiss.

Andreas didn't seem to care. He groaned into my mouth, bucking up, and his hands tightened on my hips until I thought my bones might crack. I whimpered and rode him, my hands falling onto his shoulders, craving him so deeply and desperately that I couldn't contain it, the tingling in my fingers and the pounding heat building up inside my skull—everything around me vanished in a hazy whirlwind of sensation and sparking magic, gods, magic, I shouldn't be able to—not with the potion—

And then something—*snapped*, and there was skin against skin at last, finally, Andreas's bare cock nudging behind my balls. I rose up, writhing against him, until the head of his cock pushed between my cheeks and against my slick, needy hole.

Slick? How was I…?

But Andreas was kissing me, biting at my swollen lips and fucking my mouth with his agile tongue, and his impossibly thick cockhead wedged its way inside me, a sudden and startling stretch.

"Fuck, how are you wet?" Andreas gasped into my mouth. "How are you—hang on, where did your pants—or wait, my pants—"

Good questions, but I almost had him, I almost had him—I dug my fingers into his shoulders and forced myself down onto his cock, corkscrewing my hips and taking every massive inch of him. I didn't stop until I was sitting on Andreas's thighs with my balls nestled against his abdomen. Our eyes met and held, both of us caught in the same breathless moment of stillness. A crimson flush painted Andreas's cheekbones. Within me, his cock seemed to swell, filling me until I didn't have room for breath.

I had no idea what to do next.

Andreas stroked my waist with his thumbs, circling them into the little hollows in front of my hips. A smile quirked one corner of his mouth.

He thrust up, the smallest possible movement that still jostled everything inside me, and I gasped, my eyes widening.

His smile bloomed into a grin, his eyes glittering.

Fucking smug bastard. I'd show him that two could play at that game.

I tensed my thighs and shoved up onto my knees, feeling every inch of his cock as it slowly withdrew until only the head stayed in me.

And then I leaned in close and slammed myself down.

Sensation exploded inside me, the angle of my body pressing his cock against every perfect spot, heat shooting along all my limbs and prickles of sweat breaking out all over my skin.

I went still, panting and shuddering, my body clenching and releasing around his cock. Gods, I couldn't do that again, not even to prove a point. I'd pass out and die.

"Do that again," Andreas growled, a little breathless but still completely in control, damn him. "Come on, Your Highness. Fuck yourself on me. It was your idea."

My head snapped up and my mouth dropped open in indignation. My idea? *My idea?* He hadn't exactly been arguing with me!

Wait, I'd meant to show him, hadn't I? Which meant…fucking myself on him was my idea after all.

Fucking myself. On him. I was on him, sitting in his lap, impaled.

My cock stiffened a tiny bit more. Apparently it liked the idea as much as I did, and I shivered.

And then I squirmed, squeezing around Andreas's cock, and that wiped the smile off his face. His lashes fluttered and his hands convulsed around my waist. When he bit his lower lip and gazed at me out of half-lidded, burning dark eyes, it no longer mattered whose idea it had been.

Only Andreas mattered. The way he filled me, the way he completed me. Took away that empty loneliness that I'd lived with all my adult life.

I pushed up and forced myself down again, in and out, up and down, stuffed to bursting and then painfully hollow, helpless little punched-out moans escaping me every time my hips hit his legs.

Andreas watched me silently, his body tense under me and his grip on me getting harder and tighter. His heartbeat vibrated through his fingers and thundered under my hands where I had them pressed against his chest. Every slap of my thighs on his, every slick slide of his cock in me, echoed in the quiet room. I couldn't tear my eyes from his. The pressure inside me built and built, familiar enough now that I knew I wouldn't last long…if I could come at all with my cock not fully hard, and gods, I needed to, I couldn't take it, and I slammed myself down again and again…

Ecstasy sparked and flared deep inside where his cock filled me so perfectly, as sudden as a thunderbolt. I screamed, my back bowing and my own cock twitching. I clutched at his shoulders, but my hands had gone weak along with the rest of me.

Only Andreas's grip kept me from flying off into the ether. I collapsed against his chest, eyes sliding shut, my whole body vibrating with the force of my galloping heart. Wetness spread between my limp cock and his abdomen.

Andreas let go of my hips at last, wrapping an arm around my waist and the other across my back, pressing me to him by the nape of my neck with his long fingers wrapped around the side of my throat.

The force of his thrusts up into me shook my whole body, but he had me pinned and helpless. I clung to him and let him use me, wet and tight and at his mercy.

With a low, shuddering groan, Andreas crushed me to his chest and filled me, hot and deep. I quivered around him and buried my face in his neck, breathing him in, reveling in the sensation of being bathed in him. My relief and joy had nothing to do with suppressing the effects of my cursed magic. I simply craved his come in me, marking me as his lover. How often would he need to fuck me to keep me wet inside all day and night? Every morning and evening at the very least. Perhaps once in the middle of the day.

I drifted in that hazy, beautiful fantasy as my breathing slowed and the sweat cooled on my skin, as Andreas's arms relaxed around me, cradling me rather than clutching me so tightly my ribs ached. He stroked the side of my neck with his fingertips and nuzzled into my hair. Inside me, his cock started to soften, beginning to slip out, his spend coating my thighs.

Mmm. I liked it more on the inside, honestly. But if I didn't feel like getting off his lap and washing right away, I could always just use magic to clean myself up the way I had the other night.

My thoughts stopped so abruptly they might as well have crashed into a stone wall.

Magic.

My eyes popped open as my heart lurched and sped up again.

I'd taken the potion. But not only had my body and mind demanded the satisfaction of Andreas inside me, I'd—I lifted my head and glanced down, ignoring Andreas's faintly interrogative murmur. He didn't have any trousers on. Neither did I. They weren't just torn or open, they were *gone*. And whatever slippery substance had appeared to make me ready to get fucked hadn't come from any mundane source.

"Our trousers are gone," I said.

Andreas stroked one hand up and down my back, lightly scraping his nails along my spine. Even through the fabric of my shirt it made me smile and shiver. "So they are," he replied. "I'm going to think twice before tearing your clothes in the future, if this is how you take your revenge. Any idea what you did with them? Or are they gone forever? Because I only have two other pairs in my bags. Good thing I carried everything up with us, or I'd be giving everyone downstairs quite a show in a few minutes."

His lazy, casual tone irritated me nearly as much as his touch soothed me, and the contrast annoyed me all the more. Didn't he understand the problem here? Who gave a damn about how many pairs of pants he had!

"Too bad for you," I snapped. "But I don't care where they are. I shouldn't have been able to make them disappear in the first place! I don't even know how I did it. I mean, I wouldn't be able to do it again on purpose, aside from not understanding how I managed to do it at all when I took the potion last ni—"

"You what?" He suddenly sounded much, much more alert, and his hands slipped down to my waist again as he pushed me off his chest enough so that he could see my face.

I glanced back up. Yes, that was guard-Andreas, not lover-Andreas, all sharp eyes and firm jaw and furrowed brow. And now I wished he hadn't taken me seriously after all. Five more minutes of perfect peace and contentment and lying to myself. Would that have been too much to ask?

"You took the potion?" he went on. "You wanted—that is, you needed me. Just now. I assumed you must not have taken it yet. And hang on. You used magic, unless there's another mage hiding in the corner waiting to vanish our trousers away at critical moments."

I couldn't let that pass. "Mages can't make anything just vanish. Objects can be moved with force and energy, and they can be transmuted into any other type of object, including air, the similarity or differences between the two making it more or less difficult, but you can't simply—"

Andreas's hand landed firmly across my mouth, and the words "make them disappear" vanished, ironically, into his skin.

"That's not the point," he said sternly, and his tone made me want to—well, want him. Again. Already. "The potion's not working. Right? That's a problem. If it's not working, the gods only know what's wrong with it. It could make you sick."

Oh, for fuck's sake. I hadn't even thought of that. But…no. It had tasted like the other one, and it certainly wasn't spoiled.

"Mmmph!" I said. He took his hand away. "I feel fine. This potion's incredibly difficult to make correctly, but screwing it up doesn't make it dangerous, just ineffective. Don't worry about that," I said more softly, the pinched look on his face tugging at something in my chest. Gods. I knew he had to be concerned about my well-being. He was paid to be. But this felt like more than that. Maybe I was still lying to myself after all. "Our problem's that it isn't working. That's all. And obviously we can deal with that."

My cheeks went fiery hot, and I had to fix my eyes on a point over his shoulder rather than meet his. Andreas shifted under me. The motion pulled his cock the rest of the way out, and the squelching sound and resulting gush of come didn't help with my embarrassment.

"We can," he said, voice low and gravelly. He cleared his throat. "As long as you're not in pain. Were you? Was that why you, uh, needed me?"

The chair's worn green fabric upholstery had a patch that had gotten completely threadbare on the wing. The shape vaguely resembled a fish. Perhaps if I focused on that intently enough I'd be able to admit the truth without combusting. I certainly couldn't lie. That would be unworthy of a prince. And besides, Andreas would probably know, and then he'd make me look at him and admit it anyway.

"No," I whispered. "I wasn't in pain. It wasn't time yet. The—only way to really test the potion would be to wait until I start to feel it, and then take a dose and see what happens."

"Good." Both of his hands had been resting on my back, but one of them crept down, tugging up my shirt as it went. "You must be getting cold, Your Highness. We should probably find our pants. Wherever they've gone. Or get some new ones."

Pulling up my shirt would only make me colder, but that didn't seem to have occurred to him. My breath started to come faster again, hitching in my chest, as Andreas slipped his hand under the trailing hem of the shirt and palmed the cheek of my ass, tracing delicate patterns on my tingling skin with his fingertips.

"Are you checking to see if I'm cold?" I asked, sounding a little choked.

"You have goosebumps," he said, and stroked lower, and then in, until his fingers slid between my cheeks and his palm cupped the lower curve.

I finally tore my eyes away from the fish-shaped patch on the chair, and I found Andreas's eyes fixed intently on my face. Searching, perhaps? But for what?

My goosebumps weren't from the cold. And if he kept touching me like that, my cock stirring against his stomach would tell him that without my having to say anything at all.

The words that came out of my mouth, accompanied by a glance at him through my half-lowered eyelashes, were, "You could warm me up."

Andreas's eyes darkened, the hand on my ass gripping me more tightly.

Oh, gods. I hadn't meant to sound quite so…sultry.

"I could, but don't you want to wait? It's about a day and a half, isn't it? To see if the potion works after all."

His hand had dipped into the slick crease of my ass, the index finger sliding gently inside me, teasing the ring of muscle, little shocks of sensation sparking into my insides and up my spine.

"Oh," I gasped, and squeezed around his finger. He shuddered and pushed it in all the way, and I moaned, and then we were kissing again.

Between kisses, he muttered, "It's only a few minutes. We'll start waiting however many hours, fuck, you feel—we'll wait. After this."

"Mmm," I moaned, and tipped my head back, rocking on him, his cock growing again and pushing between my thighs. "We'll—after this. We'll test it."

And then he thrust inside me, hard and fast, and I didn't give a fuck about my potion anymore.

Chapter Sixteen

Bracing myself on the headboard, I bit my lip to keep in the moans that tried to burst out with every one of Andreas's vigorous thrusts. The sun had barely crawled over the horizon, shooting a few actual golden rays through the clouds and the south-facing window of my room. Surely this wasn't an appropriate time to be fucked, was it?

But I hadn't had a chance, or the breath, to argue. Andreas had rolled me onto my stomach from where I'd been lying on my side cozily wrapped in his arms and put me on my hands and knees. Without warning, in fact, while I was still barely stirring after being roused by the servants moving about downstairs and in the yard.

I'd whimpered into my pillow as he spread my thighs and tugged my hips to put my ass in the air. My fingers clenched into the bedding as he pushed two of his own inside me, twisting and turning and opening me.

Not that I needed it much after last night.

"You're still wet," he said, and buried himself inside me.

Now he'd been fucking me for a few minutes, long enough that my cock had gotten half-hard and my lower torso had gone all hot and heavy, it could be.

"Your Highness?" Andreas lifted his head enough to nuzzle my neck. "Have you gone back to sleep? That's not a very flattering review of my performance. Or maybe it's the most flattering review. I'd have to consider the matter."

I wanted to reply with something witty, or failing that with something casual in the same lightly amused tone he'd used. Instead, all that came out was, "You should call me Nikola. Or just Niko."

He almost had, hadn't he? Only once, when we were in bed together the other night. But he'd corrected himself. Even in the throes of passion.

Andreas kissed me softly right below my ear, and then he hesitated, his breath held for a long moment before he let it out in a tickling rush. I squirmed under him, and he bit my earlobe, which for some reason sent a bolt of heat straight down into the pit of my stomach.

"When I'm committing treason," he said at last, and then stopped again. I'd gone so tense I was afraid my voice would shake if I tried to demand that he finish his fucking sentence already, so I simply vibrated with frustration in silence. When he spoke again, it was so low I almost had to strain to hear him, even though his mouth was an inch from my ear. "When I'm inside you, it seems like it makes it even more forbidden to call you Your Highness. I like it." He rocked his hips, stirring my insides with his still half-hard cock. "Do you want me to fuck you again, Your Highness?"

"Forty-two, fuck, hours," I gasped, as my spine went liquid and my eyes fluttered shut. "To test the potion."

"I came inside you five minutes ago," he said, already starting to thrust, lighting me up from the inside, hand wrapping around my limp cock and tugging on it, playing with me, massaging me. "What's another twenty?"

"Oh, gods. Andreas!"

"That's what I thought," he said, and bit my ear again.

The sun had fully risen now, the window lit up golden and the clattering and thumping from the kitchen below us growing in volume.

Hopefully it'd drown out the way the bed began to creak as Andreas knelt up and pulled me into his lap, legs splayed and ass spread to take him.

By the time he came inside me again, I'd forgotten about the potion all over again. I'd forgotten everything but his name.

"So with the bridge impassable, we need alternatives," Andreas said, addressing the small group we'd gathered around a table by the fire in the inn's small private parlor.

Sergeant Salvius hummed agreement, and Carlo and Dario nodded attentively. The sergeant and Carlo had both been part of the royal guard for decades, long enough that I couldn't remember when their faces hadn't been familiar—although they'd both gotten grayer and more lined over the years. Dario was young, and he'd only appeared at the palace a few months ago, as far as I could recall. He'd been chosen for this journey for the same reason Andreas had sent him out to ask questions the other day, and the same reason he'd been summoned to our meeting this morning: he'd been born and raised on this side of the mountains. So far he'd been quiet and unobtrusive, and he'd apologized in a way that seemed sincere for his informant's error about the bridge.

Everyone made mistakes, after all. Myself very much included.

Case in point, I'd spent the first part of the discussion trying to calculate, to the minute, how long it'd been since Andreas spent in me for the second time this morning. One hour and thirty-one minutes, based on a surreptitious glance at my pocket watch—which meant I had only forty hours and twenty-nine minutes to go before I could…

Gods, drink my potion again. That was what would happen at the end of…forty hours and twenty-*eight* minutes, now. Not Andreas tossing me onto my bed and committing multiple acts of "treason" while calling me *Your Highness* in that low, intent tone of his.

"Your Highness?" I jumped, gasped, and blinked back to the reality in front of me to find four pairs of eyes fixed on me. The words sent a flush of heat from my hairline all the way down to…all the way down. If anyone noticed, I had no idea how I'd explain it. Illness or magic gone awry, probably, and then they'd all think me even more of a strange weakling than they already did.

"Forgive my inattention," I managed. "I was preoccupied."

Again. I'd be lucky if I remembered ten words of this conversation, damn it all.

Andreas smiled, and if he kept doing that I might end up bending over the table and begging.

Forty hours and maybe…twenty minutes, if they'd been talking for a bit without my noticing. Until I took my potion, obviously. Then again, it might not work. I'd have to have an alternative cure available just in case.

"Understandable," Andreas said. "I asked if you were happy with the plan. I know the delay here isn't ideal, but it makes more sense to me than all of us forging on when we may need to backtrack, in the end."

If I'd had the slightest notion what the plan might be, possibly I could've given him a coherent answer.

Instead, I fell back on the last resort of absent-minded royalty since the beginning of time, and nodded regally, waving a languid hand in a gesture of approval and saying, "You have my complete confidence."

"Thank you, Your Highness," Andreas said, and then added, "Dismissed. Depart at once, and best of luck. Ride safely."

All three of the men rose, bowed, murmured the usual polite things, and clomped their heavy boots out of the room in a group, shutting the door behind them.

Andreas waited until their footsteps had faded before turning to me, one eyebrow raised and a smile quirking the corner of his mouth. "You have no idea what the plan is, do you, Your Highness."

He didn't make it a question. He didn't need to.

The flush on my face turned into full-on burning, but I lifted my chin and stared him down. This was his fault. If he hadn't spent all night and all morning with his hands and mouth all over me and his cock inside me,

I wouldn't have been so distracted.

"No, but since apparently you're in charge of the expedition, any commentary of mine would've been moot in any case. You only asked me to be polite in front of the men, I saw no reason to ask any questions."

I only realized how sharp my tone had been when Andreas's expression changed, going from amused to serious to annoyed as I spoke. And worst of all, I could've sworn he passed through genuine hurt on his way to being irritated with me.

"Your Highness, if you want to direct the journey, then with all possible respect, you need to either pay attention to the decisions being made or at least ask when you—"

"I'm sorry, forget I—never mind," I said, shoving up out of my chair and making for the door, flustered and with sudden prickles in my eyelids. Pathetic, gods I was pathetic. "I'm certain you made the right decision. Whatever decision you made."

Swift footsteps rang out behind me as I put my hand on the latch. Before I could open it, Andreas had caught me by the upper arm and spun me around, stepping so close he put a foot between mine and crowded me against the door.

He leaned down, bracing his other elbow on the wall beside me and caging me in. I couldn't look away. Gods, those eyes. I vaguely recalled trying to convince myself they weren't beautiful when we first met, since I'd been sulking and determined not to see anything good in him. Now, I couldn't imagine anything more gorgeous than those coppery flecks, the dark intensity of his gaze, and the firm set of his jaw and mouth to complete the picture.

"Your Highness," he said softly, and then sighed and shook his head. "Niko."

Something twisted in my chest, something painful and beautiful. Tilting my head up and falling into his kiss felt like the most natural thing in the world. The hand on my arm slid around until it rested between my shoulder blades, fingers splayed, drawing me closer.

Andreas's tongue flicked my lower lip as he pulled back, one last taste.

"Niko," he said again, and my knees almost buckled. I slumped back. Andreas moved with me, hand trapped between me and the door. Gods, I ached for him again. It'd only been—a lot less than forty hours and however many minutes. "Do you want to hear what the plan is?"

I nodded, not trusting myself to speak. Yes, I did, and wrapping my arms around him and spreading my legs and possibly accidentally disposing of what was left of our wardrobes—which I wanted even more than an explanation—probably wouldn't be the best move at the moment, seeing as we were in a semi-public place with half the village drinking ale in the taproom on the other side of the door.

"Carlo and Dario are going to get a look at the bridge for themselves, just to make sure, and then they're going to ride further north, where there may be a ferryman with a boat capable of getting us all across despite the flooding."

He paused as if waiting for some sensible and intelligent comment from me. Well, he'd be waiting a long fucking time. My cock had stirred almost to half-mast, my hole practically hurt it felt so fucking empty, and every second that I spent breathing in his heat and rich scent made me more lightheaded. I nodded slightly.

"All right," Andreas went on. "I'll take that as approval. But it means we'll be here for a few days waiting for them. I know it's cutting it close for how much time we have left to make it to your meeting. But there's no point in riding out in this weather and on these roads without any certain route."

A few more days. Here, in this inn, with Andreas. And nothing whatsoever to do.

Oh, gods. That wouldn't be a recipe for trouble at all.

It was time to admit it to myself: if I wanted to last four hours, let alone forty, I'd need to barricade myself in my room with Andreas outside it, tie myself to the bed, and knock myself over the head with a wine bottle.

The way his eyes kept flicking to my lips suggested he might be in similar straits.

And now I couldn't think about anything except barricading the bedroom door and drinking the wine, only with Andreas on my side of the door, and as for the other part…

"Whatever you're thinking, stop," Andreas said harshly. "Just the look it's putting on your face is going to fucking kill me."

Gods. *He* was going to fucking kill *me*, because now I knew that the only thing more unbearably attractive than Andreas in full, commanding control was Andreas as desperate for me as I was for him.

I could tease him.

If I dared.

I smirked up at him, fluttered my eyelashes, and said, "If you really want to know, I was—"

"I don't, because we're not even really alone—"

"—thinking about you tying me to the bed in our room."

Andreas stuttered into silence, his mouth dropping open. The hand on my back went rigid, the fingers digging in.

"You were thinking," he said, leaning down so slowly that the urge to bolt and run gathered in prickles of sweat at the base of my spine, "of me tying you to the bed. With anything in particular, Your Highness? For any particular purpose?"

I knew him well enough by now to recognize his purposefully mild tone, the way he was trying to sound unaffected. But that rasp to his voice gave him away. That and the way his chest had started to rise and fall like he'd been in a footrace. If I tilted my hips forward a tiny bit—oh, gods, yes, he was hard, so long and hard that he was about to lose another pair of trousers. My cock brushed his. I had to bite back a groan.

"If you want me to use that, tell me," he said firmly.

Another flutter of my eyelashes, since it seemed to either annoy him or make him want me, or possibly both at once. "Tell you what?"

Andreas's eyes widened. "Oh, for—fuck," he growled, and yanked me into his arms, bending me back over one of them, everything whirling around me, and crushing his mouth over mine.

The world floated away, unimportant and hazy. I needed him inside me, needed his kiss, his hands on my skin, his heat surrounding me—

I nearly levitated out of my own body as a heavy knock sounded on the door. Andreas yanked me upright and we sprang apart, my heart trying to rabbit its way out of my chest.

"Yes? What?" he demanded, sounding less than friendly.

There was a short pause before a female voice said, "Begging your pardon, sirs. But we found two pairs of pants out in the snow this morning, and your men say they're yours, they think. We washed 'em and all. For future, you want them washed, you can put them in the hall, not out the window. Just saying. And I have them here."

A heavy, fraught silence fell as all the blood in my body rushed away from my brain and into my cheeks. Andreas reached up and rubbed at his temples. His shoulders quivered. He was laughing, silently but so hard that his whole body shook. A hysterical bubble of some emotion I couldn't quite define as amusement rose up in my throat. Horror, perhaps. Wonder, very likely. Utter mortification, most definitely.

I cleared my throat as best I could, but my voice still came out oddly high and thin as I said, "Thank you. Can you leave them in my room, please?"

"Happy to," she said. "And if you have more washing, you can—"

"Yes, thank you, we get the point!"

Andreas doubled over, wheezing, his hands on his knees.

"Humph," came through the door, and then soft footsteps whisked away.

"Oh, fucking gods," he choked. "Fuck. Bloody buggering fuck." He lifted his head, showing me red cheeks, glittering eyes, and a ridiculous shit-eating grin. "You sent them all the way—"

"Shut your gods-damned mouth right now," I snarled, "or I swear by all that's holy I'm going to magic you out the window, head-first."

"I beg your pardon," he said, voice thick with laughter. "I'll, uh, I'm going to see if Carlo and Dario have left. If they need any further instructions."

He opened the door, dashed out, and shut it quickly behind him.

An instant later, I winced as he positively roared with laughter, the sound receding as he walked away.

That absolute bastard. Had he no shame at all?

I fumbled my watch out of my pocket. Now I only had thirty-nine hours and fifty-eight minutes until I'd be able to test my potion's efficacy. At least keeping off of Andreas's cock for that long would be easy now that I wanted to slap his stupid face more than I wanted to kiss it.

My pants.

And Andreas's pants.

In the inn yard.

I dropped into the chair nearest the fire and leaned my elbows on my knees, head hanging down. The gods really did seem to take special pleasure in toying with me.

If I ever got my hands on Ennolu, I'd throttle him. Right after Andreas.

Chapter Seventeen

By dint of hiding in my room, I managed to avoid Andreas completely for the rest of the day.

Of course, he didn't seek me out, either. I tried very hard not to take that personally. But when a knock on the door made my heart skitter and my cock stir, I knew I was in trouble. The sinking disappointment that followed immediately was even worse. When I called out an answer, one of the guards poked his head around the door and told me that he was here to collect Andreas's things, since Dario and Carlo's departure and some rearrangements by the innkeeper meant he could have his own room.

I sat stiffly in my armchair by the fire while he took Andreas's saddlebags, trying desperately not to remember what Andreas and I had done in this same chair. Twice. Vigorously.

"All set, Your Highness," Ludo said, and retreated out of the room.

Leaving me alone. Without Andreas, who apparently didn't mean to return at all. Who'd rather send someone else to bring him his things than even be in the same bedroom with me. Was he embarrassed about the maid finding our pants now that he'd had time to think about it? Or had my burst of temper driven him away?

I had to admit it: it was a lot less satisfying to hide from someone when he wasn't trying to find me.

In a fit of dudgeon, I rang the bell and had a maid bring my supper to the room rather than go downstairs and face either Andreas or his conspicuous absence.

Damn it, I wanted to smack him. Shake him. Shout at him. Strip off his trousers and climb on his cock and ride him until he lost his mind. No, no, fuck, I didn't want to do that! Not at all. My watch sat on the table, and I did another calculation as I spooned up a bit more stew. Thirty and a half hours now, give or take a few minutes, because my head spun when I tried to be more precise than that. I was too annoyed for mathematics.

But that meant I only had to make it until the wee hours of the morning after tomorrow. No problem. Spending the entire night and the next day and most of the next night alone would be fine.

I gritted my teeth and forced down another lump of turnip.

By the time the maid had cleared my tray and built up the fire for me, I'd worked myself into a state. I slumped into my chair and stared into the fire, hating myself and Andreas and Ennolu and everyone involved in constructing that stupid bridge so low down to the river—I mean, why shouldn't they have bloody well built the pilings up another ten feet? Didn't they have competent stonemasons on this side of the mountains? Queen Lessandra, who ruled this part of the isthmus and whom I'd met twice on state visits, had seemed clever enough. Apparently she had no interest in her kingdom's infrastructure.

My watch ticked on, the fire burned down, and finally I heard footsteps in the corridor and the low-voiced rumble of a couple of my guards passing by on their way to bed. A moment after they'd gone, a distinctive tread followed: Andreas. I strained my ears, keeping perfectly still and holding my breath, cursing the faint crackle of the fire.

A door opened and then closed. And I was pretty sure it was the door directly across from me. Right there, only…about twenty feet from me, if I assumed that room was a similar size to mine.

Oh, gods, if I'd started counting the floorboards between me and Andreas, I really had a problem.

Fuck. I had to see if the new potion worked. Because this was exactly what I'd been afraid of, wasn't it? Andreas had made me angry and then walked away. And yes, my irritation had already waned, and if he'd come to my door and apologized for laughing in the face of my embarrassment I'd have accepted it and forgotten about it by tomorrow.

But that was this time.

What if he'd given me a much stronger and more lasting reason for staying away from him? And I didn't have a potion to use instead. And then I'd have two choices: wait until the pain forced me to crawl at his feet and beg him to fuck me, or go and crawl to him sooner, albeit more figuratively, swallowing my pride and pretending it wasn't eating me up inside. I'd always be at a disadvantage without a potion. Always vulnerable.

So I had to wait the…twenty-six hours or so.

Andreas would be undressing right now. First his boots, lined up neatly near the fire to be toasty by morning—but not too near, as he'd explained to me one of the nights we'd stopped on the road. You didn't want the leather to dry out and crack. And then he'd yank his tunic over his head, leaving him in the chain mail shirt he always wore—which clung lovingly to his muscles in a way I'd never imagined metal could cling. Once he'd gotten that off, he'd only have his thin linen singlet on top. That garment left his shoulders bare and highlighted his rangy strength.

Then his trousers. The singlet and his drawers would both be rumpled after a day's wear. The outline of his cock would stand out very clearly through the cotton drawers.

Gods, that cock. I didn't even need it inside me so much as I simply wanted to touch it, make Andreas moan…taste it.

I sat bolt upright in my chair.

If he didn't spend inside me, it wouldn't affect my magic at all one way or the other. He could fuck me and then pull out before he finished, of course, but he might mistime it. It'd be much safer if I licked and sucked and pleasured him while he ran his long fingers through my hair…

The sounds of my ragged, rasping breaths pulled me back to my own bedroom, where I was alone and not sucking anyone's cock.

Clearly the potion hadn't worked so well in any case, since I'd magicked away our pants yesterday. Right? And I could feel my magic now, trickling through my veins—not the unchecked flood I'd have expected without the potion, and possibly not enough to be usable, but present and accounted for. As if it worked to some extent, but possibly wore off faster than the other formulation.

Did I really need to test the potion further?

Yes, of course I needed a real test to confirm it either way, and I was just making excuses.

Damn it.

I stood up, sat down again, stood up and paced, and cursed myself for the way I couldn't stop trying to talk myself into Andreas's bed.

No, I didn't need him. Not in the slightest. And I'd tell him so. Right now, because why wait?

A moment later I burst out of my door and then through the one directly across the corridor, mouth open to tell him exactly what I thought of him and his stupid cock—and skidded to a sudden halt as a shining and extremely sharp sword appeared, pointed right at my chest.

"Oh," I gasped, looking up from the blade, already being withdrawn, to Andreas's bare chest and grim face. "That's actual treason, I think."

He'd already slid the sword back into its scabbard before I finished speaking. "I was about to open my door for the night so that I could keep an eye on yours," he said. "I needed to change clothes first. And then there was a commotion, and then I thought—I was afraid you were in danger. Apparently you were the commotion." He leaned the sword up against his dressing table and shrugged. "Forgive me."

Oh, thank the gods, he'd given me an opening.

Speaking of openings. I spun around and slammed the door behind me, and then whirled on Andreas again.

"That's not what you need forgiveness for!" I said, mustering all the indignation that'd temporarily fled with its tail between its legs at the sight of a half-naked Andreas with a sword in his hand. My powers of rational thought had gone with it, which probably accounted for the next words out of my mouth. "Take your pants off before I send them out into the yard again."

Andreas crossed his powerful arms over his equally muscular chest and stared me down, and well, there went the last of my ability to think. "I thought you were avoiding me."

I gaped at him. "How did you—yes, I was avoiding you, and that's never stopped you before, I need to point out. But how *did* you know?" I hadn't said a word to him. If he knew me well enough to understand my mood, and if he'd simply been respecting my apparent desire to be left alone…it was rather lowering to realize that almost all of my anger had been for his distance, without much left for the way he'd laughed at me and my absurd lack of magical control.

He shrugged again, the motion flexing those arms and that chest in an incredibly distracting way.

"You walked right by me with your nose in the air on the way to your bedroom earlier. I followed you up the stairs, and you shut the door in my face. And then you called down for supper for one."

Well, all right. Yes. I had done those things, but I'd assumed he'd ignore me and come into the room anyway if he damn well pleased. Past experience with Andreas suggested that if I dug in my heels and argued about what I had or hadn't done, he'd get that gleam in his eye and give as good as he got, and it would go poorly for me, prince or no. It might be more dignified to simply…not discuss it at all.

"I needed privacy," I said loftily. "But I'll let it pass."

Andreas's lips twitched. "How generous of you, Your Highness."

Oh, for fuck's— "Take your pants off, will you?" I snapped.

"Your wish is my command," he said smoothly, and reached for his buttons. "But you haven't told me why you're angry yet."

My breath caught in my throat as the buttons slipped out and his trousers opened, revealing the thick jut of his cock, already hard and straining the linen of his drawers. For me.

So I sounded a little strangled as I replied, "Because you laughed at me." And then I stopped, horrified. I'd been letting it go, hadn't I?

Andreas's face softened and his hands stilled. "I didn't laugh at you," he said, and he was deathly serious, without a trace of his usual sardonic edge. "I thought I was laughing with you. At how ridiculous it was. I felt guilty for laughing at the maid, but I didn't—you really thought I was laughing at *you?*"

When he did laugh at me, which he had often enough—although, honor forced me to admit, only when I deserved it—it made me go all hot and molten inside, eager to argue and win or to fight him and lose, and either way to end up under him. That was what I'd wanted even before I had an excuse to act on it. I'd denied it to myself, desperately. But I couldn't deny it anymore.

And when he looked at me like this, like he cared about my feelings, cared for me…well, that gave me a whole new set of desires.

To smile into his kiss, caress him, gentle him. To fall to my knees and show him how I could care for him in turn. Show him how sweet I could be.

The sincerity in that steady dark gaze cleansed me of the last of my anger and my self-consciousness. He hadn't been laughing at me. He'd said so. Andreas would never lie to me.

And he wouldn't laugh at me now, either, even if my inexperience made me awkward. Could anyone be elegant and poised kneeling on the floor and crouching to suck a cock? If so, I wouldn't be one of them.

I met his eyes, trying not to blush but knowing I'd failed by the burning heat spreading up my neck and cheeks.

"I did think that," I said. "It was—I didn't have control of my own magic. It's humiliating. But I don't doubt your word. And I'm not angry anymore."

"How could you possibly—Niko." He stepped forward, slowly crossing the room to me. "How could you be expected to have control over your magic when you've barely ever had a chance to use it?"

When I'd told him to address me by name, I'd more imagined him doing so mid-coitus than in conversation. Guards didn't call princes by their nicknames just standing there and talking, after all. And although he had his clothes half off, this didn't feel like foreplay. Lovers would do this, wouldn't they? Real lovers. They'd dress and undress, talk, argue or resolve an argument, casually share the same bedroom and the same living space.

And they'd show each other affection and understanding, especially when one of them had unreasonable expectations for himself and took it out on his lover.

I knew damn well who I'd be in that scenario.

Through a tight throat, my eyes stinging, I managed to say, "I don't know. It doesn't make any sense that I'd know what to do, does it? But I expected—more, I suppose. Of myself."

Andreas had come within a foot of me now, but I couldn't bring myself to reach out, even though he drew me in so irresistibly that I found myself leaning, wanting his heat and his strength so badly. The moment I touched him it'd be irrevocable: this helpless need, this desperate desire, this connection that I'd never expected to have with another man.

I'd never be able to lie to myself again. And without those lies, how would I live?

"If I tell you what I think of that, Your Highness, I'm afraid you'd think me impertinent. Disrespectful, even." He lifted his hand, and when he laid it against my cheek, gently cupping my jaw and stroking his fingers along my temple, the ground seemed to shift sideways under me and my eyes fluttered closed. I tingled where his skin met mine. I opened my eyes again and found him studying me with so much intensity my breath caught. He drew a deep breath of his own, his chest hitching. "If you didn't use your potion you'd be able to practice as much as you wanted. You'd never accidentally send any clothes out the window again. But you'd be welcome to do it on purpose. I wouldn't complain."

Andreas flashed me a smile that didn't reach his eyes, and every line of his big body had gone rigid with tension.

Could he possibly mean…? My heart kicked into a gallop, so hard and fast that he must've been able to feel it through the skin of his hand.

He hadn't wanted me when my potion bottles broke in the first place.

Had he? He'd been so reluctant. And my mother paid him to take care of me.

If any other man in his position had hinted that he wanted to become my lover, to replace the potion as my source of magical balance, I'd have strongly suspected an ulterior motive. Possibly several. Career advancement and promotion, money, power, influence…not that I could offer much of the above, really, but most commoners would wrongly assume I could.

Andreas would never use me that way.

And he'd demonstrated, over and over again, that even if he hadn't wanted me at first, his desire had grown. Of course, that didn't mean part of his offer wasn't motivated by kindness. Perhaps he just wasn't certain that he was making the right decision. I knew he couldn't be afraid *I* wouldn't want *him*; I'd come to his bedroom and told him to take his pants off.

The fear, in fact, was all mine. No matter how much I trusted him, and no matter how much I wanted him, I simply couldn't rid myself of the cold, nervous lump in my chest that formed every time I imagined turning my life over to another man. Even Andreas, whose presence and voice and touch had become so necessary to me that everything felt wrong and off-kilter when he wasn't there.

"That sounds very pleasant," I said, through a throat so dry that every word scraped painfully. Pleasant, gods. *Pleasant* was strolling through the palace gardens on a sunny day. *Pleasant* was a midmorning cup of tea. What Andreas had so quickly sketched for me sounded like a paradise even Ennolu couldn't provide. "But I need the potion, Andreas. Maybe— not all of the time. But I need it. Right now, I need to know that I have it and that it works when necessary. Do you understand?"

He sucked in a deep breath and let it out slowly, slowly enough that the silence made me want to scream. "You don't trust me."

Pain spiked through my chest. After all he'd done for me, I couldn't possibly let him believe that. "I do! Gods, Andreas, I do trust you, I trust you more than anyone—"

"Don't," he said, and leaned down to press his lips to mine. One brush of skin on skin that left me silenced and tingling, and he pulled back and said, "You don't have to make me feel better. You don't trust me enough, and why should you? Even if I had a right to be upset about it, I wouldn't be."

I wanted so badly to tell him that he did have a right, and that I trusted him completely, and that the flaw of my birth, my tainted magic, had given me another: a lack of faith that had nothing whatsoever to do with him.

"I came in here with a plan," I said miserably. "Aside from yelling at you."

This time Andreas's smile did light up those beautiful eyes. "If that was the plan that involved my pants coming off, it sounds like it might be a winning strategy to me."

Thank the gods, we could change the subject. But that meant I had to—fuck, I still had no idea what to do. I'd gotten too distracted. And the idea of my mouth on his cock left my mind spinning in circles. Kneeling on the floor would work, but what if...

"Lie down on the bed," I said, hoping I sounded even slightly authoritative. "Just lie down. And let me—let me," I stammered, sounding not authoritative at all.

Andreas nodded, let me go, and backed up the few steps to the bed. "I serve at the pleasure of the prince," he said, winked, and lay back on the pillows, folding his arms behind him and spreading his legs enough to showcase the thick ridge of his cock.

My mouth went dry and my own cock valiantly tried to become fully erect, pulling all the blood from my brain in the process.

And now I had to figure out what to do next.

Luckily I'd always been a quick learner. I swallowed hard and stepped forward.

Chapter Eighteen

Andreas's body was so much more intimidating approached this way. Something about the angle. When he'd been on top of me, and even when I'd been riding him, looking down at the length of his muscled torso and at his cock pointing at me had been…well, yes, also intimidating.

But like this, as I tentatively placed a knee on the bed between his legs and leaned down? He seemed twice as big.

All of him, from his bulging biceps and his sculpted chest down to… all the way down to all of him.

Could his cock actually be that thick? I'd had it thrusting roughly inside me again and again, so I really ought to be an authority on the matter.

"If you don't know how to take someone's pants off the mundane way, I can always provide some helpful—"

My gaze flicked up from his daunting equipment to his gleaming eyes and sly smile. "Shut the hell up," I growled. "Or the pants stay on."

Not that I'd follow through with that threat, of course. I was about a heartbeat away from throwing caution to the wind and trying to magic them off to parts unknown.

And he seemed to know it was a bluff, because he pressed his lips together, somehow laughing at the same time, and shrugged. With his arms still behind his head.

No one ought to have that kind of coordination.

I certainly didn't, and it'd be likely to show as soon as I touched him.

But no quailing now.

I reached out and stroked him with a finger through the fabric of his drawers, base to tip. The cloth was body-hot and slightly damp where it stretched over his cockhead. Andreas sucked in an audible breath as I circled my finger around it, fascinated.

But I couldn't stand the tease of it any more than he could, and I took hold of the waist of his trousers and drawers and tugged them, Andreas obligingly lifting his hips until I had the clothes bunched down around his thighs. His cock stood up almost straight, with the weight of it pulling it down toward his stomach.

The thick base of his cock had a slightly different texture and color than the upper part of the shaft and the gleaming head: darker, purplish, the skin less smooth. His heavy balls hung down below, all of it surrounded by auburn curls.

My fantasies had never really included sucking cock. Perhaps it had been a failure of imagination, or a failure of my potion-stunted libido, or a failure of those stupid books that hadn't prepared me for anything, as it turned out.

But it had definitely been a failure of some kind, because my mouth watered and my tongue tingled with the desire to see how all those textures felt. The warm, spicy scent of him rose up the more I bent down.

Gods, I wanted—

"What are you doing?" Andreas's sharp-toned demand stopped me short, an inch away from licking the base of his cock.

I glanced up to find him staring down at me, eyes wide. Fuck, I wanted to lick every single inch of his big body, and it took me a moment to focus on what he'd said.

"What do you think I'm doing?"

"I told you I wouldn't," he said, sounding harassed beyond belief. "I promised you."

"Promised me? When did I ask you to—"

"You didn't ask me! But I'm not going to do this to you, Your Highness. It's not right when you're not—we're not—you shouldn't. I told you. That's an act of, of, for someone you choose."

A crimson blur obscured my vision for a moment as fury rose up and choked me. My inexperience didn't make me incapable of deciding for myself what I did and didn't want, or what was right or wrong. How dare he tell me what I ought and ought not to do? Aside from the times when I loved it when he told me what to do, of course.

But this wasn't one of them. Telling me how to please him, or how to take him when he chose to please me, weren't the same as telling me whether I was allowed to do it in the first place. And if he didn't know the difference, then I'd damn well teach him.

"You're not doing anything to me," I said. "I'm doing it to you."

Before he could argue, I swooped down and sucked the head of his cock into my mouth.

And then I froze, because I hadn't thought this far and I had no idea what to do. Andreas's cockhead filled my mouth, thick and delicious, like a salted sweetmeat. He groaned and shifted under me, and I braced one forearm against his thigh, hand on his hip.

"Fuck, Niko," Andreas said, low and strained. "You can't—I can't—" He broke off in a cry as I swirled my tongue around, licking him inside my mouth. "You shouldn't!"

I pulled off with a pop and a flick of my tongue that made his whole body shudder. The pit of my stomach twisted into a knot of need. Andreas stared down at me, mouth open, face and torso all flushed and gleaming with sweat.

"You really don't want me to suck you?" I asked him. "I really shouldn't?"

Andreas blinked at me. "Fucking gods," he panted. "Fuck. You have no idea what I'm going to do to you when it's my turn."

My blood felt like it stopped circulating for a second, my whole body going cold. "I need to test my potion. Andreas, you can't just—if I don't want—"

"I'm not going to fuck you! I'm going to lick every part of you until you're screaming. Unless you want me to fuck you, and then I'll fuck you until you scream too. Are you sucking me off or not, you little tease?"

It was my turn to stare, completely nonplussed. Not only had he understood exactly what I was afraid, of…he wouldn't do it. Never. No matter how much he liked to be in charge. *I serve at the pleasure of the prince.* He might tell me what to do, he might call me a little tease, but…he meant it.

And as long as he served at my pleasure so generously, I'd be his to command, no matter how treasonous his orders might be. Especially if they were treasonous. He probably knew it, too.

"Yes, Andreas," I whispered. "I'm sucking you off."

"Not that I'd noticed—oh, fucking gods," he said, as I bent again and kissed the head of his cock, a soft, breathtaking brush of my lips against the silkiest skin I'd ever felt. "Fuck. Your Highness. Niko—" He broke off in a groan that vibrated all the way down to my toes, and I lost myself in the taste of him and the heat of him, my own cock throbbing in the constriction of my trousers.

One of his hands slipped behind my head and wrapped around the base of my skull, and I moaned around his cock.

He didn't shove me down. He didn't need to. I wanted it as much as he did, his cock thrusting down my throat and filling it, Andreas using me until I couldn't do anything but take what he gave me. Even though I could barely fit more than a couple of inches of his shaft into my mouth, I pushed down, trying to unhinge my jaw and take him deeper, his cockhead lodged on the back of my tongue and in the opening of my throat, too thick, I started to gag, tears running down my cheeks—

"Stop, Niko." Andreas's fingers wrapped firmly in my hair as he pulled me off, gently but inexorably. I gazed up at him, panting, face damp and probably all flushed and blotchy. He'd propped himself up on his other elbow to get a good view of me, and his eyes were wide but his jaw had set in that stubborn jut of his. "You'll choke."

I didn't mind choking. But ironically, I was having too much trouble getting my mouth to work to tell him so.

Andreas petted the nape of my neck. "Open your mouth, Your Highness," he said. "And don't look away from me." He pushed down lightly, and I lowered my head, keeping my eyes up. Dark and glittering, his gaze consumed me as I wrapped my lips around the head of his cock again. "You can please me just like this. Use your tongue."

Oh, it was so much easier to do what he told me rather than desperately try to do it right on my own. When I lapped at the head of his cock, salt and sweetness made me salivate, and I slurped and sucked, sloppy and clumsy, and his fingers tightened on my neck, his cock twitching in my mouth.

I wrapped my tongue around him. He thrust up, just enough to bump the roof of my mouth. Our gazes held. For the rest of his life, he'd always have this picture of me in his mind: face red and lips all stretched and shiny, tears at the corners of my wide eyes, whimpering around his cock. I couldn't keep looking at him, I couldn't, but I did, because he couldn't look away from me, either.

"Niko," he whispered, eyes still fixed on my face, his breath hitching. I gasped as my whole body tightened, and I rutted into the bed, two thrusts before I spent helplessly in my drawers with a garbled moan around his cock.

Andreas caught me under my arms and yanked me up, everything spinning around me as he flipped us over and crushed me beneath him, kissing me frantically, hard and wet and desperate. I flailed, but he grasped my right hand and dragged it down, wrapping it around his shaft with his hand around that, using me to work him in a frantic rhythm.

At last he broke away from the kiss and groaned into my neck, his body shuddering as wetness dripped down over our hands.

I went limp and let my eyes slide shut, giving in to the weight of him on top of me, the softness of the bed beneath me, the dampness of the sweat and come all over us both. My free hand had found its way to his side, and I traced his ribs with my fingertips. He shivered and kissed my throat. Hair tickled my chin and nose and got into my mouth, and I tried to spit it out without making any disgusting sounds.

Andreas kissed my neck, sighed, and lifted his head. I opened my eyes to find him smiling at me in a way that had me melting all over again. "Your hair's longer than mine. Imagine how I feel."

It wasn't even particularly funny, but I dissolved into laughter anyway, and Andreas grinned and kissed me. Everything else went hazy, the world drifting away.

The world came back to me with a jolt some indeterminate time later, when I realized my trousers were undone and Andreas had a hand down the back of them, fingers teasing into the crease of my ass while he sucked a mark on my collarbone.

Nothing had ever felt so incredibly fucking perfect in my life.

At this rate, he'd be inside me within three minutes.

I stared up at the ceiling for a moment, the smoke-stained rafters and the water spots from a (hopefully) long-ago leak, and squirmed and gasped as he slid a fingertip inside me.

"Just my fingers," he murmured against my skin, and destroyed any chance I had of arguing with him by moving his mouth down, licking a path to a nipple that was already peaked and eager.

Oh, and he'd helped me out of my shirt, too, hadn't he? Apparently his kisses were a far more powerful drug than anything that apothecary had been able to dispense. They'd distracted me from anything else.

"And my mouth, once I get there," he added, and bit me. My hips thrust up of their own accord. "My mouth, and my tongue. I could fuck you with my tongue every day and never get tired of it. But I don't need to fuck you. I'll come all over your pretty ass. You can take as much of your potion as you want, Niko."

I didn't want to take any of it, and that was the problem. What I wanted was for Andreas to put his tongue and his fingers and his cock in me every day, more than once, as often as he wanted, to the exclusion of any other activity.

If he did that for a period of weeks or months, I might eventually grow bored with it.

Possibly.

Not likely, though.

"Will you promise me?" I asked, knowing as I did that the greatest danger would come from me, not from him. His finger slid deeper, setting off bursts of sensation that had sweat breaking out on my forehead and my breath catching. More, I needed more, and I'd be begging soon…

Quick footsteps came from the corridor, and then a brisk rap on Andreas's door. "Sir? Dario's back."

I barely had time to go cold all over in shock and dismay before Andreas had practically levitated off of me, getting to the door and bracing a hand on it to make sure it stayed closed. I hadn't locked it when I shut it behind me, had I? Gods, I could be so stupid. And if he locked it now, that'd be an obvious sign of something odd going on.

"Already? Is something wrong? Where's Carlo? I'll be out in a moment, I'm dressing," he said, sounding like an alert and competent military commander who hadn't at all just been planning to fuck my ass with his tongue.

If he used that tone while he told me he meant to fuck my ass with his tongue, I'd melt through the bed. I had to press my lips together tightly to stifle a moan. Now that he'd stopped the guard at the door from entering, Andreas was gathering up his shirt and coat with a soldier's efficiency, and watching the play of his muscles didn't help me calm down.

"Carlo stayed upriver to supervise preparations for getting us across. Sounds like they're not set up to take so many horses." Now I recognized Salvius's voice. "Dario returned at once because the ferryman who's willing to take us wants to go across tomorrow, which means we may want to ride tonight to reach the ferry by morning."

Andreas sat down in the chair by the fire and began to pull on his boots, frowning down at them. "Why the rush?"

Not that I wasn't happy to hear we might have a way across the river after all, but that was my question, too. The ferry would wait. Andreas's tongue seemed much more urgent.

"Ferryman's convinced that it's going to rain again by tomorrow night. Dario brought a note from Carlo, too, and it looks like it says the same. Should I knock on His Hi—lordship's door, or ah, is that not necessary?"

Oh…fuck.

"No!" Andreas grimaced and stood. "I mean, yes, it's necessary, but no, I'll do it. Wait with Dario downstairs. I'll be there directly, and probably his lordship too."

"Right, sir," Salvius said, and his footsteps retreated.

Silence fell, pressing down on me like a physical weight. Andreas's jaw set, and he shook his head and buckled on his sword without a word.

I swallowed hard. "They know, don't they?" I said, my voice thin.

Andreas hesitated, hands clasped around the hilt of his sword so hard that his knuckles had gone white.

"Almost certainly," he said at last. He didn't meet my eyes. "Damn it to hell. I hoped they—fuck. I was too careless."

My vision blurred. He was ashamed of the men knowing he'd taken me to bed. Because I was a dawn mage? Because of my rank? Or worst of all…just because of me?

At least now I wasn't aroused anymore. And my skin was covered in goosebumps. When had it gotten so cold in the room?

"Do you want to come down," Andreas said abruptly, "or shall I report once I've seen Dario and read the letter?"

My shirt had to be around here somewhere. I fumbled until I found it, my fingers clumsy as I turned it right-side out. The numbness in my lips and tongue made it difficult to speak, but I managed, "Make sure no one's in the hall and I'll slip across and dress. I'll be down in five minutes."

Andreas nodded. A few horrifyingly awkward, silent moments later, I'd gotten myself clothed enough to pass at a glance, dashed across, and shut the door of my own room behind me. My stomach churned with nausea, and I collapsed against the door and closed my eyes.

Fuck. Fuck, fuck, *fuck*. I couldn't even feel clearly, let alone think, too confused and sick to pull anything coherent out of my whirling mess of conflicting desires and fears. Andreas, the potion, the conclave, Andreas, his hands and mouth on me, the light in his eyes when he kissed me, the way he wouldn't look me in the eyes at all when he realized the men he commanded had guessed that he had me in his bed. The needy, helpless ache in my stomach and chest when he smiled, when he called me *Your Highness* in that low rasp of his, when he told me in such shameless detail how he meant to take me. The way I so often laughed and wanted to hit him simultaneously.

Or how I'd gone from resenting his authority over me to craving it.

How even though he'd clearly rather cut off his own arm than publicly claim me, I'd be willing to let him bend me over in the yard of the inn if he wanted to.

He liked me, didn't he? Well enough to fuck me and smile at me and kiss me. But not enough, apparently, to stand beside me and endure the laughter and the whispers and the jeers that a guard fucking a royal twilight mage would inevitably draw from literally everyone. And how could I blame him, really? He wouldn't be treated like a fellow soldier anymore by his comrades, and the nobility might not accept him. My mother would… it didn't bear thinking about, because if she had even the slightest inkling of what Andreas had done to save me from my magic, even though he'd done it *to save me*, she'd want his head on a pike over the front gate of the palace, aesthetics be damned. I might be able to convince her he hadn't taken advantage of me, but it'd be a close call.

Come to think of it, that might have had something to do with his horror at the idea of anyone knowing about us.

He'd never risk his career and his friends, and even his life, to have me. No matter how much he might like me or enjoy my body, a man like him, who could have anyone, would choose someone who'd be less troublesome. It was only sensible.

For fuck's sake, when had I started imagining an impossible, perfect future with him by my side?

A hot trickle down my cheek brought me back to the here and now, and I blinked rapidly to clear my stinging eyes.

Thank the gods I had the potion, although I had to pray it'd work when I needed it. Maybe if it didn't, Andreas could tell the guards that he had no choice but to fuck me, and then they wouldn't laugh at him quite as much.

Wearily, I pushed off the door, feeling as if I'd aged thirty years in the past five minutes. This tight, twisting sensation in my chest keeping me from pulling in a full breath had to be embarrassment and shame, nothing more. I couldn't let it be more.

Andreas's lips on mine, the smile in his eyes, the way he'd said my name...

I had to bite my lip to keep in something between a moan and a sob.

The conclave. The river. The journey. I could focus my mind on that, treat Andreas like the paid guard he was and not like the man I—fuck.

I laid out fresh clothing, packed my things, and washed as much of my body as I could with a cloth and a basin, scrubbing at my skin as if I could scour away any trace of Andreas's touch along with the more tangible evidence he'd left behind.

And then I drew in the deepest breath I could, straightened my spine, set my features in the mask of a prince who didn't at all want to fling himself on his guard's chest and beg, and went downstairs.

Chapter Nineteen

Dario's explanation clearly didn't completely satisfy Andreas, and he was frowning as we dismissed Dario to go and get a hot drink after his long ride.

"He's overeager, I think," Andreas muttered. "He wants to redeem himself for his damn fool blunder with the bridge. Not that I didn't blunder too." He still wouldn't look me in the eye, gazing down at Carlo's letter in his hand as though it would spontaneously sprout more information if stared at hard enough.

"Carlo's steady and reliable," I said. "And he agrees with Dario." The letter had indeed urged us to take this opportunity to cross the river if I still wanted to try to get to the conclave. Carlo had sent Dario back while he remained to help get the ferry ready, as Salvius had said.

But Dario's enthusiasm and Carlo's good judgment left me cold— literally as well as figuratively, an icy shiver racing down my back as I thought about mounting up in the dark, about the nighttime ride, about so many horses and men on a crowded boat crossing a roaring torrent of water.

Damn it, that was simple cowardice. And my alternative would be going home with my tail between my legs to admit defeat to my mother, who'd lecture me about my recklessness anyway, praise Andreas for bringing me home safely, and reduce me in his eyes—and mine—to a childish idiot. He already saw me as an embarrassment.

No. If I wasn't a man now, when would I be?

I tried very hard not to notice how much my motivation for going on resembled Dario's urge to prove himself, and firmly tamped down my reservations about the plan.

With (I hoped) manly (but entirely feigned) confidence, I said, "Unless you can give me an incontrovertible reason why we should turn back for Surbino, I expect us to be on the road as soon as possible. And wanting to keep me wrapped in cotton wool in a locked box to make my mother happy doesn't count as an incontrovertible reason," I added waspishly, before I could stop myself.

Andreas straightened his shoulders, hands clasped behind him, and for a moment I was transported back to the day we met in the palace stable, when Andreas had stood in this same posture, that of a soldier showing respect for a prince he didn't particularly like. The last of the warmth went out of me.

A muscle ticked in his jaw. "Your wish is my command, Your Highness," Andreas said, bowed curtly, and strode past me, already giving orders to Salvius as he passed. His voice faded in and out as my temples throbbed. "…horses watered…his lordship's saddlebags, take particular care with…"

My saddlebags. The potion. Damn it. I'd probably be on a boat tomorrow when it was time to take it, and if the pains came on early, which they very well might given the unprecedented ways in which I'd been treating my condition…it was too unpredictable. My bags might be put away in a hold, the boat might be moving too much for me to get it without spilling it everywhere, and I simply couldn't bear the thought of breaking down and starting to scream and beg in public, in front of my guards. It made my flesh crawl to imagine it.

Which meant testing the potion to its limits would need to wait.

I slipped upstairs and quickly unpacked the bag in which I'd stashed the bottles, my hands shaking as I pulled one out and yanked out the cork. The taste of the first swig made me grimace and nearly gag, but I choked down a second anyway. Gods, it tasted so much worse now that I had Andreas's cock to compare it to as an alternative.

With everything stowed away again, I left my bags for whichever of the guards Andreas had assigned to take them down, and went to the taproom to see if I could find some tea before we left.

We rode out an hour later, the moon peeking through the clouds enough to cast deep shadows beneath the trees lining the road and limn the mud under the horses' hooves with a silvery gleam. Andreas rode beside me, his silence almost a tangible thing, more eloquent than speech would've been. The tightness of his lips and the set of his jaw, the tension in his broad shoulders, and the way he kept his gaze anywhere but on me said everything.

Dario spurred his horse a little bit ahead to lead the way. The others were strung out behind us on the narrow road, keeping to the edges to avoid the worst of the sticky mud.

At this hour of the night the road was deserted. We didn't pass any other travelers, not even a hunter or a messenger. Wind rustled and whispered around us, rattling the bare twigs of the deciduous trees and shushing through the evergreens. Wisps of cloud passed across the quarter moon. An owl hooted, and another answered cheerfully in a slightly higher timbre.

Even the fucking owls were happily mated, damn them, and they probably didn't have queens for mothers either.

The monotony of the ride and the rhythm of Fluffy's hooves lulled me into a fugue, helped along by my exhaustion. Gods, I'd have gone to bed long since if I'd stayed at the inn.

I might even have gone to bed in Andreas's arms, my head tucked under his chin, his hand resting on the swell of my ass, everything right with the world.

My heart gave a sad, unsteady little lurch and my eyelids drooped.

"We'll stop here for a few minutes," Andreas said, and I forced myself upright, trying to appear as if I'd been alert the whole time and not slumping in the saddle. I glanced over and found him turning his head quickly, as if he didn't want to be caught looking at me. "I think I hear a stream."

Dario called back, "There's a better spot another little ways ahead, sir, I stopped there earlier. The stream goes closer to the road, and the horses can drink without our having to pick through the trees."

"Your Highness," Andreas said, pitching his voice very low, "if you need to rest now—"

My cheeks burned in the chill of the night. "I'm fine," I snapped. Damn it, he'd seen me falling asleep. How pathetic could I be? All of the soldiers in the party were wide awake. "I can ride as long as you can, thank you."

It took the startled, ringing silence following that announcement for me to realize how I'd sounded. Someone behind me snickered and then quickly coughed. My head went light as all the blood rushed…somewhere, and my cheeks probably glowed. Bright spots swam in front of me in the darkness.

"We'll go on for now," Andreas said, his tone so dry it could've soaked up all the water in that stream we were going to find. "Lead the way, Dario."

"Yes, sir," Dario said.

Silence fell again. I didn't hear any more laughter from the men, but that could've been because Andreas had twisted around in the saddle and glared over his shoulder for a long and quelling moment.

And then we were riding together, not speaking, with everyone else carefully not speaking, and if I hadn't suppressed my thrice-damned magic down to nothing again with a fresh dose of that thrice-damned potion, I'd have exerted every iota of power I had to open the ground beneath me and let it swallow me up forever.

At long last, Dario reined in. "We're here! The stream's on the left. Your Highness, if you'll allow me?" He waited until I'd come up beside him, and then waved a genial hand toward the stream and bowed like a butler inviting a guest to the dining room.

"Thank you," I said, and I spurred forward as he fell in behind me, only too glad of an excuse to get a little farther away from Andreas. "You stopped here earlier? Is the water running clear, or is it muddy?"

"Clear enough, Your Highness," Dario said, his voice a little strained. Gods, I hadn't meant to sound as if I'd blame him for a dirty forest stream. He needed to calm down. At this point, I didn't care about the damn bridge, and it'd been an honest mistake anyway. "Would you like to dismount and let me water your horse?"

I nodded at him and jumped down, slightly more stiffly than usual given the way the muscles pulled between my legs. How long would it take before my body no longer bore the marks of Andreas's possession of me?

No, it wouldn't take long at all. It was my heart that wouldn't recover.

My boots squelched into the soggy ground, and I bent down, trying to see if there was anywhere to step where I wouldn't sink in even deeper. The hell? There was almost no grass at all, only churned-up earth with a few bits of green mushed in, hoof marks and boot marks and…far too many hoof marks and boot marks for one man.

"It looks to be a popular spot for watering horses," I said, and looked up at Dario, who stood still beside me and didn't answer. His face shone pale in the moonlight. The hair rose on the back of my neck. "Either direction they went, we'd have seen them at the inn, wouldn't we? In the village." Something was wrong, I could feel it, and I needed… "Andreas!"

"Sir?" Salvius cried from behind me, drowning me out. I spun on my heel and found Andreas on foot leading his horse, turned away from me to look at Salvius. "Sir! I thought I saw—"

Salvius broke off in a cry as a torrent of mounted men burst out of the forest around us in a sudden pounding of hooves and loud whinnies, shouts of challenge and the flash of swords. Andreas already had his own sword drawn, and he spun and ran for me. I caught a glimpse of his glittering eyes and bared teeth, and I took one stumbling step toward him—but something caught me around the middle and jerked me off the ground, knocking the wind out of me, and I shouted and struggled and fought, dizzy and disoriented, as I was flung face-first over the back of a horse. The saddle's pommel gouged into my stomach. I shoved an elbow up and into my captor's torso, and he grunted and cuffed me hard in the back of the head. Stars exploded in my vision. My magic, I had to—but it wouldn't come, I was a heavy lump with no power in me at all, spreading my fingers and nothing, nothing!

Everything was chaos, too fast and too loud, the horse spun, my head spun an instant later and snapped back and my neck radiated agony, I couldn't see—

"Andreas!" I shouted, and twisted around, scrabbling at the horse's tack for any leverage I could get, desperate to find him, for him to find me. "Andreas!"

I thought I heard my name in reply, and then the legs under my torso kicked the horse into a gallop, and I lurched and slid, only held on by a hand around my belt. The hard tug of the belt against my gut made me gasp and gag, eyes watering—and through the blur I glimpsed him, only for an instant, fighting two mounted assailants at once with a crowd of others circling and fighting my guards. Moonlight flashed on their mail and swords—and on Andreas's sword, slipping through the air like water, like the moonlight itself. One of the enemy shrieked and toppled from his horse, and another spurred forward in his place.

Everything went silent and still as my eyes met Andreas's, bright with fury and agony and desperation. I thought I saw his mouth shape my name again. And then he went down, a sword flashing over him.

A jolt, and I was slamming up and down against the side of a horse and choking back bile, arms and legs bouncing and flailing.

Andreas. They were killing Andreas and all my men. I'd chosen the potion over trusting him to take care of me, and If I'd had my magic I might have been able to save him. Or more likely die with him, but at least I wouldn't be a helpless prisoner, tears whipping away unheeded with the wind.

Oh, gods, I'd probably seen Andreas dying. He'd said my name, and then he'd been—cut down quickly, if they were merciful, stabbed through the heart or with his throat cut, glassy eyes reflecting the moon as he bled out into the muck.

Or face down, drowning in it, gasping in mouthfuls of the same mud the horses were kicking up into my face and my eyes and into my nose—and I did vomit then, retching and spasming upside-down and barely able to breathe, until I hung there limp and sobbing and half-conscious, my eyes opening on the horse's heaving flanks and mud and more mud and the horse's sweat and the pounding pounding pounding of hooves…

Andreas. I couldn't even whisper his name through my raw throat. Andreas.

I never lost consciousness. That would've been a mercy, and the gods were clearly not inclined to be merciful. But at last, at long last, when I thought the heavy throbbing in my head and the cracking of my neck and the pain in every limb and the pressure on my lungs would kill me, there was an authoritative shout, and then my captor reined his horse in.

"Get him down," a familiar male voice said, and I struggled again, completely uselessly, as I was dragged off the horse and slung onto the ground, landing hard on my hands and knees. My head hung down as I gasped and retched again. Mud. Under my palms, between my fingers, under my shins, seeping into my boots. Frigidly cold and squishy. Andreas had to be dead, in mud like this.

Someone else's filthy boots appeared a few inches from my nose. "Get up, if you please, Your Highness," their owner said.

Dario. That was Dario's voice.

And suddenly I understood, the events of the past days and weeks twisting, resettling, and taking on a new shape, like an optical illusion resolving into a recognizable object.

The traveler he'd found who had recent knowledge of the bridge hadn't been misinformed, he'd been paid to lie. Dario had taken employment with Surbino's royal guards for this purpose, probably, part of a long-planned plot to…I didn't know what yet, but someone who wanted the best for me wouldn't have murdered my escort, kidnapped me, and tossed me on the ground like refuse. My saddlebags on the pass through the mountains, the way the strap had torn. As if it'd been sabotaged. A bid to make me more vulnerable? To force us to turn back?

Or simply delay us?

And the ferry…if there even was a ferryman, Dario had certainly never bothered to speak to him. It had been a ploy to lure us into an ambush.

It hardly mattered. Andreas and all my men had died for nothing, with Carlo the first victim of Dario's betrayal, his letter forged—Andreas and I would have no way of knowing his handwriting from anyone else's.

Carlo's family and friends would never see him again. None of my men's families would ever see them again. And it was all because of me. Nothing else mattered but that.

I lifted my head and shoved up off the ground, rising to my feet.

No, one thing mattered, and it burned in me, deep down, stinging and searing and agonizing, giving me the strength to move.

I swayed, caught myself, and looked into Dario's eyes. "I'm going to kill you," I said. "Not an execution. Not a trial before Surbino's judges. I'll kill you myself."

His teeth gleamed white in the moonlight. "Go ahead, Your Highness. By all means. Kill me with your mighty magic."

A red flash obscured my vision for a moment, all my muscles going rigid, hands clenching. Gods, I'd never understood what hatred meant before this moment. The urge to fling myself on him and choke the life out of him, gouge out his eyes, make him scream…but there were several men behind me, another three behind Dario. A whole troop. And even if it had been just the two of us here alone I'd have been outmatched.

I quivered with frustrated fury, but I kept myself still. "Perhaps I will," I ground out. "When the moment's right."

The bastard actually threw his head back and laughed, and several of the men around us chuckled. My skin burned, my fists shook, I'd kill them all, but I couldn't, I couldn't, and I reached deep inside where my magic lived and tried to pry it out, but there was only a void.

"No, you'd have used it already if you could," he said. "To save your precious Andreas, hmm? That fucking traitor," he snarled, and spat on the ground, his eyes glittering with hatred that almost equaled mine. "He should've died on the pass. That would've been a fitting end for him, crushed on the rocks. Not killed in an honorable fight."

"Honorable—you—it was an ambush, you coward, and if you had any honor you'd have fought him yourse—" Dario struck like an adder, my ears ringing as I tripped and fell to the ground again, mud squishing under my arm and hip, only understanding he'd backhanded me across the face when I tasted blood and reached up to feel the imprint of his knuckles on my cheek.

This time I couldn't get up again. Not right away. Through the buzzing thump of my own blood I could distantly hear Dario's men talking in low voices, the jingle of the horses' tack, the stamping of their hooves.

His voice cut through clearly, though. "I wouldn't dirty my sword with him," Dario said, and I laughed, because I knew damn well that in a fair fight it'd have been Andreas's sword, not Dario's, that came away needing to be cleaned.

A boot struck my thigh, pain blooming into agony, and I curled in and cried out, not bravely at all. At least Andreas wasn't there to see me cringing and crawling. I'd have hated that. My head dropped into the mud, cheek wet and cold, and I squeezed my eyes shut and whimpered. Maybe Dario would kill me. But then I couldn't kill him. Coherent thoughts took so much more effort than they should have.

Dario left me there, walking away to give orders that I vaguely heard and comprehended. The mountains. A pass through the mountains…not the one we'd taken from Surbino. The northern pass the landlord at the inn had thought we were making for in the first place.

The pain in my leg subsided enough that I could gasp half a full breath and force my mind to work. The first mountain pass, where that fucking son of a bitch thought Andreas should have died, although it didn't matter, because Andreas was…my chest spasmed with unbearable anguish, and I turned my face down and got a mouthful of slimy grass and filth for my trouble. I spat it out, choking. The mountain pass. The rope. That hadn't been an accident either. Carlo had blamed himself for it, but it had been Dario all along.

Traitor, he'd called Andreas a traitor, when he was the one who—no, he wasn't a traitor, was he? He was a spy. A foreign agent. He'd claimed to be from the east, but his total lack of an accent should've made that suspicious from the beginning. And now that he didn't need to hide anymore, he sounded northern. All of his men did.

Northern. He had to be. Andreas had served Duke Treviso in Calatria, hadn't he? And then left the service of his heir, Duke Lucian, to join Surbino's army. And it seemed that Dario hated him for it.

We had to be on our way to the Duchy of Calatria through the northern pass. Nothing else made sense. I would be a hostage, a political prisoner. Locked up in a gilded cage if I were lucky, held to ensure my mother's compliance with—what, though? We didn't have any ongoing disputes with Calatria. Not for decades.

And anyway, if that had been the plan, Lucian's men probably wouldn't have been beating me or leaving me to shiver on the ground. They'd have been treating me like a royal prisoner and not…this.

I knew where we were going and who had abducted me, at least. But the rest of it remained opaque. Andreas would've been able to figure it out. If he were here, he'd have been defiant, bold, strong and sure. Biding his time.

Not groveling in the mud.

But everything *hurt*, and I was racked with shivers, and I hated Dario so much that my teeth ached, but my head spun too much to do anything at all and I hadn't slept or eaten or drunk.

I'd stay alive. I could do that much. I'd stay alive until Dario was dead.

I clung to that thought as I lay there, icy cold and horribly alone. For Andreas, I'd stay alive until Dario was dead.

Chapter Twenty

The second day of my captivity found me curled in a shivering ball on the rocky ground, aching in every limb, in a low-ceilinged cave halfway to the summit of the pass. My captors huddled around a fire a few feet away. A brutal wind howled through the boulders, and eddies of snow twirled frantically in hypnotic patterns outside the cave mouth. We hadn't stopped moving at all the first night, and we'd pushed on throughout most of the following day, taking a couple of hours of rest here and there. Dario had called a halt here in the evening as the weather closed in ominously.

Now it was morning again. I watched in grim satisfaction as Dario and one of his men, apparently his next in command, argued with low voices but sharp gestures near the cave mouth. Dario wanted to go on. The other thought it would be suicide to try to make it to the top of the mountain in what could become a real blizzard.

Since their troubles were my only source of satisfaction, I savored it as much as I could. Hopefully they'd all fall off a cliff and be smashed to bits and turned into chunks of bloody ice.

I cared very little if I met the same fate as long as I knew they suffered. Andreas was dead. The thought occurred to me every ten seconds or so, a new and piercing grief each time. When I remembered the heat of his mouth on my skin, the rough clasp of his hands around my hips, the timbre of his voice and his laughter, I could sink into it for a moment. And then the pain hit again, and again, like lashes, and I shook with sobs until my ribs ached and my eyes swelled shut.

At least I could pretend I had Andreas for a few minutes first.

When I returned to reality, prickly ropes dug into my wrists, not so tight as to numb my hands, but tight enough that my elbows and shoulders ached constantly. My arms were in front of me so I could scratch my nose and drink water when it was offered to me, a small mercy. Although Dario had a habit of lifting me by my arms, using his height to pull me all the way up to my toes, something he couldn't have done with my arms behind my back. Both of my cheekbones throbbed now, since I'd spat in his face the first time he'd done it.

In between bouts of weeping and half-consciousness, I'd nearly given myself a stroke straining to reach my magic, closing my eyes and holding my breath until my lungs burned. It should've been long enough for some of it to have returned, given what I'd experienced at the inn—and the horrible thought that it had been my proximity to Andreas rather than any weakness in the potion that had allowed my magic to return more quickly had started to worm its way into my brain.

But Andreas wasn't here now.

Only once, about an hour before, I'd felt a twitch of…something. A spark. But it had vanished as I tried to grasp it, and I'd slumped back against the rough cave wall, panting and drenched in sweat.

Now the sweat had cooled. My teeth chattered as I tucked myself as best I could under the thin blanket one of Dario's slightly kinder men had tossed over me when he dropped me on the ground like a sack of potatoes.

The men seemed hungry, actually. I didn't think Dario had planned for such an arduous trip through the mountains, and they were grumbling. So no, not like a sack of potatoes. They'd have treated that with care.

Moldy potatoes, maybe. All bruised and withered and useless, destined for the garbage heap.

I still didn't know what they wanted with me, precisely. One of the men had said the name *Tavius*, but while that name rang a very faint bell in the back of my mind, I couldn't pull it to the surface. Some agent of Duke Lucian's, perhaps?

Most of the time I didn't particularly care if this Tavius meant to kill me. But when I thought of Mama, of Philippa and Amara and Franco, I cared. My gut twisted into a knot and I couldn't breathe, because their grief…if my death caused them a tenth of the horror and despair that overwhelmed me when I imagined Andreas lying cold and gray on the road, flies buzzing on his eyes and mouth…at those moments, I knew I had to fight to live and to spare them that. And I would fight, probably. When the time came, I'd give it my best.

But bound and helpless and frozen and weak and hungry, there wasn't much I could do. And while my life might be important to my family, which Calatrian asshole had decided to try to end it really wasn't particularly relevant.

A violent gust of wind shrieked through the cave, bringing with it a snatch of the argument: "…to scout the path ahead," Dario was saying. "They have two hours, no more, and then we move regardless. You're not in command here."

I opened my eyes a slit and watched as Dario stomped away from his officer back toward the fire. The curled-lip glare the officer leveled at Dario's back suggested that he might not be in command for much longer if he turned his back on the fellow somewhere a bit more private.

Good. Let them kill each other. Bastards.

I tried again to touch my magic. It glimmered faintly and winked at me, shadowed and distant and unreachable.

The officer called out to some of his men, and they rose slowly from beside the fire and joined him at the cave mouth, near the horses. I couldn't hear what they said, but their sour expressions and unenergetic preparations to mount up and ride out told me enough.

Scout the path ahead. So those three had been chosen for that unenviable task. Maybe they'd all be caught in an avalanche and die screaming. The thought almost made me smile.

They led their horses out of the cave a few moments later and disappeared into the storm, leaving Dario, his officer, and the two other men sitting by the fire in tense silence.

I shifted on the rough ground, trying to dislodge a pointy rock that'd embedded itself in my hip. Gods, my legs hurt. Shooting pains in both calves, and intermittent stabbing sensations in my knees and my feet. They'd hobbled me with a rope between my ankles, the loops loose enough that it shouldn't be causing me any discomfort other than the knowledge that I'd been treated like livestock. Squirming only bought me a scrape on my lower back from that same damned rock and another twist of the knife in my left knee.

Fuck's sake, I shouldn't be that stiff, in that much pain, with sweat beading my forehead and my body growing hotter just from—I stared out at the snow, horrified into stillness.

The pain and the perspiration and the irregular rhythm of my heart weren't the result of being treated roughly by Dario's men, or of hunger, or of my damp clothes.

My magic had started to turn on me again. How had I not even thought of that? I curled in on myself again, forcing my breath to even out, holding it in and letting it out slowly. Fucking hell. When had I…it'd been late in the evening when I took the potion. Possibly around eleven. And then it'd been a night and a day and another night. The weather made it impossible for me to estimate how long the sun had been up, but it couldn't have been more than thirty-four hours since I'd taken the dose.

Of course, I'd known it would be unpredictable. A different formulation. A different strength. And I hadn't been particularly precise when I took it, either, too angry and upset and reckless.

If I had my watch I could—

Oh, gods. No.

My watch.

Which I'd packed away in the same saddlebag that held the potion, which had been on Fluffy.

Who'd been left behind.

I didn't have my potion.

My helpless little moan echoed in the quiet cave, in harmony with the lower-voiced groan of the wind.

"The fuck is it now?" Dario said harshly. "Shut up. Prince Nikola. None of us want to listen to your fucking whining."

My teeth nearly pierced my lip, but I kept in the next sound that was rising up from my twisting gut. Gods. Did I tell him or not? I lay there, panting as silently as I could, starting to twitch in every limb. It was coming on fast. If I didn't tell him I might die from the curse, or he might beat me when I couldn't control my screams anymore.

That might kill me faster.

Now that it'd come down to it, I found that I didn't want to die. Not like that, anyway. Not in agonizing, humiliating misery writhing on the floor of a cave, filthy and disgusting and pathetic.

I didn't want to die at all. Even without Andreas, I wanted to live.

Apparently the human body and the human soul shied away from the void even when there was nothing to live for.

Horrid laughter wrenched out of my chest, shaking me, mingled with the cries I couldn't suppress anymore. Pebbles skittered out from under my kicking feet, grit in my hands and my cheek where I'd rolled away from the wall and fallen to the ground.

If I told him, what would he do? Cut my throat to save himself the inconvenience of watching my magic rip me apart from the inside?

Except that he'd said he needed me alive.

And without the potion, there'd only be one way for him to keep me that way.

No, gods. No, I had to lie to him. He couldn't know. I couldn't bear that.

Heavy footsteps crunched on the small rocks littering the floor, and then a hand grasped my shoulder hard enough to make me cry out, flipping me onto my back. I blinked up through a blur of tears into Dario's furious face, his blond brows drawn together and thin lips compressed as he glared down at me out of bloodshot eyes. He looked almost as shitty as I felt, and I wished I could appreciate it more.

"If you don't shut up, I'll shut you up," he growled. "What the hell is—" Dario stopped abruptly, mouth hanging open. "Oh, fuck," he said after a moment, and passed his hand over his face. He spun around. "Where are the prince's bags?"

The wind whistled. The fire crackled. A horse whickered softly.

"The prince's bags," Dario repeated slowly, his voice deadly. "His saddlebags. That have whatever medicine it is that keeps him from going crazy and dying!" He whirled back to me as I began to laugh again, high and thin, my voice cracking. "So help me, if you don't shut up I'll fucking put my fist down your throat!"

He cursed and shouted, demanding answers from the men, and I howled with laughter, rolling onto my side again, my blood starting to boil with fever, delirium overtaking me. I didn't even know why it was funny. I knew they hadn't brought my bags. Someone would've mentioned it by now.

"Damn you, you're all useless!" he shouted, and turned back to me.

I saw his boot coming, and I tried to dodge, but he kicked me hard in the hip, and my laughter choked off in a sob. I fell silent at last, racked with pain and my vision going blurry, staring up at him.

I'd never seen anything more terrifying than his face: his narrowed eyes and the hard lines around his mouth. He hated me. He'd hated Andreas, and he hated me, and he'd be happy to see me suffer. I had to be alive to suffer. Lucky him.

"Well, since my fucking incompetent subordinates didn't get your medicine, you'll need something else," he said, suddenly calm again. I tried to crawl backward, away from him, as my flesh tried to crawl off my bones. "Is it going to kill you? This evil magic of yours. Your royal curse. You going to die, Your Highness?"

"No," I whispered, knowing how useless it was. "I'll be f-fine."

Dario grinned, showing far too many teeth. "Oh, you shouldn't lie to me. Because I know you're lying to me." His foot shot out again, my upper thigh this time, and the pain arrowed up and in, white-hot. I moaned and shook, everything going hazy. "…wants to fuck the prince of Surbino, eh? See if a royal ass feels any better than a plain one?"

"No," I gasped again. "No!"

"You don't get a choice," Dario snarled. "You took it from that traitor Andreas. You'll be begging for more, I bet. Well? Who's volunteering?"

"Not me," said one of the men, after a pause. I thought it might be the officer. "Not lookin' to be cursed myself."

A low mumble of agreement followed. Through Dario's legs, I could see one of them flicking the fingers of his left hand in a warding sign, the same one more rural citizens of Surbino used sometimes when I passed by.

"You really are fucking useless," Dario said. "All of you. Fine. I'll do it myself. And don't try to watch, you want some fun, you have to fuck the little bastard yourself."

Dario lunged for me, and I shouted and kicked and fought, but he backhanded me across the face and grasped me by the wrists, jerking them over my head and pulling me deeper into the cave. The three men stared for a moment, their eyes glinting orange and black in the firelight, before they shrugged and turned their backs.

"Please," I cried, "please help me, don't let him—fuck!" Dario dragged me over a sharp rock, and it sliced into my back and down my leg.

Dario pulled me around a corner of the cave and caught me around the chest, flinging me face-first onto a blanket, apparently his bedroll. I landed hard with the wind knocked out of me, dizzy and nauseated, and tried to fight, bucking as he landed on top with his body pressing down on my ass, between my legs. I screamed for Ennolu or Dromos or anyone, even the soldiers, to help me.

"Shut the fuck up, shut up," he panted, tearing at my trousers. "You don't want to die."

"You were too much of a coward to face him yourself, you worthless—"

"Shut up! He's dead and you're under me, you little fucking cunt." He got his hand around the back of my neck and shoved me down onto my face. Stars exploded behind my eyelids.

I tried to scream, but my mouth opened on his musty blanket, and I gagged and coughed, my hands trapped painfully under me, my magic searing through every vein and nerve, Dario's other hand shoving my thighs apart, his touch sickening, horrific—and through my own cries and the pounding of my blood I thought I heard something else, a shout, a familiar deep voice raised in command, a voice I loved more than any other on earth.

Rage cut through my terror and despair, as hot as the cursed fever boiling my blood and brain. I'd sworn I'd kill Dario, that I'd live until he was dead.

"Niko!" Andreas's voice again, imaginary and impossible, tormenting me with hopeless yearning, while Dario yanked my trousers down over my ass at last and put his cold hand on my crawling skin. Between my cheeks. Touching me where only Andreas had touched me, removing the imprint of Andreas's callused hands, so gentle for how big they were and how much damage they could do if he wanted.

All of my fury and agony and the swirling magic inside me, all oily and tainted and deadly…it all compressed down and down, a weight like lead in my stomach and chest, crushing my organs and pushing the air out of my lungs, and then up and out, a cursed torrent, rushing out of me uncontrollably, everything inside me consumed in the flames of my hatred for Andreas's murderer.

My magic screamed in triumph as it found its victim. And Dario shrieked, high-pitched and inhuman, his weight tumbling off of me. I struggled to my side and craned my neck, blinking the dirt and sweat out of my burning eyes.

Dario crouched behind me, moaning, clutching his right wrist in his left hand, staring down with his eyes wide in shock.

I stared too, in pure disbelief. His right hand and forearm had shriveled down to almost nothing, like shiny red parchment wrapped around gnarled, twisted bones, blackened patches of burned skin flaking off and drifting down.

"Oh, gods," he wailed, "gods, what did you do to me? What did you—" He looked up, eyes wild. "What did you do to me?"

I had no idea what I'd done to him, or how. But I smiled at him, baring my teeth in a snarl.

And then I heard it again. "Niko!" But this time, there were pounding footsteps and the clash of metal on metal, and a cry of pain, and—

My heart stopped. My lungs froze.

I'd lost my mind. Ennolu's curse had driven me mad.

Because the footsteps drew close, and then—there was Andreas, skidding to a halt behind Dario, looming there all tall and grim and beautiful with his naked sword dripping blood.

Chapter Twenty-One

I stared up at Andreas. He couldn't be real. He was dead. He had to be. I'd seen it in my mind so many times in the last two days that it felt like I'd witnessed it. I hadn't been able to see anything else but his eyes, glazed and empty. But here were those eyes, deep coppery black, fixed on me with agonized intensity, as if he couldn't see anything else either.

My mouth formed his name, just the way his had mine when I was taken from him. But my throat was too tight to let out a sound. Everything faded away, even the pain from my bruises and cuts and the curse of my magic, and my heart raced desperately, vibrating through every vein until I thought I might float up off the ground.

Dario turned and looked up, shouted, scrabbled for his sword, screamed as his ruined arm tried to move.

Almost casually, Andreas set his sword down, seized Dario around the throat, and lifted him, flinging him out of the alcove. I heard a thump and clatter and a moan as he hit the ground.

"Secure him," Andreas called out.

"Aye, sir," came back. Salvius's voice. He was alive too, and that was a blessing, but…

"Andreas," I whispered, finding my voice at last. "You're dead."

"No," he said, voice hoarse, and—it was his voice, it *was*, and then he was kneeling beside me and pulling me into his arms, his hands so gentle, his body so big and warm and alive. "Not dead. Sweetheart. I'm sorry. I'm so sorry, it's my fault you're hurt—gods, Niko—"

I managed to get my bound arms up and looped around his neck, and I buried my face in his chest and fell apart, shaking like a leaf in the wind, teeth chattering with the force of it. Andreas clutched me close and rested his cheek on my hair. His torso heaved with something like sobs, it felt like, and his whole body trembled, a match to mine.

Andreas. He was there, and he could take the pain away, and my magic surged toward him, frantically eager.

I couldn't help my moan.

Andreas pulled back as far as he could with my wrists behind his neck, bending to peer into my face. His brows drew together, the lines there joining the fine ones around his eyes and the deeper grooves bracketing his mouth. He looked exhausted beyond measure.

"You're not just hurt," he said, voice tight, "you're—gods. Fuck." He twisted his head around. "Salvius, His Highness's potion, now!"

He turned back to me, stared into my face for a moment, and then muttered another curse and bent down and pressed his lips to mine, hard and fast, as if he couldn't help himself. That kiss seared me down to my bones, a shock through every vein and nerve, the magic of it finding its way to the center of me and twining with my own, his heat and life calling out to mine like a lodestone. My magic clamored for more of him. Pain twisted through my arms and legs, and I cried out into his kiss.

He tore his mouth away, eyes wild. "I'm sorry, I know it's not the right—but that's all I could think about, was this. I could kiss you forever," he said, and gently lifted my arms from around his neck, sitting back on his heels and pulling my hands into his lap. I whimpered at the loss of his warmth, lurching forward to chase it. Just lurching, really. I could hardly keep myself upright. It didn't matter how much I wanted to feast my gaze on him, my eyelids kept sliding shut, even as my whole body spasmed with magical turbulence. "Let me get your clothes—there," he said, as he tugged my trousers back into place gently. "And I need to get these fucking ropes off of your wrists. Damn it. Salvius!"

Gods, I couldn't believe he had my potion. Somehow he'd survived and killed his assailants and followed me and rescued me, and he'd even managed to bring it, but… "I don't need the potion when I have you," I mumbled.

A smile flashed across Andreas's face before he bent down to examine my wrists more closely. A knife gleamed in his hand, and he began to carefully saw at the ropes, one hand tenderly cradling my forearms. Gods, his fingers on my skin. I wanted to kiss his hands. I would, later, when I had the leisure.

I could kiss any part of him as much as I wanted now. He was alive.

My heart lurched and leapt, beating far too fast because of my curse and faster still because of Andreas.

"The potion's better right now. I'm not going to take you here on the cold ground. On that bastard's blanket where he was going to—" His hands tightened, and the knife tore through several strands of the rope at once. "I was already going to kill that motherfucker. Kill him twice. But your wrists, damn it to hell. I'm going to kill him slowly. Over the course of months."

The rope came loose at last, and he tugged it off and tossed it aside.

"You're going to kill him for my wrists? Not because he tried to, to rape me?" The words tasted like sawdust and ashes on my tongue, shockingly hard to force out. Andreas hadn't even been able to say them, had he?

Andreas looked up sharply, agony in his dark eyes, those coppery flecks glinting, his hands gone still and tense.

"That's what I'm killing him twice for," he said, very low. "The first time for everything else. The second time for that. Slowly for every mark on your perfect skin." He passed his thumbs over the abraded welts on my wrists, and I winced even at that gentle contact. Amidst all my other miseries I hadn't even noticed how raw and sore they'd gotten.

Andreas let out a harsh sound and bent down, touching his lips to the wounds. "My darling," he whispered, barely audible. My chest squeezed, breath rushing out of me as those words lanced through me and settled inside me, a desperate yearning layered on top of the way my body ached to have him take away its pain. "Niko, you don't know how much I—"

And of course, that was the moment Salvius chose to stride into the alcove, my potion bottle in his hand.

"Your Highness, here's your—oh. Gods. Um, sir, I have the—Your Highness, we're all more relieved to find you than you can imagine," he finished in a rush, and he sounded touchingly sincere, although his face had gone the color of a ripe beet. "Sorry to interrupt."

Andreas lifted his head. I blinked at him, heart pounding, with no idea what to expect. If he tried to pretend this was nothing but a guard's concern for his prince, my heart might break in half.

But his hands didn't even twitch, his grip on mine steady and strong.

"Leave the potion, please," he said mildly. "And tell the men to secure the prisoners for the journey and make ready to go. We're not staying here one more minute longer than we need to. Move my saddlebags to someone else's mount to take some weight off. His Highness is riding with me."

Andreas was speaking to Salvius, but the light in his eyes, and the smile that curled one corner of that generous mouth, were just for me.

The soft, helpless, gut-punched sound I let out probably would've horrified me if I'd had the strength for it. But the last of the rage and terror had drained out of me at last, leaving me hollow and weak, lightheaded and near to fainting, with the sharp aches and pains of bruises and scrapes starting to make themselves known again all over me. I'd hardly slept or eaten in days, I'd been dragged up a mountain tied over the back of a horse, beaten and kicked, brutalized and almost raped. The pain from my magic wasn't quite as bad this time as it had been in the past, as unpredictable in this as it had been in every way lately, but hot sparks shot through my feet and down my spine, the fever growing.

But with all of that, Andreas didn't care if the men knew he wanted me, that I belonged to him—and that was enough to compensate for all of it. Andreas had called me his darling, and he was alive. My vision went sparkly-gray, and the world started to tilt sideways, a nauseating slide into the abyss. Or perhaps that was me. It didn't matter. Nothing else mattered.

Well, mostly. I wanted to know if they'd found out what happened to Carlo, and how they'd survived the ambush, and if Fluffy was all right… but the words wouldn't come, and I thought I might throw up, or die…

Andreas's arms closed around me, a wall of strength and safety, and I fell, fell, fell into him, his worried voice a distant hum.

Something was at my lips, and I heard Andreas's coaxing tone and opened my mouth obediently. My potion, and as it trickled down my throat, herbal and bitter, the sharp spikes of magical pain in my body subsided to a low murmur, leaving me with the throb of bruises and the burning in my wrists.

Everything went sideways again and I tried to open my eyes. I managed a fleeting awareness. The stubble on Andreas's jaw in front of my face, and beyond that the cave, horses, men moving around, bustle and snow and stamping feet and deep voices.

I tried to cooperate as he and someone else got me up on a horse in front of him with my legs hanging off to the side, but I thought I might have kicked Salvius in the nose.

And then we were moving, the horse's rolling gait nauseating me all over again, and someone was carrying me away, Andreas…I moaned and struggled.

"No, sweetheart, I have you," Andreas said, and clutched me tight against his chest.

Andreas. His voice, his arms holding me close, his cloak tucked around me to keep out the frigid, searching fingers of the wind and the chill spray of sleety snow, and the rest of the world with them.

I turned my face into his shoulder and inhaled deeply, his spicy heat and the scents of steel and leather. He probably wouldn't have smelled particularly good to most people, since he obviously hadn't much more time to bathe than I had. But I could've breathed him in forever.

The first part of the journey passed in disconnected snatches of consciousness: a glimpse of gray sky, cold water at my lips, which I guzzled greedily, and then more motion. My bruises ached and throbbed. We stopped again for a few minutes, long enough for Andreas to coax me into sleepily eating a few bits of bread and cheese and swallowing another drink of water. And always, through riding and stopping, Andreas held me fast, anchored and safe.

I still couldn't muster the strength to speak, much less formulate coherent questions, and exhaustion pulled me under again. The last thing I heard was Andreas's voice, words I couldn't quite parse. But he said my name. I grasped the front of his tunic in one hand. His hand wrapped around it, fingers sliding between mine.

I woke from a deep sleep to find myself on a horse, wrapped in a heavy cloak, unable to move, and I couldn't—Andreas—

"I'm here," he said. "I have you, Your Highness." I felt as much as heard his voice under my ear, and I subsided, panting, the sheen of sweat on my face and neck instantly chilled in the icy cold of the pre-dawn.

A faint peachy-gray glow filtered through the—trees, yes, those were branches above me. Ugh. My vision moved more slowly than my head.

"Where are we?" I said, wincing at the stickiness of my lips and tongue. The cloak wouldn't—but Andreas pulled on it, and at last I could sit up a little and look around me.

Trees. Leaf detritus. Slushy snow and mud. Hardly enticing. I shivered and curled closer to Andreas, even though I knew by the way the men were dismounting and rummaging their saddlebags that we'd be stopping for a bit, which meant getting down myself.

"Time for a rest, Your Highness," Andreas said. His voice sounded thick, a little slurred. Off. I was suddenly wide awake, my heart galloping. "I have you, don't worry."

I sat up all the way, bracing myself on his shoulders and hitching one knee up onto the saddle so I could look him in the face. He was breathing hard, eyes glittering, a deep brick-red flush coating his cheekbones, his lips chapped and flaking. And although we'd been riding for the gods only knew how long in the cold and damp, when I reached up and put my hand against his cheek, it was burning hot and bone dry, like paper before a fireplace.

"Andreas. Andreas, look at me!"

He blinked, slowly refocusing on my face from where he'd been staring off over my shoulder. "Your Highness, you shouldn't ride out alone," he said, and his eyes rolled back in his head, his arm going limp around me.

Chapter Twenty-Two

For a frozen, horrified moment, I simply stared at him, time stretching into infinity around us, the men's voices and the calls of birds and the horses' whickering fading to a murmur.

And then everything came rushing back in, unbearably loud and fast. Andreas slumped and tipped to the side, inexorably falling from the horse as I desperately caught him in my arms, sliding with him, shouting for Salvius—and a cry of alarm went up, men rushing forward to catch us as we tumbled down.

We landed in a heap with me sprawled on top of Andreas and a sharp pain in my knee where it'd struck a branch embedded in the mud. Someone I didn't know, a scruffy soldier in studded leather armor, crouched at Andreas's head, holding it up off the ground. He'd probably kept him from snapping his neck and saved his life.

I laid my hand on Andreas's cheek again. It seared my palm—even hotter than it had been a moment ago. Salvius skidded to a stop behind the soldier, mouth open, eyes wide.

"Oh, gods," he said. "He said it was nothing, that it barely went through his mail! No one more stubborn than our command—"

"He was wounded?" I choked. Of course he had been, because no one, no matter how skilled a soldier, could've come out of that fight unscathed. And then he'd mounted his horse and ridden after me, saved me, when he… "In the ambush. He was wounded. And he—fuck. Fuck!"

For an instant I almost passed out again, a wave of vertigo nearly carrying me away. I closed my eyes, sucked in a deep breath, focused on the rough several-days'-growth of Andreas's beard beneath my fingers.

I found my center at last and opened my eyes. A circle of men surrounded us: Salvius, the soldier I didn't know and three others in similar armor, and Ludo and Piet, two of the men who'd come with me from Surbino.

No Carlo. No Rinaldi, who must've fallen in the ambush. Their loss cut deep. My fault. Dario's fault too, of course, and that of the bastards he'd commanded and whoever had given all of them their orders. But if I hadn't insisted on this journey…

Gods, I couldn't break down. Because everyone had their eyes fixed on me as they waited for me to tell them what to do. And Andreas… unable to help myself, I reflexively glanced down again, instinctively seeking his strength and decision and judgment.

I'd never seen him less than entirely competent, exuding power and command. But he lay still, mouth slack, breathing far too fast, fevered and helpless. At his side, his hand lay empty and bereft, limp in the dirt, the fingers curled as if searching for his sword hilt. Or for me.

Terror constricted my chest and wormed its way into me, clawing at my insides. I couldn't lose him.

I'd placed my trust in him, put my life and my body and my soul in his hands.

Now it was my turn. Andreas needed me. Rising to the occasion wasn't optional.

I looked up. "Do we have any kind of canvas, a shelter? Move him under those trees and set something up, light a fire, and make camp as comfortably as you can. We're not going anywhere for a while." They stared at me. "Now!"

All at once, they burst into action, a flurry of talk and motion. Salvius began to repeat the same orders I'd given, only more loudly. I lurched to my feet heavily, sliding my hand down to grasp Andreas's. The curled fingers stayed lax and loose, but I gripped him hard enough to hurt, willing him to feel my touch, to know I was there.

Ludo and two of the soldiers maneuvered Andreas onto his cloak and lifted him, bearing him off toward the scant shelter of the trees, with me trotting alongside, my gaze fixed on Andreas's face. It was gray where it wasn't hectically flushed.

I had to let go of him for a moment as the men carefully laid him down on a hastily assembled pallet of blankets. As soon as we lost that point of contact, I went cold and numb all over. He wouldn't really die if I didn't touch him, but…fuck, it had to be my imagination, I knew it did, but my fingertips twitched to the rhythm of his heartbeat, too rapid and too weak. His labored breaths rasped in my ears and strained my own lungs even though I couldn't possibly hear him over the hubbub around us.

"Your Highness, we'll have a fire lit in a moment," Piet said, rising from next to Andreas's legs. "Hot water? You'll want that, I'm thinking. And we'll have something to keep the drizzle off in a few minutes."

He bustled off without waiting for an answer, and I dropped down to my knees beside Andreas, taking his hand again. Did he feel somehow weaker? That had to be my imagination too. You couldn't tell that from holding someone's hand. But he hadn't opened his eyes since he collapsed. Except for the fevered flush, he looked like a corpse.

I shook my head and scrubbed my free hand over my face, swallowing hard around the lump in my dry throat, and then started to pat at Andreas's body, looking for any sign of a bandage or blood or…anything at all. But he was wearing his mail, and Salvius had said the cut had barely gone through it, but I couldn't even find the rent in it.

"Salvius!" I called, and a moment later he crouched down beside me. "Where the hell is he wounded?"

"Along his right side," Salvius said. "He said it was only a scratch. He wouldn't wait for anything."

Wait for anything to follow me, Salvius meant. Andreas lay here now, desperately ill, because of his devotion to me.

Tears stung my eyes despite my determination to stay in control, and I blinked them away, hoping Salvius wouldn't see them.

I carefully laid Andreas's hand by his side and started to tug at his tunic. How many times had we torn each other's clothes off, with or without magic, his hot mouth at my throat and his deep voice murmuring his desires in my ear…gods, not often enough, not nearly enough, and I'd give anything to have that again. To have it forever. But right now I had to get him undressed for a much less pleasant reason, and it was a lot harder without his cooperation. Finally I shoved his damp, heavy wool tunic up far enough to expose his chain mail shirt.

And there it was: a jagged rent in the side of it, only a few links snapped. It looked like nothing at all.

It took Salvius's help to get the mail pushed up out of the way, both of us grunting and cursing, and me so impatient I could've screamed.

At last I could see the final layer, Andreas's linen undershirt. It bore a dark, seeping stain, with what looked like a lump of bandages beneath it, no doubt applied by Andreas himself.

Even in the cold, the smell hit me like a slap to the face.

Ripping the undershirt up the side and peeling it back revealed another one of Andreas's linen shirts, pressed to the wound in a wad. It was stuck to his body, damp and crusty and foul, and I had to turn away for a moment, eyes watering, and gag.

And then I slumped there, shoulders shaking, as if I'd had the wind knocked out of me by an actual blow.

A few years ago I'd spent some time shadowing a physician in Surbino, attending at surgeries and in examinations. And I'd done my share of reading, too, medical texts and more abstract studies of the structure of living things. After all, it was possible that someday I might be able to use my magic for healing.

So I knew what that smell meant. What Andreas's high fever meant.

I'd been praying to the gods, to Ennolu and Dromos and the minor deities and anyone who'd listen, that he might only have some slight infection in the wound. That he might have contracted some kind of cold, or the grippe, that had struck him harder due to exhaustion and his injuries and the weather, and being chilled and damp for days on end, and that the small hole in his mail meant the wound would necessarily be minor.

And perhaps it had been, at first, before he'd neglected it and left it to fester, quite possibly with part of his clothing or some other detritus embedded within.

I'd been far too hopeful. Without a physician, and probably even with one, Andreas would die. The only thing that could save him now would be healing magic—strong magic, wielded by someone who had experience and practice. One in a thousand mages could save his life, probably.

Which didn't include me, because I had neither the experience nor the magic. Andreas had given me a large dose of my potion about eighteen hours ago, I estimated. He'd been too gallant to fuck me there on the same grubby bedroll where Dario had meant to rape me, and so he'd end his life here on a grubby bedroll by the side of the road, and I'd dribble water into his mouth to keep him from going mad while he died. That would be the extent of my usefulness.

"Good fucking gods," Salvius muttered at my side. I jumped, having forgotten he was even there. "Pardon me, Your Highness. Fuck."

He knew, too. I could tell by the tone of his voice.

"Yes," I whispered.

Silence fell between us for a long moment. Salvius sighed, shifted his weight, sighed again. I couldn't look at him. I stared at Andreas's chapped lips and stubbled jaw until my eyes ached. Someone, I couldn't even be bothered to see who, had started setting up a makeshift shelter over me and Andreas. A fire had been lit a few yards away, and the men conversed in low voices, discussing their food supplies and setting a watch. It felt like a dream, far away and detached from reality. This couldn't possibly be real.

"They'll get you hot water and the cleanest cloths we have, Your Highness," Salvius said quietly, sounding desperately uncomfortable and awkward. "I think you'll be the one with the most knowledge of physicking, won't you?" I nodded, the only answer I could muster. "But in the meantime—I need to know what your orders are, with the captain down for the count. For now," he added quickly, because I'd let out a choked sound I couldn't suppress. "Just for now. We've two prisoners, that fucker Dario and one of his men, and they'll need to be untied if they're going to eat, although they can drink without. We killed the others. And—"

"Wait," I said. The others. Shit. That had penetrated even my fog of misery. "There were—there were three more, in Dario's party. He sent them ahead to scout the pass. I'm sorry. I forgot to tell Andreas." My voice broke on his name. "They weren't back yet when you arrived, and they may be coming up behind us at any moment."

I half expected Salvius to chastise me, but he only nodded and said, "We'll post a lookout, not to worry, Your Highness. We've enough men to handle it, as you must've seen? We were offered a few reinforcements by a fellow—actually, he's the reason we're not all dead. That and the captain's right arm. Came along and helped, he was suspicious of all the movement in his woods, he said. I think he might be a highwayman, but he has a right small army. And a very fancy coat. And that's another thing. He'll be wanting his men back, and here we are stopped and needing to keep 'em for now. We were meant to go to his headquarters, only we can't go on yet."

Oh, gods. What the hell did he—a *fancy coat*?

I blinked at him, trying to work my way through his torrent of words. Salvius wanted me to…everything buzzed, like a swarm of bees between my ears. Too much. I wanted to snap at him, to tell him to figure it out himself, because wasn't he Andreas's second in command? Andreas still hadn't moved. Imaginary or not, his thready heartbeat thrummed through me, insistent and impossible to ignore for even a moment, overwhelming anything else I needed to do or think about.

But Salvius's face was pale under its decades of weathered tan, showing his exhaustion as clearly as if he'd complained about it. Which of course he would never do.

And he wasn't in command here, was he? I was, with him now my second instead of Andreas's. Without a queen here to decree otherwise, a prince would always outrank a sergeant. Damn it. How the hell did Andreas make keeping everyone organized seem so effortless?

I couldn't exactly ask him. But maybe this was all I could do for him, really: take over his responsibilities without shirking, or whining, or letting the men down. Make him proud of me even though he might never wake to know he ought to be.

"The—prisoners," I said haltingly, and sucked in a deep breath. I slipped my hand back into Andreas's and clutched it tightly. He might not be able to help me, but strength seeped into me through his skin. "Give them water and don't let them die of exposure, but they can wait to eat. They're in no danger of starving to death."

They were in a lot more danger of my ordering Salvius to interrogate them without any attempt at gentleness, but that could wait, mostly because I didn't want to listen to screaming, even Dario's, with my head pounding like this.

Salvius smiled, the creases around his mouth deepening. "If it were up to me, I'd cut their throats here and now. I won't be shedding any tears for them being a mite hungry. And the men we've borrowed?"

That needed more thought than I had to give. I glanced back down at Andreas, sprawled on the ground as if he'd never move again, and then up at Ludo and Piet, who were diligently tending the fire. Steam curled from the pot they'd hung on a hook. And now that I paid a moment's attention, Andreas and I had started to dry out a bit; the canvas they'd strung over us between two tree branches was keeping the drizzle off.

Primitive, but better than nothing. And moving was impossible in any case.

"Tell our allies—ask them if they'd be so kind as to wait for now. Or, no, we could send one on with a message. He could tell this master of his we'll be another day. He could ride to the nearest town and look for a physician first, couldn't he? Or a mage who has any healing skills at all."

That would be useless. We both knew it. But I could pretend, at least, that a miracle might be possible.

"Aye, sir. I mean, Your Highness. That's an idea," Salvius said slowly. "Can I promise more pay? On top of what Andreas already offered. Because it's a ways to ride, and no guarantee it won't be a hopeless errand. Begging your pardon for saying so, Your Highness."

Pay? If they were highway robbers, why hadn't they simply, well, robbed us? But that didn't matter if they kept on not doing it.

"Whatever it takes. I leave the details to you. As long as he rides fast."

Salvius nodded. "One of them can go at once, Your Highness." He stood, grunting as his knees creaked. "Damn it," he said, and strode away.

That summed it up well.

And it also seemed to bring my immediate responsibilities to an end. Hadn't Andreas often been busier than this? Well, sometimes. He'd seemed to have plenty of time to hold me down and fuck me.

I bit my lip until it bled, but I managed to keep the next wave of tears inside, huddling there as silent and still as Andreas until at last Piet brought me the pot of boiled water and a pile of almost-clean linen shirts.

"I'm sorry, Your Highness," he said softly, setting the pot down on the ground. "They're the best we've got. I'll boil some other things for bandages. But we used up all the actual bandages we had in our supplies, you know. For bandaging."

Piet had one of his own around his forearm, and the same weary, gray pallor as everyone else in our party.

"Thank you," I said, for lack of anything more meaningful.

Piet cast a frowning glance at Andreas, opened his mouth, and closed it again. "I'll bring you a bite when we have it ready, Your Highness," he said, and retreated to the fire.

I had to let Andreas's hand go to start cleaning his wound, but I raised it and pressed a kiss to his knuckles first, not even caring if anyone saw me. His skin burned my lips. I lingered longer than I should have, pushing as much strength and will into him as I could.

And then I gently laid his hand down, moving his arm away from his body to give me room to work, and picked up one of the cloths.

It took painstaking effort, repeated soaking and loosening, to get Andreas's attempt at a bandage off of him. But it peeled back bit by bit, revealing swollen, shiny, reddened skin, and as I pulled off more of it, patches of deep purple, the color of a rotten plum.

My vision blurred as I delicately sponged Andreas's wound, a shockingly small opening between two of his ribs. At this point, trying to remove any foreign matter stuck inside would've been futile and agonizing, even if I'd had a surgeon's tools, so I cleaned off as much of the pus and dried blood as I could and then covered it with a pad of linen and wrapped his cloak over his side.

Perhaps it made me a coward, but I couldn't look at it anymore. I'd touched Andreas's body more than I had anyone's, ever, but I couldn't recall spending much time with that particular part of him. The long, lean planes of his torso hadn't been a priority for me.

They should've been. Kissing my way down every inch of his body ought to have been my only priority when I had the chance.

Instead I'd wasted precious hours wringing my hands over my independence and my self-respect—as if a life alone, without Andreas, could possibly be preferable to kneeling at his feet and begging him to be kind to me, if that's what it took to make him want to fuck me every day. Or even to look at me.

Andreas had stirred slightly while I worked, little twitches in his fingers and a restless toss of his head. Not so much as a flicker of his eyelids, though, and no sign that he knew I was there. It'd be better for him if he never woke, I knew. An infection like this was an agonizing way to die. But I still sat there, unmoving, all my limbs gone cold and stiff, staring at his face as if I could force him to open his eyes through willing it alone.

If he fought to live, if he would only smile at me…I whispered helpless pleas to Ennolu, praying as I never had in my life. By taking my potion all these years, I'd thwarted Ennolu's will and circumvented his plans for me. But I wouldn't, not anymore. I'd do exactly what he expected of me. If he would hear me…

My body ached with the force of my longing and my grief and my rage, every muscle taut, my lungs burning with my held breath, my mouth open in a silent rictus. If he'd made my magic stronger before, why wasn't it working now? It must have been my imagination, or the dosage I'd taken of my potion had been wildly uncalibrated. Or perhaps Andreas had to be conscious.

Either way, nothing happened no matter how I prayed.

Someone set something down beside me, probably Piet leaving me food. But I didn't think I could ever eat again. The day went on around us: a light rain pattering on the canvas overhead, an icy breeze whispering down through the clearing from the snowy mountains, the whinny of a horse, Salvius giving orders to change the watch. Andreas remained the same, unmoving and dying.

I'd clutched his hand to my chest, both of mine wrapped around it, and I curled down and kissed it, again and again, my tears as hot as his fever-parched skin.

Until now, I hadn't put a name to the inescapable feeling welling up inside me and turning my chest to lead. If Andreas had woken, I'd have told him, thrown myself on his mercy, given myself to him without any reservations at all. Been his slave, if that's what he wanted.

But he wouldn't wake. He'd never hear me say it.

I turned his hand over and pressed a kiss to his palm, the salt of his skin lingering on my lips and mingling with my tears. "I love you," I whispered. "Andreas. I love you."

Chapter Twenty-Three

For a moment the world felt like it held its breath.

And then I gasped at the sudden pain: my fingers and my lips burning as if they'd been shoved into a fire, the flame chasing up my arms and down my throat, licking along my veins, burning, burning, bright in my magical vision. The potion I'd taken sizzled and spat, seared out of my blood, firecrackers exploding along my nerves and down to the tips of my fingers and toes.

Everything went sparkly-crimson and twisted upside down, my magic slamming into me with the force of an avalanche and sucking me under, my lungs full, choking, and that sound was my scream as my blood went white-hot like molten lead.

I shouldn't have had any magic, or at most a trickle, but there it was—all of it. Pulsating and writhing as if it had a life of its own, suffusing my flesh and glowing through my skin, the last little floating particles of the potion popping into nothingness as they fled the conflagration.

Andreas's hand still burned in mine. I turned my attention to him, his body and soul filling my senses. They seemed to pulse at the same frequency as my magic, in perfect harmony. Or like a lock and a key, made to fit only one another.

Harmonious completion. No matter what I'd experienced recently, I'd truly believed that it had to be nonsense, mealy-mouthed spiritualism without any basis in reality. The kind of useless mumblings that took time and attention away from real research into twilight mages' curses.

But now…the total destruction of my potion. As if the natural resonance of Andreas's soul and my love for him had truly amplified my magic until it took on a strength I'd never imagined, hypnotizing, mesmerizing, tempting me to simply lose myself in it.

But there was something else there with us, and when I saw it I went cold all over.

A gaping black void swirled in the middle of him, the raging infection in his torso like a rabid animal's hungry maw devouring him from the inside, his glorious vibrant life dimming and being sucked away.

For a moment I lost my bearings. The pull of the darkness spun me sideways, dizzying and disorienting. But then I seized my magic like a drowning man reaching for a rope, tugged myself upright, drew my strength inward, and *focused.* There it was, the source of the foulness: the infection itself, tiny busy motes that swirled and oozed in mesmerizing patterns and multiplied too quickly for even my magical senses to comprehend. The complexity hit me in a tremendous wave of sensory information, like hearing the colors of a texture at an ear-splitting level, a roar of energy surrounding me, the cacophonous music of the world that no mundane ears could ever detect.

But beneath that I could feel that harmony Andreas made with me, the way the rhythm of his body and his mind moved in complementary counterpoint to my own. His pattern.

And I clung to that, keeping hold of it in the overwhelming chaos of motion around me as I sank deeper into that space beneath what we could touch and see without magic, far outside of what humans were meant to know.

In that moment, I understood why Ennolu hadn't wanted us to have this power: I teetered on the edge of madness, and it *hurt*, gods, it hurt down to the core of me, like a galvanic shock through the marrow of my bones.

But I could see it now. Andreas's life, and his imminent death, and what had to be done to preserve the one and prevent the other.

I could see it all.

Of course, that didn't mean I had the skill or the strength to do a damn thing about it. I'd never gone this deeply into the world below the world, the gods' domain of magic. I didn't belong here. No human did.

And yet it was mine to use, if I could find a way. I'd paid the price for it all my life.

I sucked in a deep breath, not even sure if it was into my lungs or just my mind's interpretation of them, and let my power flow in and fill me to the brim. Calm. I had to stay calm and focused, because there were two tasks to accomplish, both fiendishly difficult, and all the while, my blood sizzled and burned, and I knew my physical body's voice was screaming…

First the infection, and there had to be more subtle ways to remove it, but I was running out of time, and I couldn't, I couldn't find the shape of it, and I was panicking, because I was losing Andreas moment by moment—and so I gathered everything I had, pictured the way the magic had spontaneously incinerated the potion in my blood, and threw everything I had at the edges of the void where the infection proliferated in a seething mass. My magic struck, a burst of pure energy. The flash of brilliant light and heat and screeching noise nearly swept me away, my vision blurring and the ever-present throb of pain flaring into agony for a moment before it died down again, leaving me panting and wobbly.

It took a long few moments to clear my magical vision of the crimson-cloud haze that'd descended over it.

When I blinked it away at last, the infection was shriveled and dead, detritus around the edges of his wound.

But Andreas was still dying, his life still fading.

Gods, I didn't understand, I'd fixed—and then I realized: it wasn't the infection itself that had been killing him. It was the poison it'd pumped into his blood.

I chased the poison frantically, trying to burn it out the same way. But there was too much of it. It'd infiltrated his entire body, and as I reached out tendrils of magic, tracing down his veins, I was spread thinner and thinner, weaker and weaker, my magical strength running out even more quickly than Andreas's life. Matter, the substance of the world, could be transmuted to another substance, and energy to energy. I could make more of his life with my magic, but it would only work if I destroyed the poison, and if my magic ran out…

But that wasn't all I had, was it?

I had my own life.

My own reservoir of glowing, beautiful life, the wellspring of my thoughts and the motion of my body—and my love.

It meant nothing at all if Andreas died.

Without thinking, without hesitating, I opened myself to my magic and let my life flow out of me unstintingly. It rushed through Andreas and lit him up from the inside, carrying away all the taint in his blood with irresistible force.

I grew weaker, weaker, my vision starting to gray out, but I clung to consciousness with every bit of my remaining strength. Andreas was almost cured, if not healed. His wound would still be open when I'd finished, but it'd be clean, a small cut that would only need a few days of bandaging to fade to a harmless scar, one of many on his soldier's body.

Almost. If I could hold on for one more moment, he'd live…as everything went dim and distant around me, I felt the glow of his life flaring anew, his fever abating, his body surging with strength.

I love you.

Everything went dark.

"…never said he's the most skilled mage you'd find—"

"As if you're in a position to judge, you utterly ignorant, stupid son of a—"

"Enough, both of you."

Andreas.

Where…how…I didn't even know if I had a body, let alone what state it was in. I could barely comprehend that I had a mind.

But I'd have known that voice, so deep and sure and reassuring, even if I'd been dead.

A distinct possibility, actually. Did I have a body? Seriously, I'd begun to find it disturbing that I couldn't tell.

"I beg your pardon," said the first voice, a smooth, faintly sardonic baritone. "Lord Cyril likes to stand upon his dignity. If he wants to be argumentative, he should go further from your prince's sickbed. And if he wants to be known as a competent mage, he should learn how to be one."

"I told you he's alive, what more do you want from me?" demanded the second voice, lighter and more pleasant than the other, but very sulky.

Prince. Sickbed. Alive. Well, that at least answered my most pressing question.

"Good thing we consulted you, then. The fact that he's breathing and has a pulse never would've been enough for mundane idiots like us to—"

"Don't include me in that, even though *mundane idiot* probably describes me fairly, I'll admit," Andreas said. "I want no part of this argument, if you please. I appreciate all the assistance you've rendered, Ser Enzo, more than I can possibly ever tell you. And you have my word of honor that—"

"*Ser* Enzo? *Ser?* Are you joking? He's a common ruffian, and if you had any honor at all you'd be rescuing me from—mmmph!"

"My apologies," Ser Enzo said, over Lord Cyril's muffled but shrill protests. Did he have a hand over his mouth? Rescue? Was he this Enzo's prisoner? If he was, Andreas didn't seem concerned about it, so I could safely ignore it too. "We'll leave you alone, but there's someone in the hall if you need anything. I'll take Lord Cyril out of earshot, I promise. Yours, anyway, I'm stuck with him."

The sounds of a scuffle faded, presumably as Enzo dragged Cyril away, and then a thump and click suggested the shutting of a door.

A deep sigh filled the ensuing silence.

Andreas again.

Andreas…and a door? We'd been on the ground by the side of the road.

It all rushed back, too quickly and too forcefully, too much—the fight, screaming, being carried away, Dario's rough hands, pain and terror and grief, Andreas's wound all blackened and deadly, and then all my magic and my life pouring out of me and leaving me a shriveled husk…in the present, a faint sound, a soft whimper…

"Niko," Andreas said, voice hoarse with some strong emotion. "Niko, sweetheart, can you hear me? Are you in pain? Fuck, what do I do," he muttered, and that clearly wasn't directed at me. "Damn it. Niko?"

Awareness of my physical body had started to filter back in: warmth, glorious, unexpected warmth, wonderfully soothing after my last memory of being crouched on the frozen ground and dying.

No, none of that, because I was warm now. And Andreas…and it figured that the first real sensation I'd get back would be the wetness under my eyelids as tears started to slip out. And the arid stickiness of my mouth. Andreas. Alive and well enough to tell that pair of annoying fellows to shut up.

And to say my name in that tone that set my—yes, I could feel my heart again, and it was racing.

My eyes stung even more. Which meant I'd become conscious of them, hadn't I? So I ought to be able to control them.

Heavy though they were, I fluttered my eyelids open.

Pale, heavily stubbled, his brow deeply furrowed, and with purple shadows painted beneath his eyes, Andreas was still the most beautiful thing that I'd ever seen. Gloriously alive, with a look in those coppery eyes that stole my breath and left my chest aching. I seemed to be lying under a heap of blankets, with Andreas sitting in a chair beside the bed and leaning in to peer at my face. Sunlight gilded his auburn hair, which stuck up in wild tufts as if he'd been running his hands through it for hours.

Sunlight through a window, and a soft, warm bed.

Gods. When Andreas had been incapacitated, I'd tossed him on the ground under a tree with icy drizzle falling on us and cleaned him up with a guard's not-very-clean undershirt. Apparently when it'd been my turn to be unconscious and useless, he'd managed to find me a cozy bedroom. And better weather to boot.

No wonder my mother had put him in charge.

"You're awake," Andreas said, as I blinked up at him. "Finally. Fuck. I was starting to—we're going to have words, Your Highness. As soon as you're well enough that I won't feel like a monster for shouting at you."

Shouting at *me*? Aside from the way I'd tried to doctor him in the middle of a rainy forest, what could he possibly be angry about? If anything, I'd be shouting at him, because he was the one who'd let his wound get to the point of gangrene. We wouldn't have been there at all if he'd taken better care of himself! His *words* wouldn't be a one-sided argument, and if he thought they would, he'd be thinking again.

I licked my lips, trying to get my mouth and my throat to function. Gods, I had to tell him that he shouldn't be angry with me and that I'd done the best I could, and berate him for being so fucking stupid, and tell him how much I loved him and that I'd rather have been dead than lose him.

Instead, all that came out, in a hoarse little whisper, was, "Why aren't you in bed with me?"

Andreas's eyes widened. "Why—what—I didn't want to presume," he said. "You weren't awake to tell me you wanted me." Before I could reply, he'd stood up, flipped back my blankets, and climbed in beside me fully clothed, the bed jouncing under us.

He wrapped his arms around me and pulled me against his chest, his warmth and scent enveloping me and sending a shiver of pure pleasure down my spine. I melted, my eyes practically rolling back in my head.

"How do you feel?" he asked abruptly. "Because that half-pint mage said he didn't think there was anything physically wrong with you, just severe magical exhaustion. Was he right?"

"I think so," I said. "Unless something happened to me while I was unconscious. I had some bruises. But I feel like they've healed." And now that I thought about it…had that been a side effect of my magic being amplified by Andreas? "I think maybe—"

Andreas cut me off with a ferocious kiss that stole my breath and left my lips stinging when he lifted his head again, his eyes blazing. "The only thing that happened to you while you were unconscious was you," he snarled. "You nearly died! You tried to kill yourself saving my life, you—you—I'm going to wring your neck!"

Oh, gods. Right. I had done that, hadn't I? And Andreas, who'd sworn to protect me, who'd been willing to die for me, who'd almost died again in the process of rescuing me, probably hadn't been very happy to…what, wake and find me nearly dead myself by his side?

That hadn't even crossed my mind while I'd been doing it, that he'd probably rather die than have me sacrifice myself for him. Even if his feelings for me didn't extend that far, his dedication to his duty certainly did.

I swallowed hard, my eyes widening as I took in the hard set of his jaw. That expression never boded well.

"Wringing my neck would be counterproductive, wouldn't it?" I quavered. "And genuinely treasonous, and I think we've established there are better ways to commit—"

Andreas's mouth descended on mine again, hot and demanding, his tongue sliding between my lips and teasing me open, showing me what he meant to do to me. One arm slid under my waist, and a moment later he'd rolled us, me on my back with Andreas pushing my thighs open with his knees.

"Andreas," I gasped, tearing my mouth away long enough for one word before he was back to kissing me. I tried again. "Let me finish a—" He bit my lower lip, and the sting of it arrowed straight down to my hardening cock. I arched up, moaning, and he bit me again, lapping at the indent he'd made with his tongue. "A sentence!"

He lifted his head and stared down at me, eyes wild and face flushed. "You said you preferred this kind of treason. I'm either going to throttle an apology out of you or fuck an apology out of you, but it's one or the other."

Oh, gods, he couldn't be serious. I opened my mouth to argue, but whatever I would've said withered on my tongue. A muscle ticked in the angle of his jaw, and his eyes had gone flinty.

Andreas had never been more serious in his life.

My heart thudded painfully and my cock was rock-hard. Everything else below my navel had gone all hot and molten.

Apparently parts of me didn't mind being threatened when the threats came with Andreas between my legs, looming over me and glaring down at me as if he meant to put them into action instantly.

Silence fell for a long moment.

"Niko," he said at last. "I was delirious. And then I was unconscious. And then I felt you, somehow. In my mind—in me. It was, gods, I can't even describe it. You were so beautiful. Ennolu himself couldn't be that beautiful. And then you went dim, and you screamed, and I woke up with a start, covered in sweat, with you collapsed on my chest. My wound was healed to a little cut, no infection at all. And you wouldn't wake up. I thought you were dead."

His voice broke, and he turned his face away, a tremor going through his arms and his broad shoulders.

"Andreas, look at me." He shook his head. I could only see his heavily stubbled jaw, the corner of one eye. A drop of moisture clung to the tips of his eyelashes.

Oh, gods. He was crying. For me. My stoic, calm, in-control Andreas had tears in his eyes. Tenderness welled up in me so suddenly and irresistibly that I went lightheaded.

"I'm sorry. I'm so sorry," I said, voice thick. He was too strong for me to pull down if he didn't want to be pulled, but I wrapped my arms around his body and tugged anyway, lifting myself up so I could kiss his cheek, press my lips to his neck, mouth along his Adam's apple. "I'll never do it again. I promise, I'll never—frighten you like that again. I'm sorry. You have my word."

He shook in my arms, and his breath hitched.

Obviously he needed more from me. "I promise that if I have the choice, next time I'll let you die," I said, and maybe, just maybe, a touch of asperity had leaked into my tone. No matter how guilty I felt, I was still angry too. "I'll say, well, too bad, and walk away and have a cup of tea."

He huffed out a breath and finally turned his head, and I dropped down onto the bed again to look up at him, tracing my hands up his back and then down his arms, fingertips sliding over muscles as hard as boulders. Red-rimmed eyes gave him away, but he'd composed his expression again except for the faintest quirk at the corner of his mouth.

"Do I detect a hint of sarcasm, Your Highness?"

I blinked at him and fluttered my lashes. "Isn't that what you wanted me to say?"

"Sarcasm aside, you should. If there is a next time. Better me than you." Andreas cocked his head, examining me. "But I could've sworn—" He bit his lower lip, worrying at it, a wrinkle between his brows, everything about him uncharacteristically hesitant. "Never mind. I was imagining it."

No, I wasn't letting him off the hook that easily.

"Tell me," I said, and gave the words all the royal authority I could muster. He raised one eyebrow, unimpressed. Fuck. All right. I licked my lips, shifted my weight down the bed and squeezed his hips with my knees, and said, "Please tell me?"

"Niko," he breathed. "Fuck. I shouldn't—gods damn it. I thought I heard you say you loved me," he said in a rush. "And if that's—if you—you didn't. I probably heard you wrong. But that's what I want you to say." The expression in his eyes could've melted granite, and he looked steadily into mine. Unflinching and unwavering, braver than I could ever be. "Maybe it'll take the rest of my life, but I'm going to spend it trying to make you say it. That you'll do what I ask you to do and keep yourself safe, even if it's at my expense. Because I want you to. Because you love me."

Chapter Twenty-Four

Because you love me.

When I'd said it, I'd been desperate with grief over the thought that he'd never hear me.

He'd heard me.

And now half of me wished I could pull the blankets over my head, sink through the floor, run away and hide. All my fears came rushing back in: dependence, humiliation, shame. The risk to my own self-respect would be only the half of it. Bearing the mockery and jeers of everyone at court and in the city of Surbino would be newly dreadful, too. A dawn mage who took a potion wasn't nearly as attractive a target for prurient humor as one who used his powers and maintained them the old-fashioned way.

But Andreas was gazing down at me, lips pressed into a tight, anxious line, eyes shining with hope and longing.

I'm going to spend it trying to make you say it.

His whole life. Would I care if people pointed and laughed if I had Andreas by my side? Not nearly as much. Would they even dare?

Would my mother allow it, or would she try to drive him away?

I found that I didn't care a whit for that. If my mother threatened Andreas or forbade him from being my lover, or tried to forbid me from having him in my bed and in my life, I'd leave Surbino with him. Phil and Amara would talk her round eventually, anyway, because we'd miss each other terribly. But I'd go without hesitation, and there was nothing she could say that would intimidate me into doing otherwise. She could hardly hang Andreas in the public square with me screaming and carrying on in the background.

"All right," Andreas said, and I started. I'd hesitated too long, and now—his jaw had that stubborn jut again. Oh, no. "You already said you're sorry, so I guess I don't need to fuck an apology out of you. But I can get started on fucking you until you admit you love me. Or until you fall in love with me. Either way."

"Andreas, I—oh, gods, what are you—fuck," I groaned, and threw my head back, any other words fleeing into the ether as he bit my right nipple hard enough to send a lancing, unbearably perfect sting through my chest and down, lodging behind my balls.

His tongue traced down over my ribs, and then he bit my hipbone and my hands flailed, landing in his thick hair and tangling there.

A kiss to my inner thigh had me shivering, and then—

"No, no wait, I haven't bathed in so long—"

"Not when you were awake for it," he murmured against my skin. "There's a healer here. A grandmotherly type. She cleaned you up. I think she has a bit of magic of her own and used that too. Any more questions?"

I squeezed my eyes shut, but it didn't remove the very unappealing image of someone's grandmother washing me.

Andreas lifted my balls and nuzzled behind them, breath hot against my hole.

And suddenly I no longer cared about anything else, including elderly witches.

"Tell me you love me," Andreas said, and spread my cheeks with both hands.

I opened my eyes and whimpered helplessly as I almost spent then and there, my cock jerking. Andreas, bent down between my legs, eyes devouring me and hot mouth about to do the same, was enough to have me on the edge of madness.

He kissed my hole, tongue flicking into the center of me, hot and wet and coaxing. "Tell me you love me," he said again, the words burrowing into my body, a low vibration.

"Please," I gasped, and he thrust his tongue into me, spearing me open, my rim stretching and giving way for him, desperate for him to fill me. "Please, Andreas, please," and then, on a wail, "I love you!"

"Fuck, gods, fuck," he said, and sat up, leaving me blinking up at him, bereft, the air of the room too cold on my wet flesh.

If I hadn't loved him so much, trusted him more than anyone else on earth, I'd have been terrified of the expression on his face. He looked like he wanted to eat me alive, focused on me with an intensity that had me desperate to—spread my legs, it turned out, because I'd wrapped my hands around the backs of my knees before I even knew what I was doing, pulling myself open for him.

His hands moved too quickly for me to follow, tearing at the buttons of his trousers, while his gaze dropped between my legs.

"You can't say things like that and expect me not to fuck you until you scream the roof down," he said. "I hope whoever Enzo put in the hallway isn't a prude."

"You told me to say it," I protested. "You made me!"

"You meant it." His tone suggested I'd be sorry if I denied it. "And I'll make you say it again. Just to be sure." He lunged, and I craned my neck around to find him rummaging on a shelf above the head of the bed. "I knew she'd left this up here," he said, and sat back on his heels with a jar in his hand.

When he pulled the stopper, the scent of sweet herbs wafted out. Some salve for healing, no doubt, but he put it to a much different purpose, taking out his cock and slathering it from tip to base, slick and glistening.

"I almost forgot how big you are." I hadn't meant to say that aloud.

Andreas grinned, predatory and bright. "I won't let you forget again," he growled, and leaned down, bracing one hand beside me and using the other to rub the remaining salve into me and then guide his cock where he wanted it.

The head kissed my hole, gently pressing against my rim. I couldn't see anything but his eyes, pools of black surrounded by a gleaming ring of bronze. He held me completely spellbound, his natural magic so much stronger than anything a mage could've produced to put me in thrall. My whole body quivered, empty and wanting, my hole clenching around nothing.

And then he thrust, all at once, one long, heavy slide of his thick cock so deep into me that it punched the air out of my lungs.

For a long moment he didn't move, buried in me, throbbing in me, letting me feel every inch of him.

"Tell me again," he said, and kissed me, lips catching on mine, tongue teasing the roof of my mouth and then pushing in to claim me.

Contradictory, because I couldn't speak with him taking my mouth like he owned it. And I couldn't speak at all impaled on that massive cock.

But I moaned into his mouth, and that seemed to be enough for him, because he started to thrust, hollowing me out as he pulled his hips back and filling me to the brim when he shoved back in, kissing me, opening me, making me his.

He tore his mouth away from mine and bit at my throat. "Your Highness," he rasped against my skin. "My love. *Mine*," and he pounded into me deeply, every stroke lighting me up the way my magic had illuminated him, sparks flying inside me until I screamed the roof down, just as he'd said I would, my throat raw.

I clawed at his shoulders, fingers digging into his tunic, and arched up, cock painfully hard and throbbing, balls achingly tight.

One more thrust that felt like it turned me inside out, and I clenched all my muscles, squeezing him and drawing out a groan, and came all over us both, soaking the front of his tunic and spattering my own skin.

I collapsed, shuddering, my breath coming in gasping sobs.

Andreas bit down on my throat, the sting of his teeth making me convulse with an aftershock almost as strong as the first wave of pleasure.

He went rigid, his cock swelling in me, heat spreading from the head of it to fill me up inside.

He released his mouthful of my neck and dropped his head down, sweaty forehead on my shoulder, his whole body heaving. When I opened my eyes, I couldn't see anything but his black-clad shoulder blotting out the rest of the world.

Exactly as it should be. I never wanted to be without his protection again—although the longer I tended to my cursed magic this way, rather than with a potion, the better I'd become at protecting myself.

And him, too, when he needed me.

Andreas was so strong in every way, so muscular and brave and skilled with a sword, a respected commander with a clever mind and a quick wit. But when I slid my hands down over his chest and wrapped my arms around his back, stroking along his spine with one hand and burying the other in his hair, he shivered and thrust into me one last time, pressing a kiss to my collarbone. As if my touch was enough to make him weak.

"Niko," he said softly into my shoulder.

I closed my eyes and let myself sink into the bed, everything else spiraling away. I had Andreas in my arms and inside me. We were both alive. And beneath my lingering exhaustion, I could feel my magic beginning to stir again, like a delicate little shoot rising from the roots of a plant that'd been dormant under the frozen ground.

We were alive. My magic would recover. Everything else could wait. Maybe I'd take a nap with Andreas wrapped around me, and he could fuck me again while I was still half asleep, whispering in my ear, making me moan into the pillow...

Footsteps in the corridor heralded a soft rap on the door, and my eyes popped open, all my relaxation fled.

"Sir! There's dinner ready, and they want to know if you'd like it here or if you'll come to the hall downstairs." That was Salvius, and he sounded nearly as worried as when Andreas had been dying. "I can sit with His Highness if you'll take a breath of air. Ten minutes, sir. I promise I'll come for you if anything changes."

I stiffened, braced for Andreas to leap out of bed and rush to make sure Salvius didn't see or hear anything untoward. Although Salvius's implication that Andreas hadn't left my side for so much as a moment suggested…

Andreas didn't really move, simply lifting up enough to prop himself over me on his elbows and turning his head to call out, "Give us a few minutes, Sergeant. And I wouldn't open the door, if I were you."

There was some muttering from outside the door, Salvius's voice and another man's. And then a startled laugh.

My face went boiling hot in an instant. Apparently whoever Enzo had left outside had functioning ears and had taken it upon himself to give Salvius a report.

"Um," Salvius said through the door. "I'm glad, uh, His Highness is awake. Give a shout when you want dinner, then! Um. Sorry to disturb you, sir. Your Highness. Food's hot!"

There were a few more murmurs of conversation from the hallway, and then Salvius's footsteps retreated.

"I forgot there was someone out there," I muttered, covering my eyes with my hands. It didn't help. "Oh, gods. I won't be able to hold my head up. I sounded like, I sounded like a slut."

"Mmm," Andreas said, and kissed me softly, his mouth lingering. "I'll be able to hold *my* head up. Every man here's going to envy me. You sounded incredible. Delicious."

The edge of laughter in his voice was just too much. I pulled my hands away and glared up at him—and yes, he was grinning, eyes gleaming.

"How nice for you," I groused, and his grin widened.

It was infuriating. But—he hadn't moved, had he? No jumping out of bed, no frantic efforts to make sure no one knew what we'd been doing. In fact, he'd lain here calmly, on top of me and still inside me, and as good as admitted it.

"Last time we were interrupted—you panicked," I said. "You were ashamed of me. But now you—and you haven't even said you love me! If you—"

"I love you," he said evenly, eyes fixed on mine, so bright and intent. "More than life or breath. More than enough to tell everyone you belong to me, if that's what you want. Last time, I didn't want you to be embarrassed. That wasn't for my sake. I was just as much in love with you then as I am now."

"But, but," I sputtered, as a warm, quivering sensation I'd never even imagined bloomed in my chest. It felt like bubbles. It felt like joy. A smile had spread across my face, so wide that my cheeks were hurting. "How could you think I'd be embarrassed to be with you?"

Andreas raised his eyebrows. "Getting fucked by your personal guard? I can't imagine why that would embarrass you, Your Highness. Besides, you were. Don't try to deny it."

Gazing into those eyes, I couldn't possibly try to deny anything. Lying would be impossible.

And besides, I didn't want to. I never wanted anything between us but the truth again.

I still had to take a deep, shuddering breath and force the words out. "I was, but not because of you. Because of what I am. Andreas, you know what everyone thinks of twilight mages, and dawn mages in particular. It's—I've used the potion because I didn't want—I hate what I am!"

That came out too harsh and too vehement, and tears stung the corners of my eyes.

I'd never said that out loud before. I'd hardly even allowed myself to admit it directly in the privacy of my own mind.

Andreas leaned down and kissed the words from my trembling lips, soothing me, loving me. "You saved my life with what you are," he said softly. "Even if I didn't already love you, you'd own me for the rest of the life you gave me just for that. I'd follow you around like a faithful dog until I died."

My chest felt too tight, too heavy, like it might crack in half. I put my hands on his shoulders and dug my fingers in, never wanting to let him go.

"You can do that anyway, if you want to," I choked out. "Please."

He shook his head, laughing a little. "Right," he said, his voice thick. "I'm afraid you won't be able to get rid of me, sweetheart. I didn't exactly fall in love with you at first sight, but no one else ever compared to you, either."

"At first sight?" It was my turn to laugh. It released something in me, something hard and frozen, and I could breathe again. No one else had ever compared to me. He loved me. He truly loved me, and I could breathe. "Even my little sister thought I was too hard on you when we met, and she usually takes my side in everything. No one could've fallen in love with me like that. Not even a saint."

I had a sneaking suspicion that *I'd* started falling in love with *him* that day…but having nothing but the truth between us from now on didn't mean I had to tell him literally everything in my mind, did it?

Andreas bit his lip, closing his eyes for a moment and then meeting mine again. "That wasn't my first sight of you. You were—I'm sure you don't even remember. I know you don't, or you'd have said something, I think. But you saw me at Bossale, when you reviewed the fortress a few years ago. I saw you, anyway. I never forgot you."

Bossale. He'd been part of the garrison there when I visited? Impossible, because surely I'd have remembered someone like Andreas.

But I hadn't. To be fair, I'd spent much of my life trying not to notice beautiful men, because I knew I couldn't have any of them.

"You really noticed me?" I hated the needy, hopeful tone of my voice, but…Andreas had noticed me. He'd thought about me for *years*. I wanted to hear more. Much more, infinitely more, preferably while he fucked me again.

Andreas grinned and shook his head. "Not a chance, Your Highness. No fishing for compliments. I fell in love with you while you were turning up your nose at me for doing my job, and that's bad enough. I don't need to humor you by telling you about pining for a prince I knew I'd never even be able to touch. You're—fuck," he gasped.

I smiled up at him smugly and clenched my muscles again, squeezing his cock where he'd only started to slip out of me, still half erect. Gods, he was getting hard again. I could feel him lengthening inside me.

"Humor me a little bit?" I rotated my hips. "You can touch me as much as you want. Commit all the treason you like."

"Fuck," he said again, sounding breathless, and thrust once, shallowly, stirring my insides and making me whimper. "Is it treasonous to say I love how wet it sounds when I fuck you with my own come?"

I gaped up at him in wide-eyed shock as that hit me in the pit of my stomach, my cock hardening so quickly I went lightheaded. "How can you say—gods, Andreas—"

"Like I've told you from the beginning, well worth being hanged," he said, and swooped down to claim my mouth, hot and hard.

I had one last thought, that I really hoped the poor bastard outside our door had left to go down to the hall for dinner, and then I didn't think about anything else at all for a long, long time.

Chapter Twenty-Five

We crested the highest foothill above Surbino on a bright, breezy, chilly day two weeks later, the icy mountain wind at our backs and the softer, balmier sea air sweeping up to meet us. The city looked exactly the same as it had a lifetime ago—although since that lifetime had comprised only a little over a month in total, including the journey home, it shouldn't have seemed so shocking.

But whether or not my home was the same, I'd changed irrevocably in that month.

Without a word, Andreas and I both reined in, with Salvius, Ludo, and Piet coming to a halt a few feet behind.

I glanced over at Andreas and found him gazing at me, not at the view of the gleaming gold and white city with its brightly colored tiles and the sparkling silvery river and sea beyond. The little smile playing around the corners of his lips and the light in his eyes suggested he didn't feel like he was missing anything.

My cheeks flushing, I turned back to the city, gripping my reins tightly and focusing on the palace at the center and the burgundy pennant above the flag of Surbino that indicated the queen was in residence.

If I pretended I wasn't two seconds from flinging myself off Fluffy and into Andreas's lap, maybe I'd be able to control myself and not do it at all.

Fifteen days since Andreas had told me he loved me more than life. He'd told me every day since, too. And it hadn't gotten the slightest bit old. My heart fluttered, and I blushed and smiled like an idiot, and everyone around me could see how much I loved him and how helpless I was to hide it. The men were no doubt gritting their teeth with eagerness to be home and get the hell away from us and our lovestruck foolishness.

Mine, anyway. They wouldn't dare show their impatience to Andreas.

What that said about their relative respect for their prince and their commander, I didn't examine too closely—and I didn't blame them, either. The right kind of look from Andreas had me on my knees, after all.

They were definitely happy to be going home instead of going on, though, one reason why I'd made the decision I had. The day after I woke up from my magical coma, Andreas had asked me if I still wanted to try to find another way across the river and attend the second half of my conclave.

I'd thought about the bridge and the ford and the imaginary ferry and the abduction and rescue, and Andreas coming an inch from death, and I'd laughed until I was red-faced and crying at the thought of continuing the journey. There was challenging the gods, and then there was outright stupidity. Andreas had expressed his relief and agreement, and kissed me, and that was that. We'd spent a few days recovering in Enzo's surprisingly comfortable fort, in large part because Fluffy—whom I'd been abjectly grateful to see alive—had a cut on his shoulder that needed to heal. And then we'd set out for home.

"Two days still before we're home," I said. Casual conversation. I could do that. Speaking to Andreas felt awkward of late, laced with the tension of constant desire. It'd fade into comfort at some point, I expected, but for now it made every interaction difficult unless we were alone and I could tear his pants off. "It feels so long, though. I miss my bed." Oh, gods, that sounded like an invitation. Of course, it was one.

The tips of my ears burned. "Where do you think Enzo's men are? The northern pass had so much more snow than this one."

We'd paid Enzo handsomely to have a party of his men take Dario and the other prisoner to Surbino through the northern pass and then south along the other side of the mountains. Andreas had point-blank refused to take them with us. He didn't want Dario within a mile of me. But they had to go to Surbino to be imprisoned and interrogated more thoroughly. Enzo was the solution.

His men operated on both sides of the mountains and, Enzo assured us, could take the prisoners through their native Calatria without attracting any attention or letting them ask for help or escape. Discretion was definitely called for. What little Andreas had gotten out of Dario suggested that he might not have been working for Duke Lucian at all, but against him, in the employ of one of his relatives, perhaps attempting to cause conflict with Surbino and use it to usurp rulership of Calatria. The details of the plot hadn't been forthcoming, and we had no interest in attracting attention from anyone in Calatria before we could get enough information for my mother to evaluate the diplomatic implications.

I was relieved by what we'd learned, though. If Lucian hadn't been involved, then it wasn't an act of war. And the last thing I wanted was to be the cause, even indirectly, of more death.

Andreas had spent one more hour questioning Dario, spoken to the men intended to form the escort, and seemed satisfied to send them on their way. And having approved the outline of the plan, I left the details to him.

Which meant it was just the five of us going home, relaxed and taking it at an easy pace, spending more than one night in some places along the way if the weather was unusually unpleasant for traveling.

Andreas and I shared a room every night.

I was exhausted and well-used every morning, and the way he looked at me when I grimaced while getting into the saddle nearly sent us right back to bed.

But we were almost home. Where we'd have my own bed, soft and warm and private. Andreas could spend whole days between my legs. I could spend hours on my knees, on a soft rug in front of the fire.

A shiver went down my spine, and it had nothing to do with the cold wind.

"They might even be there before us," Andreas said, startling me out of my fantasy. "They seemed like they were used to hard travel, and they're surely not going to be taking the journey easy for their prisoners' sakes. They're planning to rough it, actually. Sleep out in the woods and avoid towns."

He sounded deeply pleased by that, and I couldn't help laughing. "They're lucky not to be traveling with you."

"Very, very lucky," Andreas growled. "But I'm going to petition the queen to let me have a hand in continuing the questioning. So he won't be lucky for long. That is, unless she throws me in the cell next to his."

I glanced over at him.

He was looking at me again—or possibly still looking at me, smiling as if the possibility of being locked in a dungeon didn't trouble him in the least.

Gods, he loved me so much. I swayed toward him. One kiss, and then—

A loud throat-clearing behind us had me sitting stiffly upright in the saddle again, biting my lip and red-faced.

Andreas grinned and shook his head.

Fine. I didn't like it, but I could wait until we stopped for the night.

"That won't happen," I said. "I won't let her. She's going to lose her mind when she hears what happened, but she can hardly blame you." And it was true: at least her fury at my kidnapping would distract her from thinking Andreas might have taken advantage of me. A silver lining, I supposed. "She won't blame any of you," I added a little more loudly, because I knew they were all listening anyway. I got a murmur of what sounded like thanks for my trouble. "Leave my mother the queen to me."

"Gladly," Andreas said with force, and behind me, Salvius laughed. "Let's go, Your Highness. We're burning daylight. If we ride hard for a bit, we can reach that inn we stopped at before. With the bathing room?"

Oh, gods, my eyes rolled back in my head at the thought of sharing that enormous bathtub with Andreas, and my face must've been a sight. Andreas laughed and nudged his horse into a trot.

We all followed, with Surbino glimmering up ahead to show us the way home.

The last two days of the journey were easy, especially compared to what had come before. It didn't stay sunny, but a bit of rain and a muddy road felt like the minor inconveniences they were rather than misery-inducing obstacles.

My standards had changed.

And I was ready to face my mother, too. I didn't care if she threw a truly royal fit, tried to punish Andreas, tried to confine me to the palace until I was old and gray, or even ordered us all shackled to a wall. Maybe I'd grown up a bit, having faced the first real hardships of my entire life. Maybe knowing Andreas's future rested on my ability to have a spine had given me courage. And maybe simply wanting something, needing something, more than I craved Mama's approval had finally given me a sense of proportion.

After all, what did it matter if she raged at me? Granted, I was one of four people in the kingdom who could face the queen's potential fury without much fear for the consequences, but…I *was* one of them. And I was a grown man, with my magic finally at my fingertips. I'd even used it to spark our campfire the other day when we stopped on the road for lunch. Just like that, without setting my pants aflame, or making them fly off my body, or anything.

Of course, it all depended on whether or not Enzo's men reached Surbino before we did. I'd written her a letter, to which Andreas had appended his official report, and we'd entrusted the packet to the leader of the party.

She might have had a bit of time to digest what had happened before we arrived, if they got there first.

Or it might be better for us to explain events in person.

Either way, I expected my very first look at her would tell me one way or the other.

As it happened, I didn't even need to see her to know. We approached the city gates in the middle of a steady downpour, with visibility limited to a few feet in front of our faces—which were half hidden by the way we all had our hats pulled down as much as possible.

But the gate guards swarmed out to peer at us despite the rain, and they let out a shout of recognition, everyone running around like a kicked anthill.

My heart sank. Clearly Enzo's men had arrived before us, and my mother was not in a calm frame of mind about it.

Half the city guard, it felt like, escorted us through the bustling lower city and up the hill to the palace gates, marching in a formation around us. Typically we would've ridden around the side of the palace to the stables, dismounted there, and used a smaller entrance.

But not today.

As we approached, there were far more of the palace guard than usual lining the front steps, clearly forewarned by a messenger sent from the city gates.

And heedless of the rain, my mother the queen strode out of the main doors, Philippa beside her. Beneath the trappings of her royalty— the golden circlet nestled in the elegant coif of her light-brown hair, the sweeping green silk of her gown, all spotted with rain already, her jeweled rings and the array of royal guards around her—she was my beloved mother, her eyes shining with love and worry and relief.

All at once, I wasn't so much a grown man with a mage's powers and a soldier lover, who meant to stand on his dignity and assert his rights to independence. I hadn't even realized how much I missed her.

I didn't wait for anyone to take Fluffy's reins. I simply leapt down from his back and raced across the graveled carriage drive, running up the marble steps and flinging myself into Mama's arms.

"Niko," she said, "oh, thank the gods."

She held me tightly, stroking my back and kissing my cheeks, and I had to bend down and press my face to her shoulder to hide the tears. My mother felt small in my embrace; I'd grown used, of late, to having my arms around someone much larger than me. But Phil had come up from the other side and flung her arms around us both, laughing and crying, and the sensation of oddness vanished in pure happiness.

Mama kissed me one more time and pulled back, slipping her arm around me and pulling me toward the doors. The guards arrayed on the steps were grinning, and she waved a hand at them and said, "Get in out of the rain, gentlemen, and have a drink to toast Prince Nikola's safe return. And make sure his escort has the good stuff," as we passed, earning herself a flurry of bows. Phil had better be taking notes for when she became queen.

My escort. Andreas. Where the hell had he gone? I craned my neck over my shoulder and caught a glimpse of him standing by the horses, gazing after me. He nodded, smiled, and turned away, giving orders.

Gods, I had said I'd handle the queen, but…an odd shudder went through me, a terrible dread that somehow everything that had happened between us had vanished now that I was home and we were in our proper places.

But I didn't have time to stop, to call out to him, because my younger siblings were running toward me in the main hall, both laughing and crying. Even the usually sullen, mustachioed Franco hugged me and whooped and ruffled my hair.

They hustled me into our mother's private study, tugging at my wet coat, telling me everything: Amara's twisted ankle, an ambassador who'd tried to negotiate for a tariff on the weather, the head palace chef's disastrous attempt at a rabbit pie with cranberries, how worried they'd been when they had my letter.

"Thank the gods I put Andreas in command," my mother said, as she shoved me into a chair by the fire. "The thought of what would've happened to you if I'd allowed you to be in charge makes my blood run cold. Honestly, Niko, you ought to have a governess still!"

She glared down at me, her fists on her hips, reduced by motherly worry to looking almost like a regular woman in a temper, and not a queen.

At least she was directing it at me and not Andreas. If he'd bothered to come with me, damn him, he'd have been relieved to know he wouldn't end up in a dungeon after all.

Hadn't I had such good intentions about standing up for myself at last? And that had gotten me through one hug from my mother and thirty seconds of scolding. Fuck.

I straightened my shoulders. "Mama, it was hardly something I could predict—"

"I told you this journey was a terrible idea, far too risky at this time of year and for a member of the royal family. You'll be home for a while, Niko." Gods, I couldn't listen to this. Impatience boiled up, a pressure in my chest and my throat, raging for release. "Under Andreas's supervision, I think, because he's certainly proved his—"

"Andreas is my lover, not my keeper," I said loudly. "I've stopped taking the potion. And I won't be under anyone's supervision. I'm nearly thirty, and I've had enough!"

In the ensuing silence, the faint pop and hiss of a damp log in the fireplace echoed like a thunderclap. My mother's eyes went wide as she stared at me, a deep crimson stain spreading over her cheekbones.

"Phil," Amara said, and I looked over to find her holding out her hand in the universal gesture for *give it to me*. "Now, or you'll find some excuse."

Philippa shifted uncomfortably, her eyes darting to our mother. "You know I don't carry any silver with me when I'm in the pal—"

"Then admit in front of witnesses that you owe me, because I don't trust you to—"

Franco burst out laughing, at the exact moment that I realized what my horrid harpies of sisters had done.

"You placed a bet on—how dare you?" I demanded, and popped out of my chair, because the top of my head felt like it might pop off if I didn't. "A bet? On whether I'd—Andreas and I would—*how dare you?*"

The room exploded in protestations and argument, Phil denying it, Amara shrilly reminding her it'd been Phil's idea, Franco howling with mirth, and my mother scolding all three of them. And me, too, although I didn't really understand why. Well, I understood. But it still seemed unfair.

A brisk knock at the door cut through the din. Everyone fell silent, royal training overcoming even the heightened emotions of a family quarrel. You never knew when it might be a member of the council or a gossipy courtier on the other side of the door.

"Oh, what now," Mama muttered. "Yes, come in!"

The door opened to reveal Andreas, wearing his most controlled and stoic expression—not surprising given that he'd surely overheard the entire royal family of Surbino shouting at each other like tavern brawlers.

But when his gaze shifted to me, which it did almost instantly, a slight smile teased the corners of his mouth, and his eyes lit up.

And even though I knew my whole family was watching me, I couldn't help my own smile of relief that he'd followed me—and of pure, helpless love.

"Oh, gods," Amara muttered, glancing from Andreas to me and back again. "Phil, you owe me double."

"Amara!" Philippa and my mother said in shocked unison.

Franco started laughing again. "Captain, do you have any brothers?" he said. "One younger, and one much, much older, because Philippa's about a hundr—"

"I strongly advise you not to finish that sentence," Andreas cut in. "Princess Philippa could order me to string you up by your toes, brother or not. And besides, you may not be in a position to judge aesthetics, going by your mustache, but the crown princess is known as far as the other side of the mountains for being beautiful and brilliant, too."

Franco stared at him, turning an awkward shade of red.

"Well, he has my approval," Phil said briskly, going rather pink herself.

"It would help if he troubled to present himself properly to his queen," my mother said, extremely dryly. "My approval may or may not be forthcoming."

Oh, for the love of the gods. Andreas stood there all straight-backed and honorable and perfect, the crown's most devoted servant, and my adoring lover, and the only thing stopping us from going to my rooms and ordering a hot bath and some lunch and then falling into bed was this nonsense.

Andreas squared his shoulders, clasping his hands behind his back. A soldier being dressed down by the queen, not a man who loved the queen's son.

And that wouldn't bloody well do at all.

"Mama, I don't need your approval," I said, tearing my eyes away from Andreas with an effort and turning to face her. She opened her mouth, eyes flashing, and I continued quickly with, "No, I don't. Not for how I conduct my personal affairs. Andreas isn't a criminal, he's no threat to me or to Surbino, and you have no reason to interfere. Besides which, I won't tolerate it. I love you, Mama. And I owe you all my respect and fealty. But not in this."

The whole room seemed to be holding its breath. I knew I was.

My mother drew herself up to her full height, only an inch or so less than my own, with her carefully arranged hair and her crown bringing her higher—and her royal poise making her larger than life.

At last she sighed, shook her head, and—smiled. Something in her eyes made my chest tighten—gods, seeing my mother's sadness beneath her self-control always hurt—but she smiled.

"Very well," she said. Very well? "Close your mouth, Niko, it's very unappealing. Captain, come here."

My siblings stood aside to allow Andreas to pass by, and then he was right there. I could almost feel the warmth of him, smell the enticing scent of his skin, leather and steel and soap and pure Andreas. My fingers itched to reach out to him.

He bowed deeply, only rising after a pause long enough to show the most profound respect. "Your Majesty, if you'll allow me to present myself," he said. "I'm ready to give you my report at your convenience."

She chuckled. "Better late than never for the proper formalities, I suppose. At ease, Andreas. I had your letter, and Niko's. That was all highly informative, enough for now. Although I will expect you in the council chamber at nine o'clock tomorrow morning, ready to give your full report and your assessment of Calatria's involvement in this affair.

In detail."

"Yes, Your Majesty," he said.

She nodded. "And in the meantime, we will expect you to supper tonight. Ensure that Niko arrives on time, if you please."

Andreas's eyebrows went up, and it might've been my imagination, but I thought he went a little pale under his tan. His Adam's apple bobbed. "Yes, Your Majesty. Ah, forgive me. Will I be, that is—"

"Sitting at the table wearing something that hasn't seen weeks of travel, if you please. Both of you." She turned to me, a glint in her eyes that had me frozen like a rabbit in the sights of a silk-clad hawk. "You're nearly thirty, as you say, and perhaps the queen has no right to interfere in your personal affairs," she said pleasantly. "But as your mother, I look forward to hearing all about how the two of you became...close. Not to mention your plans for the future. A wedding, for example. Any son of mine will observe the proprieties."

Or else hung in the air unspoken, as clear as if she'd shouted it.

A muffled squeak and a hissed admonishment sounded like Franco had started laughing again and at least one of our sisters was shutting him up.

Oh, gods, I'd be lucky if Andreas didn't run screaming. He'd come from Calatria to take service with Surbino. He could go somewhere else just as easily. Enzo would probably appoint him his second in command in an instant.

My heart in my throat, I finally dared to look up at him.

And I found him smiling blandly, calm and unruffled once again. As if the idea of a wedding didn't worry him as much as supper with my family, for fuck's sake! Then again...he had a point there. The prospect of that supper, choking down bites in between telling my eager family how Andreas and I had become...close...was turning my stomach in an entirely unappetizing way.

"Niko?" my mother said. "Are you quite well?"

Beneath the sarcasm, I detected a real note of concern. I opened my mouth to reassure her, but Andreas got there first, cutting in smoothly with, "I beg your pardon, Your Majesty. But would you allow me to escort Prince

Nikola to his rooms? It's been an arduous journey. He needs his rest."

"Rest," Amara huffed. "Right."

"Amara!" Philippa and my mother said.

My eyes met Andreas's, and I read the same level of "fuck this" in his that I knew shone from mine. A hot, giddy, floaty sensation bubbled up in my chest.

"If we're going to be able to come to supper, I need a nap," I said, never breaking Andreas's warm gaze. "Now. We're going. Right now."

And without waiting for permission—because why should I, after all? I was one of four people in the kingdom who didn't need to worry about being hanged for it—I seized Andreas by the arm and all but dragged him away, elbowing Franco aside when he didn't move fast enough.

"Thank you, Your Majesty!" Andreas said hurriedly, and then in a lower voice, "Your Highness, I can't just—"

"Yes, you damn well can," I hissed. "See you at supper!" I called out.

With my free hand, I yanked the door shut behind us, getting one last glimpse of my family's faces: my mother wearing a bemused expression that meant we'd be hearing it later, but that Andreas wouldn't be in a cell anytime soon, Philippa shaking her head but smiling, and Amara and Franco gaping. Good. Let those two see their older brother setting a good example, for once.

The click of the door echoed in the quiet hallway.

I looked up at Andreas, and I found him gazing down at me, his eyes soft, his smile…well, foolish, really. Besotted. He didn't show any sign of wanting to run away and join Enzo's band of ruffians.

But I had to be sure. "You know supper's going to be—no matter what methods you mean to use to interrogate Dario, my mother's going to do worse. Andreas, you don't have to—"

He caught me around the waist, crushed me against his chest, and kissed the breath out of me, my lips bruised and my body bent back over his arm. Right there in the hallway outside my mother's study.

When he lifted his head, he gazed down at me with that light still shining in his eyes. "I love you, Your Highness," he said. "Now come upstairs. I have treason to commit before you take that nap."

I couldn't help my nervous glance at the study door. "My mother might hear you!"

Andreas shrugged. "Then we should probably go upstairs," he said, far too calmly, and only grinned at me when I glared.

Damn it, I couldn't exactly argue, could I? Not when he was so obviously right. Especially not when I wanted to be alone with him at least as much as he did.

He wrapped his arm around me, and I leaned my head on his shoulder, and we went upstairs, heedless of passing servants or guards.

We even took a nap, Amara's skepticism be damned.

Eventually. With Andreas's arms wrapped around me from behind, his cock nestled between my thighs.

And I'd never slept better in my life than in my own bed, and with the man I loved. I was truly home at last.

Epilogue

Two Months Later

Pacing the terrace outside my bedchamber wasn't nearly enough to burn off my anger, frustration—and creeping dread.

Damn it all to hell. I ran into the wall, slapped it with my open palm, cursed when it stung, and spun and paced the other way. I paused for a moment at the other side, leaning out over the parapet and scowling at the gorgeous pink-tinged honey-gold of the sunset pouring over the early springtime flowers beginning to bloom in the garden below. The plash of a fountain and the chirp of an enthusiastic bird seeking a mate only added to the overall peaceful beauty of the world around me.

Fucking stupid beautiful world.

Fucking Andreas.

Gods, I hadn't even thought about my curse for months, not since we came home. I hadn't needed to. Andreas spent every night in my bed—our bed, really, because I was pretty sure he'd moved into my rooms a few weeks after we returned. We hadn't discussed it, but three or four black tunics and an equal number of black trousers had appeared in a neat stack on a shelf in my dressing room, and a small chest full of swords, knives, armor, and undergarments occupied a corner of it. That seemed to be the extent of Andreas's possessions.

And every night that he spent in our bed, he fucked me. Without fail, without question, as if he could never get enough of me. Sometimes I protested, claiming exhaustion or an early morning the next day, simply for the pleasure of being firmly overruled, flipped onto my stomach and pinned, Andreas's low voice in my ear telling me *I'll take your orders anywhere but in this bed, Your Highness.*

The nights would've been enough to ensure that I never came close to reaching the limit of my curse. But no matter how busy he was with his new duties training the royal guard as their second in command, he always found the time to track me down in the middle of the day, too. When he sauntered out and went back to work, whistling and with his coat over his shoulder, I was usually still sprawled across our bed, sticky and flushed and aching in the most perfect possible way.

And my magic thrived on it. The more he filled me, the stronger I became—far beyond the vitiation of my curse. Control was coming more slowly. Much more slowly, as my singed eyebrows could attest. But every bit of practice brought me closer to mastery, and I had more to work with than I'd ever thought possible.

I'd even written a letter to those eastern priests and asked them to send me copies of their texts. Because while I didn't think I completely believed in the idea of one perfect match for every mage, there was clearly more to this than simple removal of a curse. Healing Andreas's wound even though I'd taken the potion had been one strong piece of evidence, but now I had a pattern.

So I wasn't entirely convinced yet…but my wonderings had started to coalesce into belief.

One night over a bottle of wine shared with Phil, I'd confided my secret fear: that I loved Andreas, and he loved me, because of some divine trickery, some gods-decreed magical compatibility. The very thought made my skin crawl. Not only that Andreas's feelings could be false, in some sense, but that yet another aspect of my life had somehow been determined for me.

But Phil had laughed, shaking her head and patting my hand in an obnoxiously condescending big-sister way. "Don't be silly, Niko," she said. "You were in love with him before you ever touched each other, and you were using the potion the whole time. And don't even try to tell me you weren't."

Well, when she put it that way, I found it hard to argue. Loving Andreas didn't require any outside assistance—and I'd been content to accept the idea that loving me didn't, either, especially when Andreas gazed at me with his heart shining in his eyes. He'd given me no reason to doubt him, after all.

Until two days ago, anyway.

It'd been forty hours since he was inside me, and he'd spent the last two nights in the barracks, not coming near me at all. I hadn't even seen him since he'd glared at me, tight-lipped and with a muscle ticking in his jaw, spun on his heel, and strode out, slamming the door behind him.

For fuck's sake, my mother wanted to make him a lord, not have him publicly whipped—although you'd have thought it was the latter by his reaction. But he'd been infuriatingly measured in his tone and his words as we argued, mostly, until I'd demanded to know how I was supposed to introduce him to foreign dignitaries if he didn't even have a title—and what I'd really been thinking, and had been too afraid to say, was that by Surbino's laws he couldn't marry me without a title, which he manifestly didn't want.

"I have a rank, and that's always been good enough before," he'd said, and then he'd left me.

I'd lain in bed without blowing out the candles for hours that night, and the next, waiting for him to come back and apologize.

He hadn't.

And now, I'd be in pain by the time the sun went down unless I found him, swallowed my pride, and begged.

Precisely as I'd always known would happen if I depended on someone else.

It didn't help that the hard, agonized knot in the pit of my stomach wasn't due to reluctance to humble myself. Or at least, not mostly.

It was because I missed him like I'd miss air, because my skin tingled with the need for his touch, because I felt like I'd lost a limb in his absence.

Footsteps on the stairs made me look up sharply, and I froze mid-pace, my heart skittering and my chest suddenly tight.

Andreas appeared at the head of the stairs, took two steps onto the terrace, and then stopped abruptly. The air around me felt thick and heavy. Gods, I'd usually be in his arms by now, and the distance between us seemed so dreadfully wrong.

He had his soldier's face on, hard and neutral, but his intent, hungry gaze roved over me before he looked me in the eyes again. My heart pounded. He had to touch me first. He had to, or I'd never be able to respect myself again. *Please, please…*

"I brought you something," he said, the words startling in the tense silence. "I didn't know if you had any left. The other day, I asked Gennaro to make some just in case."

He took another step forward, pulled something out of his pocket, and set it on the table by my chaise. A bottle.

My potion.

My heart actually stopped for a moment, and I reached out blindly, fumbling for the back of the chaise and leaning on it for support when my knees threatened to give out.

I stared at the bottle, throat dry. Two bottles, now, because my vision had blurred and the corners of my eyes stung horribly.

"Damn it, Niko," he said hoarsely. "Don't look like that! Damn it. You owe me an apology, because you're in the wrong and you acted like a fucking royal brat, but don't look like—fuck. I promised myself I wouldn't crack first," he muttered.

I looked up at him, blinking to try to clear my eyes. "You brought my potion," I said, too softly, too huskily. Clearing my throat didn't help. "How am I supposed to look? If you don't want to—"

"If I don't want—say the fucking word, Niko. One word from you, and I'll have you bent over that chair in two seconds!" His eyes blazed, and he took one step forward and then stopped again, as if he could hardly help himself. He had his fists clenched at his sides. "I brought that so you don't have to make up the quarrel if you don't want to. Even though you're wrong, because there's no number of fancy titles that can paper over what I am, Your Highness, and if you're ashamed of me, you should say so now. Before I—while I—" He cut himself off by running a hand over his face roughly, and when he dropped it to his side, he looked—well, as exhausted and desperate as I felt after two nights apart.

"It doesn't matter when, actually," he went on, low and quiet. "If you tire of me now, or later, one won't be worse than the other. But tell me. I'd rather not have you at all than make you unhappy. I brought the potion so you can make up your mind without feeling—you can be as angry with me as you want, and I'll fuck you if you'd prefer that to the potion. No apology required, and we can keep fighting after we're done. Or you can drink that and tell me to go to hell. It's your choice."

Andreas gestured at the bottle on the table and then put his hands behind him, standing straight, at parade rest.

My choice. He loved me enough, understood me enough, respected me enough…and of course he did. He would never use my curse against me. And I'd have known that, rationally, if I'd taken the time to think about it rather than letting my lifelong fears come rushing back the moment we had a quarrel.

Love welled up in me so strongly that I couldn't speak, could hardly breathe.

Instead, I held out my hand, praying that he'd cross the gap between us and take it.

An instant later everything went whirling sideways, and I landed on my back on the chaise, Andreas stretched out over me. I blinked and he was there, eyes fixed on mine. Searching.

"I want you to choose me," he said. "But I won't try to persuade you."

He had one arm propped on the chaise, with the other hand buried in my hair, his thumb stroking my cheek. And the weight of him rested between my legs, pressing me down, his already half-hard cock pressing behind my balls.

I almost laughed. No, not persuasive at all.

"I don't need persuading," I managed. "I don't care if you have a title, or a rank, or neither. That's not—it doesn't matter to me."

He bent and kissed the corner of my mouth, lingering, his breath hot on my skin as he took a deep, shuddering breath and let it out slowly. "Then what, sweetheart? Because you're too upset for something that doesn't matter."

I squeezed my eyes shut. He nuzzled my cheek, bent lower, softly kissed my throat, his hips starting to move.

Gods. Not try to persuade me. Right.

"Niko," he whispered. "Come on. You know I'll get it out of you as soon as I get your pants off."

"You'll get something out of—ow!" I winced and flailed as he ducked down and bit my nipple through my shirt. "All right, I—gods, that feels— you can't legally marry me without a title!"

Andreas went as still and tense as if I'd turned him to stone, his mouth open over my nipple, the fingers pressing against the side of my face digging in painfully. My words hung in the air. Fuck, fuck, *fuck*.

"I can't what?" he said at last, and lifted his head. His eyes practically bored holes in me, glittering copper and black. "Marry you. You want me to marry you. The queen said, fuck, I thought she was just needling you, talking about a wedding!"

Swallowing down the thick lump in my throat hurt like hell. "Why do you think she wants to give you a title? It was her idea, not mine, she's thinking ahead. But if you never want to, we'll never mention it again. I promise."

He blinked, stared at me, blinked again, and finally shook his head, looking more than a little dazed.

"Marry you," he said again. The corner of his mouth twitched. "If I married you, I could do any gods-damned thing I wanted to you, couldn't I? It's not treason when you hold your own husband down and turn him inside out."

"Oh, gods," I choked, as all the blood in my body rushed to my cock and my hole clenched, desperate to have him do exactly that. "I don't think that's in the high priest's homily on the purpose of marriage, though!"

"Probably not." He lowered himself down onto the elbow of his braced arm, pressing me deeper into the cushions of the chaise, heavy and hard. "But it's still a little bit treasonous right now, isn't it?"

"Mmm," I said, tipping my head back, because he thrust gently, pushing his thick cockhead against my hole, and even through several layers of clothing he felt so big, so perfect. "Yes."

"Good. I want a few more chances to ruin my prince's sweet little ass before I marry you and make it legal." He latched onto my throat, nipping my skin, flicking me with his tongue, ruining me before he'd even gotten my clothes off, and I writhed under him, whimpering. "Tell me you love me," he said. "Tell me again."

"Make me," I gasped.

His hand replaced his mouth, wrapping around my throat lightly, massaging me, as he pushed himself upright and began to tear at the buttons of my trousers with the other. The little smile that'd been playing around his lips blossomed into a wicked grin, toothy and predatory. I shivered and went still.

"Your wish is my command, Your Highness," he said, very low. "As long as you want me, I'm yours."

"You're all I want. Now show me, unless you're all talk."

Andreas laughed, and leaned in to kiss the hollow of my throat, and I moaned and spread my legs. He moved down, lower and lower, kissing every inch. As he bent his head, I saw the last of the sunset gilding the vines climbing over my balcony. Such a beautiful world.

"Yes, please," I whispered, as he pulled my trousers down, mouthing along my inner thigh.

Then I couldn't remember anything but his name, and three other little words that I repeated over and over again as he moved over me, in me, showing me how much we belonged to each other.

And that was all the magic I needed.

THE END

Acknowledgments

Thank you so much to Amy Pittel for fitting this book in around her other commitments so generously! This book wouldn't be here without her. Alessandra Hazard's edits and notes were also invaluable. Without the two of them, none of this would make sense.

Special thanks also go to Cora Rose and Jem Zee for reading this in multiple stages, encouraging me, and being lovely people.

Natana Holbrook is the best book gremlin PA an author could ask for, and Brit McGinnis is the best PR consultant. I'm lucky to have them around. Thank you!

Get in Touch

I love hearing from readers! Find me at eliotgrayson.com, where you can get more info about my books and also sign up for my newsletter or contact me directly. You can also find out about my other books on Amazon, or join my Facebook readers' group, Eliot Grayson's Escape from Reality, to get more frequent updates. Thanks for reading!

ALSO BY ELIOT GRAYSON

Mismatched Mates:
The Alpha's Warlock
Captive Mate
A Very Armitage Christmas
The Alpha Experiment
Lost and Bound
Lost Touch
The Alpha Contract
The Alpha's Gamble

Blood Bonds:
First Blood
Twice Bitten

Goddess-Blessed:
The Replacement Husband
The Reluctant Husband
Yuletide Treasure

Portsmouth:
Like a Gentleman
Once a Gentleman

Santa Rafaela:
The One Decent Thing
A Totally Platonic Thing
Need a Hand?

Beautiful Beasts:
Corin and the Courtier
Deven and the Dragon

Brought to Light

Undercover

The Wrong Rake